GLIMPSES OF DEEP SPAIN

TALES OF SPANISH LIFE FAR FROM THE TOURIST HORDES

Also by the author

Scotland the Brave
A Tragedy

GLIMPSES OF DEEP SPAIN

TALES OF SPANISH LIFE
FAR FROM THE TOURIST HORDES

IVAR ALASTAIR WATSON

Matador
9 Priory Business Park
Kibworth Beauchamp
Leicestershire LE8 0RX, UK
Tel: (+44) 116 279 2299
Fax: (+44) 116 279 2277
Email: books@troubador.co.uk
Web: www.troubador.co.uk/matador

ISBN 978 1783064 830

British Library Cataloguing in Publication Data.
A catalogue record for this book is available from the British Library.

Typeset in Aldine by Troubador Publishing Ltd
Printed and bound in the UK by TJ International, Padstow, Cornwall

Matador is an imprint of Troubador Publishing Ltd

In memory of Daniel Gastón
a Saintly Jesuit

CONTENTS

PROLOGUE

Although GLIMPSES OF DEEP SPAIN is not autobiographical, some background will be given to make clear that this book is the result of observing and working with Spaniards over a life-time.

It all began sitting on the top deck of a smoke-filled bus to Fort Dunlop at 05.30 for the early shift, the cloth-capped workers silent as they dragged through their cigarette butts. The message was clear. This is not life, but DEATH IN LIFE.

Seven months later I was in Seville. In Life Street. The contrast with Birmingham could not have been greater. This was LIFE. The beginning of a love affair with Spain. And like all true love affairs it was to oscillate between idealization and exasperation in a country that is *salado,* and where the unexpected usually happens.

After two years in Seville in the *pensión* in Life Street and one in the *San Jerónimo* hotel in Barcelona, high up on Tibidabo, where the Catalans believe Satan offered Christ the world, there followed an interval at the Shah of Persia's University in Shiraz. An idyll in those days. An old Persian palace was rented with harem; premises only.

But Spain beckoned strongly, and it was back again with a life contract as *Catedrático* – Professor – of English Literature and Director of the English Department at the Jesuit University of Deusto, while living in a hill-top croft house in the Basque country. Sixteen years of it, with progressively more distinguished students, including a fair number of brilliant ones.

But eventually it palled with the realization that the life contract had become a life sentence; that life had become like a tram going round the same annual circuit.

Time to go, before it became Death in Life once more.

Then it was clink-clank down to Málaga in a car packed with pots and pans, plates, clothes, blankets and Shiel, our Scotch collie;

not to mention a Spanish wife. And no job; no prospects.

We bought a barren hill washed by a river with a ruined house near *La Viñuela*, where we planted two thousand avocado trees, palms, cypresses and an avenue of aspens, besides grape-fruit, oranges and lemons. Then in 1990 floods carried out to sea multitudinous avocado trees by the river. All re-planted.

That there were problems with workmen goes without saying. One day, when there was a violent thunder storm, I ordered a man who was collecting avocados to go home, especially as he was using a telescopic metal pole with a bag to reach the high fruit.

Later that black morning I saw a naked apparition high up a tree.

"You keep drier without clothes and I don't need the pole," the spectre shouted down.

Our assets were down to 3,000 *pesetas* that winter, some £15, and calling at the *Banco Atlántico* to withdraw 2,000 I quipped to the pretty bank teller "Not bankrupt."

"No, not yet!" she unsmilingly replied.

But the avocado trees did prosper in spite of all, though our principal enemy is the north wind, the dreaded 'terral', that periodically blows red-hot from the sierra in summer, and in winter with gale force blasts avocados off the trees.

So we are still here after thirty years, still struggling against the winds and the other vicissitudes of country life. Our experience has been in some ways similar to the sketch *EL PARAÍSO*. Though with many compensations. There are myriad birds: golden orioles, hoopoes, nightingales, turtle and collar doves, besides the more common swallows, finches, sparrows and blackbirds. One spring Mary of the Angels climbed a tree and brought down four moribund blackbird young, the mother having been decapitated by a kestrel. She installed them in the bathroom and fed them first milk with water, then chopped olives and later meal. They would call to us when they heard us in the corridor and perch on our shoulders when astride the throne. One later died in the night, but three prospered and flew away.

For some years we had half a dozen peacocks but their propensity to fly over the two-metre fences of the plantation and across the river into enemy territory, besides the infernal noise they made at night, meant that eventually we had to find a new owner for them.

A Welsh border collie was imported as Shiel's paramour, giving birth to five handsome pups, while five abandoned mongrels found a home here. (Just as well for them: in Málaga dog pound they were lassooing and gassing vagrants in big batches as late as 2005, which Auschwitz process was publicly denounced by a brave vet. The horrifying procedure was cheaper than lethal injection.)

With luck and much hard work we have survived against the odds. Moorish towers have been built on either flank of the rebuilt house, and besides a big four-by-four to take the avocados to the international wholesalers halfway up a mountain we have a couple of old convertibles, one of them a Rolls Royce.

Not that we are millionaires. We knew that life here would be life-in –the-raw, but that it meant independence, although with the concomitant risk of failure. Yet that independence is worth more than a highly paid 'job'.

Finca Dos Mundos is a demi-paradise, but 'civilization' is ever encroaching. A peasant picturesquely described this plantation as 'an island in a sea of diarrhoea.'

It may be that one day not far off this island will be left behind with a return to Seville, that city of dreams. Where it all began.

These sketches are the result of all those years' experience of Spain. Apart from Dr. LEAVIS IN SPAIN, which is 'reportaje', they are fiction. Even if in more than one instance they are close to 'reality'.

Finca Dos Mundos, Spring 2014

A SPANISH MOUNTAIN GOAT

Don Eusebio always had breakfast at half-past nine in the Bar *Bulevar* in the *Diagonal*. But this morning he was late and his friends ribbed him the moment he arrived.

"And where were you last night, then? Ha! ha! ha!" barked out Colonel Catalá, slapping him on the back and winking at the little group of friends crowding round, guffawing hoarsely. It was no use Eusebio protesting that he hadn't had an 'assignation'. It was too well known that he was irresistible to the fair sex.

"With such a beautiful wife, I don't understand it," laughed *don* Serafín, knocking back his *aguardiente*: sugar cane spirits, literally burning water.

"No really," smiled *don* Eusebio complacently, "I have a good reason for being late. Had to deal with bureaucratic nonsense about my excursion to *Sierra Tejeda*. I leave for Andalusia tomorrow; the hunting permit should have been ready before now. In spite of a stream of faxes to the Headquarters in Málaga, nothing had materialized. But a phone call to the *Jefe* has put matters right. My permit will be sent to the Hotel *Viñuela* to await my arrival."

"What did you expect?" jeered Catalá, "good for nothing, lazy Andalusians. What time did you phone them? This morning? Well, I'm amazed they weren't asleep, ha! ha!"

"And what are you going to be hunting that you need this portentous permit, Eusebio?" inquired *don* Serafín, the enormously fat *Jefe* of Customs in Barcelona, "lynx, wild boar? Or maybe tigers?"

He roared with laughter, laughter at his own joke, swivelling his eyes slyly round the animated faces of his friends.

Don Eusebio gulped his coffee and took a quick swig of *coñac*, showing off his dazzling white teeth with a confident smile. *Don* Eusebio really was extremely handsome: about six feet tall with a clear cut, clean shaven face. Dark, slightly sallow, his features were unexceptionable; perfectly straight nose, small neat ears, deep brown eyes and elegantly cropped black hair. He wore a fashionable darkish green overcoat that chilly December morning, beautifully pleated in a slightly unconventional way that did not hide his slim athletic build. "Mountain goats," he answered genially.

That was too much for his cronies. They bellowed with laughter until all the customers in the bar stared at them with good-natured curiosity.

"Goats?" howled the chief of police, *don* Manuel, always known as Manolo, who had a terrifying scar that stretched from his left ear to his chin, so black that his attempt to disguise it by growing a beard only made it more sinister. "You mean those with enormous horns?"

This set the gang off again. They began to dance round *don* Eusebio with two extended fore-fingers clamped on each side of their temples. Colonel Catalá called for another round of drinks, which they all sank at one gulp, clapping each other on the back, reiterating:

"Beware of those horns! Ha! ha! ha!"

Eusebio winked at the head of Customs, who between dancing round with his colossal bulk, fingers aloft, and intermittently throwing his head back to drain his glass, almost fell over in spluttering glee.

Don Serafín always had a story about his conquests. His tactic was to wait to be asked, by first asking the others. Whether or not they were mere figments of his imagination was never hinted at by his eager listeners. There is no doubt that *don* Serafín, who had thirteen children, eleven fat girls and two boys, was ardent in his desires. It was known that he had taken a young English girl to Madrid in his car, which he bragged about to his pals. He had had all kinds of expectations and corresponding plans. But what he didn't let on to his cronies on his return was that when they arrived in Madrid the sweet Oriel thanked him profusely with bewitching smiles, and then suddenly jumped out of *don* Serafín's car and slipped off amongst the crowds in the Puerta del Sol. Perhaps she had heard of *don* Serafín's prodigious reputation.

But today, when it came to his turn to divulge, *don* Serafín contented himself with a knowing giggle, and glancing at his watch announced that he must be going to the Customs. The Colonel ordered another round, but both Manolo and *don* Eusebio insisted that they must be going too.

"Good hunting," croaked the Colonel, "be sure to let us see those horns."

Amid further guffaws, they all went their separate ways.

Don Eusebio, who at thirty-seven was a good bit younger than his three friends, set off along the Diagonal – Barcelona's rather pompous principal street – with his springy walk. It was Thursday. He had a lot to clear up at his printing works, from which he made a small fortune, and then tomorrow he would leave for the south.

He smiled to himself at his good luck in life as he made his way to the printer's that bright if nippy morning, nodding to acquaintances and stopping to speak to friends. He couldn't get a refrain from last night's oratorio by Handel out of his head, humming and even singing 'Hail to the conquering hero!' as he passed the somewhat surprised Catalans hurrying back to work after el *desayuno*.

"Thank God I'm the boss, the owner" he said under his breath, eyeing the scurrying executives, subordinates and secretaries with a measure of pitying condescension. "After all, it was I who built up this business from nothing, even if my father-in-law did contribute something once he could see it was going to be a success."

"Conqueror I am!" he laughed out loud, thinking of his many clandestine liaisons. Girls gave him admiring glances and he couldn't help smiling to them, especially when one or two of his ex-conquests, now married, tripped elegantly by. But he stopped discreetly for *doña* Miren, a married woman with whom he was currently having an affair; though he was aware that their brief *tête-à-tête* in the street attracted quite some interest from the passers-by. As he moved on that chorus from Judas Maccabaeus became more and more insistent.

He and Elvira were distinguished aficionados of the Barcelona opera house, having their own box at the *Liceo,* where Elvira's beauty was much admired by all, from handsome young men to middle-aged merchants and industrialists, lawyers, diplomats and government officials, not to mention aged lechers. But Elvira's virtue was known to be unsullied. She was renowned for her demure deportment and unfailing devotion to *don* Eusebio. When it came to champagne cocktails at the *Liceo*, she would be surrounded by admirers, but *don* Eusebio could confidently chat to fellow businessmen or government Ministers without anxious glances in her direction.

Doña Elvira was only twenty-nine, that almost perfect age for a woman, when she is old enough to have dignity and presence, but young enough to have still the bloom and vitality of youth. She was just about middle height, slender, with well-shaped legs and small feet, a bosom that was neither skimpy nor excessively developed, with a gentle curve under her cashmere jerseys that one could only describe as maternal.

Yet Elvira had no children. This might account for the slightly melancholy, dreamy tinge to her oval olive face. But her dark brown eyes were sparkling besides intelligent, and her Grecian nose lent an aristocratic air to her perfectly sculptured head, which was set off by glistening black tresses through which small, shell-like ears could be glimpsed. Her lips were neither full nor mean, tending to be parted by her upper teeth which jutted slightly forward, giving her an enchantingly innocent look when she smiled.

Doña Elvira's clothes were almost invariably bought from *Loewe,* as were her shoes and handbags. Everything about her denoted refinement and good taste without over-statement. Like most Latin women, and especially Spaniards, she seemed to glide rather than walk, at a confident unhurried pace; quite unlike her north European counterparts with their lumbering, awkward gait.

Everyone referred to her as *doña* Elvira, in spite of her youth, and perhaps on account of being the younger daughter of the *Marqués de Nousma*. But there was not a trace of snobbery in *doña* Elvira's character, which was intelligently straightforward with just a touch of the mischievous in her eyes and smile occasionally. But only rarely.

Although she was vivacious even, at the champagne cocktail gatherings at the *Liceo* and musical soirées with her friends, when her face was in repose, unseen sometimes by others, her expression was of boredom. When *doña* Elvira sat alone in her beautifully furnished rooms of a morning or afternoon she would leaf through copies of fashionable magazines, occasionally pausing, with a sigh, to focus on certain society photographs, and then, leaving them aside, return to an absentminded perusal of *Madame Bovary* or some similar novel.

Eusebio was not much at home, working long hours at his flourishing printing works, breakfasting and lunching with friends or those he had to maintain connections with and returning to their house late in the afternoon for a siesta. It was only in the evenings that he and his wife were together. At weekends, in the hunting season, *don* Eusebio was invariably out both Saturday and Sunday on a shoot with other aficionados, even getting up before dawn to get the unfortunate birds in their line of fire while they were only half conscious in the twilight.

But tomorrow Eusebio was setting out on a lone expedition to Andalusia, for which he had bought a magnificent new Winchester repeater. Or it was to have been a lone journey until Elvira looked at him bewitchingly as he was taking coffee after dinner and politely suggested, not begged, that he might take her with him.

"After all, *cariño*, you'll be away all weekend, and I should miss you so."

"Splendid!" Eusebio agreed spontaneously. "I only hadn't asked you because I was afraid you'd be bored with waiting in the hotel all day."

"Oh, don't worry. I shall go for walks round the beautiful reservoir and take a couple of novels with me. What do you think about D. H. Lawrence's *The Rainbow* and *Women in Love?*"

"Never read them, *cariño*. As you know, I can't speak English. Never studied it. I think the French are so superior."

"How can you say that if you've never read any English novels?"

"Well, I've read one or two in translation. Charlotte Bronte's *Jane Eyre*. Romantic melodrama of the silliest kind. Apart from that, the adventures of Sherlock Holmes complete my acquaintance with that barbarous country's literature."

Doña Elvira smiled to herself and said nothing. She knew perfectly well that Eusebio's pursuits were not very highbrow, and loved him for his unsophisticated manliness. He went with her to the opera mostly to please her. But he did enjoy casting an eye over the 'talent' from their box, and also being seen by Barcelona high society. *Doña* Elvira and he were, after all, much observed by all. She for her beauty and he for his handsome figure in 'smoking'. And when he got bored, he would slip out of the box and spend an amusing half hour in the bar, perhaps setting up a discreet 'assignation', or swapping gossip with friends.

They had a good journey to *La Viñuela,* arriving at near midnight in *don* Eusebio's magnificent Volvo Estate. He was, and he knew it, a good and fast driver, tolerating no nonsense from other road users, and immensely proud of his huge car, which he had bought only recently. It impressed all his hunting friends, who tended to turn up in rather more mundane transport. But Eusebio never boasted about it: its superior quality was reflected unspoken in its owner.

After a light supper *don* Eusebio and *doña* Elvira retreated to their bedroom suite. Elvira spent a quarter of an hour or so on the balcony, admiring the stars and the reflection of the moon on the surface of the lake. It was about one before she retired to bed, where she read the first chapter of *Women in Love,* before putting out the light and going to sleep. To the gentle snoring of *don* Eusebio.

Eusebio was up at the crack of dawn, which was not very early at that time of year, and after a quick breakfast of coffee and *magdalenas* met the three fawning Nature Reserve wardens who were to lead him to his quarry. They set off in a *Land-Rover,* reaching the high ground of the sierra after some forty minutes negotiating progressively narrower tracks. Eusebio marvelled at the beauty of the craggy mountains in the early morning sunlight, the summit of Tejeda resplendent in its mantle of snow, and looked down over the cold mists swirling above the lower peaks, enveloping the lake beside which his wife was slumbering.

He had never felt happier in his life as he trudged up the wild hills dressed in his khaki camouflage hunting outfit, the oily smell of his new rifle titillating him like some intoxicating perfume. He couldn't get the refrain from Judas Maccabaeus out of his head, and to the astonishment of the three undersized Andalusian game-keepers, spontaneously burst into loud song: 'Hail the conquering

Hero comes'. His not altogether tuneful baritone echoed round the mountain tops, while his guides nudged one another and exchanged sly grins. Eusebio sang regardless, though whether he had noticed their reaction would not have mattered. He was indifferent to the comportment of these *catetos,* ignorant and simpleminded peasants. Hr did not realize that beneath their easy-going bonhomie was a cunning that belied their ignorance and even stupidity. They well knew how to humour rich caballeros from the north who came to Andalusia in search of hunting trophies. And they hid the contempt they felt for him and his like with ready smiles and much subservient flattery. They behaved, as they called it themselves, with *mucha astucia*: much craftiness. They knew that so far as mountain hunting was concerned *don* Eusebio was ignorant, like all the caballeros they had to humour. Gonzalo, José and Paco were accomplished actors with quite some years' experience, and that night they would recount the way they took him in to their friends in the bars of *Puente don Manuel.*

Doña Elvira had a leisurely breakfast in her suite at half-past ten, admiring the view of the lake from the balcony and then reading *Women in Love* for an hour or two before going down to the lobby. Which had a series of glass-topped tables with wicker chairs and a bar on the left beside the dining-room, imposingly divided from the lobby by heavy velvet curtains. *Doña* Elvira was dressed in her favourite dark green suit, with a wine-coloured silk scarf thrown loosely round her neck and over her shoulder. Over her breast she wore a gold brooch given to her by Eusebio. It consisted of two letters *E*, one inverted so that they were facing each other as it were, with the inscription, 'One and Indivisible'. Eusebio and Elvira. She wore her glossy black hair parted in the middle and drawn back in a chignon that morning.

She put her book on the table and beckoned to the waiter behind the bar, who came running obsequliously out, having observed her admiringly with beady eyes divided by a large beaked nose. *Doña* Elvira, who was aware of his glances, smiled at him with composure and ordered a dry Martini.

The lobby was almost deserted. There was only a German

couple drinking glasses of *manzanilla* at the bar. Elvira casually leafed through the pages of *Women in Love* as though she was looking for something, and then, with a sigh, laid the book down face upwards on the table. Eusebio wouldn't be back until after sunset, and with that passing thought she pensively sipped her aperitif.

Just then the main door by Reception banged loudly and a gangling young man of about twenty-two with blond hair that was neither long nor short made his way rather noisily and clumsily to the bar, knocking against one of the chairs set round *doña* Elvira's table. He apologized blushingly in English, and Elvira smiled at a pair of big blue eyes looking at her a little apprehensively, before striding to the bar and asking in atrocious Spanish for a pint of beer. He was very boyish in manner but his expression was serious, even thoughtful.

Doña Elvira had a slight cough – always had, though she didn't smoke. Still, she was in perfect health in fact. But it caused the young man to swivel round on his bar stool. Catching sight of her novel, he asked her if she was an admirer of Lawrence.

"It's the first time I am reading him," she replied smiling in English, "but you can see from the beginning of 'The Rainbow' that he is great writer."

Noting her two language errors, without being invited the English boy came over and sat down on one of the vacant chairs at Elvira's table. He at once engaged her in a discussion of the novelist's virtues, explaining that his name was Henry and that he was on his way to Ronda on his motorcycle. He told her he was to be interviewed for a job as an English language teacher at a private institute the next morning. If he got the job he would return to Barcelona for a couple of days to pay off his pensión and collect a few belongings. Then he would go south again and start a new life in Ronda.

Doña Elvira raised her eyebrows. "So you have been living in Barcelona?"

"For more than a year, but I can't stand it. I find it stifling. It's too big, too commercialized. My colleagues at the British Council Institute are not there because they are interested in Spain. They dress up in 'smoking' and go to the opera at the *Liceo* to drink champagne cocktails," he said with contempt. "And they live in Barcelona because it's convenient for France. Such a lot of petty little snobs as I've ever known."

Doña Elvira smiled thoughtfully, and asked "What then do you like about Spain?"

"The vast wide open spaces, the sense of being in a wild, exciting country where the unexpected always happens. If you keep away from the coasts, of course, which are infested with tourists. I travelled throughout Castile and Andalusia in my university vacations and I found it exhilarating. When I returned to England I had a sense of claustrophobia and couldn't wait to get back to Spain. But the only job on offer was at the British Institute in Barcelona. I haven't told them I'm leaving, in case I don't get the job in Ronda. But if I do, I'll be off like a shot."

"So you'll go back to Barcelona for a day or two?"

"Yes, as I told you, just to clear things up and resign from my British Council post. I hope to get my Christmas bonus. Not that it's worth much!"

"And how do you come to be in *La Viñuela*?"

"Well, I got lost, missed the turning for Ronda. You see, I haven't got a map."

Doña Elvira couldn't help laughing. "You won't get lost on the way north again, without a map, will you?"

Oh no. Although the last few hours will be in the dark. I follow the stars. Orion's Belt points due north, you know."

Doña Elvira observed him with a droll smile. "And what if it's cloudy?"

Henry now laughed good naturedly and shrugged his shoulders, turning up the palms of his hands as Spaniards do. *Doña* Elvira was quietly amused, telling him in turn that her husband was out hunting and wouldn't be back until evening.

"What about a walk round the lake?" the boy asked ingenuously.

"Well, just a short one," *Doña* Elvira replied with a sparkle in her eye, telling the barman to look after her book. 'Why not?' she thought to herself. 'It will relieve the tedium of waiting for Eusebio, and this boy is obviously innocent.'

Henry impatiently adapted to the sedate pace of *doña* Elvira, holding himself back like a constrained colt being broken in.

"What is that big bird flying so slowly with those huge flapping wings?"

"That's a heron" Henry proudly told her as the great bird emitted its harsh cry, flying like a black shadow over the water.

"And those are sea-gulls, aren't they, those birds flying in V-formation?"

"Yes," Henry acknowledged, watching as the gulls changed their order in a leisurely way, as though unsure which should have precedence. "They will have come in from the sea for food from the lake, little fish, no doubt. One creature devours another. That's nature's way, isn't it?"

Doña Elvira hadn't thought about that before, perhaps because she had always lived in a big city, though the sea bit remorselessly at the strands of Barcelona, and had done all her life.

Suddenly *doña* Elvira started. A fox ran across the track just in front of them that windy morning, his brush magnificently gleaming in the intermittent sunlight that forced a passage through the contorted clouds.

"Cunning fellow" said Henry, "he'll be tracking his prey."

Then without warning a heavy shower descended, and they hurried back to the hotel.

Doña Elvira invited the boy to join her for lunch, saying she must run upstairs to change her damp clothes. Henry readily accepted, being an impoverished language teacher and having intended to make do with a stale cheese sandwich in the pannier of his motorcycle on the road to Ronda.

Doña Elvira reappeared in a scarlet woollen dress with a gold band necklace from which an emerald dangled on a plaited chain. The outfit showed off her slender form exquisitely. Henry looked startled but *doña* Elvira's elegant composure reassured him as they walked into the airy dining-room with French windows overlooking the lake. Henry looked even more startled when the beaky-nosed waiter, with a contemptuous glance at his unkempt clothes, handed him a menu. The price of one dish was as much as Henry earned in a week and he scanned the pages nervously trying to find something cheap. *Doña* Elvira laughed, sensing his discomfiture.

"Let me order for you, may I? Why don't we both have the same?"

"That would be wonderful" agreed Henry gratefully, knocking over a glass as he returned the menu to the supercilious waiter.

"We'll begin with prawn and avocado cocktail" said *doña* Elvira languidly, "then sword-fish with miniature onions and tomatoes, to be followed by roast quail with mushrooms."

"And to drink, *señora*?"

"You may bring us half a bottle of *Federico Paternina Banda Dorada* with the fish, and a half bottle of *Marqués del Riscal* to go with the quail. Oh, and a bottle of mineral water."

Henry gasped.

"Thank you, *señora*" said Beaky unctuously, recovering the multi-page menu enclosed in a leather cover. He hovered a moment, paused, and then said, abasing himself almost on one knee, riveting those beady eyes on *doña* Elvira.

"Ahem…if I may say so, *señora, ¡usted es guapísima! ¡guapísima!* You are very beautiful! Very, very beautiful!" *Doña* Elvira smiled insouciantly, thanking the waiter for his compliment, and laughing, turned to Henry.

"You see I have an admirer! Who would have thought it in this wilderness?"

"He's not the only one" rejoined Henry gallantly, but in all sincerity. He had never seen such a beautiful woman, though wisely, perhaps, he didn't say that.

Two hours later, when lunch was over, they both felt animated by the food, the wine and their cheerful conversation. Henry admitted he had no fixed girlfriend and like so many other drifters in Spain, no fixed aim in life other that 'to write a novel'. That was why he wanted to live in the wilds of Andalusia, he added rather incongruously.

After a somewhat pregnant pause Henry said sadly, "Well, I must be off."

"Just a moment," *doña* Elvira replied, a trifle breathlessly, "I'll get you a map. My husband has two or three and I think he has left one in our sitting-room."

She got up to go.

"I'll come up with you to save you coming down again," said Henry guilelessly, and so found himself in the salón of *doña* Elvira's suite. She gave him the map and then rummaged in the bedroom for a moment, returning with Eusebio's check scarf, which she had bought at *Loewe* for his Saint's Day.

"I can't have you riding off on your motorcycle in just that flimsy shirt in this wintry weather."

She put the scarf round Henry's neck, stood back and looked into those big blue eyes with the suspicion of a smile on her lips. And before either of them knew what had happened they were in each other's arms. Elvira felt a stirring in his loins as she embraced and kissed him deeply. They were both overwhelmed by sudden fervent desire that made them almost swoon.

Eusebio and the three wardens had had a long, hard slog up the craggy face of the mountain, so far without spotting their prey. They had come across timid rabbits, crazy hares, slinking foxes and grunting wild boars, but Eusebio would have none of them. He was possessed with the notion of returning to Barcelona with one and one only trophy: the horned head of that elusive mountain goat to adorn the space he had cleared above the huge fire-place in the study of his magnificent house in *Pedralbes*, that leafy enclave of the upper class high above the town centre.

Eusebio called it his study, but in fact it was more of a business office, though there was a big teak desk and a bookcase adorned with a set of encyclopaedias bound in gilt, but never opened. Like many Spaniards, Eusebio was not given to reading.

"I don't read books" he would boast in jest to his friends, "I make them."

It was here, in his den, that Eusebio entertained his clients and close friends in large leather armchairs, to his unparalleled selection of Scotch whiskies packed in the glass-fronted cupboard.

Eusebio was what you would call a man's man, intelligent but uncomplicated – except in so far as 'assignations' went. He had clear ideas of what he wanted, and everything about him was large and generous. And what he wanted now was to have his friends the Colonel, *don* Serafín and Manolo, the police chief with the terrifying scar, admire his trophy in the comfort and conviviality of that study.

Eusebio admired his wife immensely. He knew she was devoted to him, and she was a great embellishment to his life. She was admired by the high society of Barcelona not only for her astounding beauty but as an *aficionada* of the arts. She played the piano exquisitely, sang superbly, and had had more than one exhibition of her watercolours favourably reviewed in the Catalan press.

When she appeared in her box at the *opera* – and she was one of those few who went to hear the music – she was the idol of all for her queenly deportment. *Doña* Elvira would not have been a woman if she had not sensed that universal admiration with pleasure; but she had an endearing simplicity that banished any suspicion of vanity or pretentiousness.

Eusebio thought of her now as he looked down towards the *Viñuela* hotel and the lake, which were shrouded in a great bank of low cloud, like an impenetrable mist.

"*¡Don* Eusebio! Look up there" whispered Gonzalo, catching at his arm. There, standing on a crag outlined against the sky was a magnificent mountain goat, its long curved horns like two burnished scimitars in the evening sunlight. Aware of the hunters, two alert eyes were fixed on them.

"I must have that!" hissed Eusebio, catching his breath.

"Come, give me your rifle, *don* Eusebio" urged Gonzalo sharply; he positioned the Winchester over a smooth rock, taking a quick sighting, then motioned to Eusebio to get behind it. Eusebio aligned the crossed wires of the telescopic sight on the goat's heart and, holding his breath, fired. The noble animal remained silhouetted for an instant against the sky, so that Eusebio feared he had missed. But then it crumpled suddenly, tumbled down the crag, and lay with its legs thrashing contorted in the air.

"My God!" Eusebio called out, "it's mine! The head won't be damaged will it? Shall I have to put another bullet into it?" He ran forwards and upwards, his rifle at the ready, followed by the gamekeepers.

"All is well" shouted Paco, having overtaken Eusebio, "it is stone dead."

"And there are no marks on the head, *don* Eusebio, no marks at all!" exulted José.

"You are a marksman, and no mistake, sir!" wheedled Gonzalo, "only one shot, and that a dead shot!"

"A marksman!" echoed José gleefully.

Eusebio laughed modestly, clapping Gonzalo on the back.

"It's you who aligned the rifle, Gonzalo. I owe it to you."

Veritably, they had had a long hard day and the wardens had been beginning to fear they would not track the elusive creature. But now they were all joyous. To celebrate, Gonzalo produced a large *porra*, a leathern bottle of rich red wine, offering it first to *don* Eusebio, who squirted a plentiful supply down his gullet before handing it round to the assistant huntsmen, or so he thought of them.

It was almost dark now, and Gonzalo swung the dead animal over his shoulders as they set off on the journey down the mountainside. They had to go slowly, as it was more onerous than the long drag up, the escarpment being covered in treacherous loose stones. It took them more than an hour to regain the vestiges of a track, but Eusebio was in irrepressibly high spirits, once again breaking into the heroic refrain from Judas Maccabaeus, his raucous voice reverberating round the rocks. The three game wardens chuckled as they made their way down in the starlight until they got below the level of the clouds. In the silent blackness Eusebio got out his whisky flask, pressing the three to take a swig. But they refused, joking that they would tumble down the mountainside: they were not accustomed to such strong drink. So Eusebio drained the flask himself. Oh how marvellous he felt! And how he would enjoy showing off his prize to Elvira.

It was also getting dark when *doña* Elvira saw Henry off on his motorcycle. She kissed him goodbye with tears in her eyes, but warned him that it would be impossible for them to meet in Barcelona when he returned to pay off his pensión and collect a few belongings on Monday evening. She was sure, from what he had told her, that he would get the job in Ronda.

When he rode noisily away, the last rays of the sun gilding his young blond head, Eusebio's scarf half shrouding his face to keep off the cold, she stood thoughtfully gazing after him long after he was out of sight. Her lover, she reflected with some not unamused astonishment. The only one she had ever had. And yet she had thought of him as much as a son when she had put her hand on his tousled hair in the twilight once he had mounted his motorcycle. She had given way to a sudden rush of passion. She, Elvira, the paragon of good breeding and self-control. But she had no feeling of remorse.

Henry would be back in Barcelona the day after tomorrow and then gone to the south and out of her life for ever. On no account would she consent to see him in her home town. She knew that would destroy the serenity of her perfectly ordered life. A wry smile emerged spontaneously when she reflected that Eusebio had had countless affairs. After the first she had always accepted them as inevitable. And she knew that they meant nothing serious to him, that they were merely his 'recreation' and that they tickled his vanity. She had never reproached Eusebio, or even said anything about these affairs. She affected to know nothing, and Eusebio in his simple way took that for a fact, as the truth.

Doña Elvira began to shiver slightly, suddenly realizing that she was cold from standing so still in the dark. She went back to the hotel, and was glad to see that the maid had tidied the rooms and turned down the bed. She slowly undressed and having put on her embroidered cotton nightie, exhausted, she lay down and soon fell asleep.

Eusebio was late in returning. She heard the groaning of the *Land-Rover* below and the '*hasta mañana*' of the game-keepers, but when Eusebio quietly opened the bedroom door, she feigned sleep. She heard him humming cheerfully and no doubt a little tipsily in the *salón,* and then the door banged and she knew that he had gone downstairs to have supper.

In the morning they had an early breakfast at the bar, interrupted by the obsequious appearance of the game-keepers, who brought a sack containing the by now severed head of the goat, which they deposited on the tiled floor, the long horns protuberant, and a little blood oozing out of the sack. Though it had, they assured Eusebio, been sterilized.

Doña Elvira observed it with distaste and pity, but she managed to dissimulate her feelings and congratulate her jubilant husband.

"He's a great hunter. A crack shot!" insisted Gonzalo, to a chorus of applause from the two assistant game-keepers.

Meanwhile two porters brought down the elegant suitcases and *don* Eusebio tipped them generously from a large roll of bank-notes, which did not escape the attention of the game-keepers: Gonzalo, José and Paco. This was the important moment. They busied themselves with a great show of diligence loading the sack into the back of the estate car and handing his rifle to *don* Eusebio, not omitting to open the passenger door with unabashed servility for *doña* Elvira. The game-keepers then congregated round the driver's door, assuring *don* Eusebio that they wished him and his *señora* a very safe and good journey, and that they would not forget his outstanding hunting skill and his friendship. "*Muy sinceramente*" they added; very sincerely.

Don Eusebio discreetly slipped them an enormous tip, and with a joyful *hasta la vista, don* Eusebio and *doña* Elvira took the road for the north, stopping at a *Parador* for lunch on the way.

"I must have left the map in the hotel suite" laughed Eusebio, "and I can't find my check scarf anywhere. I wonder if the porters took them."

Nevertheless they had a good journey, reaching their romantic old house in *Pedralbes* in the late evening. The lights were glowing through the slats of the green wooden shutters casting welcoming shadows on the lawn and amongst the pines and cypresses in the garden. Pepita opened the door wide, embracing *doña* Elvira as though they had been away for months. She curtsied to *don* Eusebio, flashing him a smile from her dark eyes and pale lips.

"Celestino has got the dinner ready, and I have made sure that your bedroom is warm" she laughed. Pepita always did laugh whenever she said anything.

Eusebio was as eager as a schoolboy to show off his hunting trophy to his cronies in the Bar *Bulevar* next morning, leaving home early to be sure of finding a parking space for the *Volvo* estate nearby. He even took his new Winchester too. "That'll impress them," he said to himself as he parked, then called a waiter from the *Bulevar* to carry the sack into the bar.

By the time he came back the terrible trio had arrived and were already chaffing one another about last night's exploits.

"*¡Hola* Eusebio! *¿Qué tal, hombre?*" How are you, man? They crowded round him with much back slapping and embracing. And then they saw it.

"For the love of God!" exclaimed the Colonel. "But what a marvel! And you shot it yourself?"

"Magnificent!" ejaculated Serafín, beaming from his fat jowls. "Extraordinary!" enthused Manolo, the Chief of Police, bending down and running his hands over the beautiful horns. "How did you do it?"

"Well, it wasn't very easy" Eusebio explained, "it was only after a long arduous climb up the mountain that I saw it in the twilight. I drew a bead on it at once and got it clean through the heart first time. One shot only. Though my Winchester is a repeater, see?"

"Good God, man, what a beauty!" said the Colonel, taking the rifle and examining the mechanism. "And a telescopic sight and all! You're a lucky man, Eusebio, a lucky man!"

And the three raised their glasses of *aguardiente.*

"To your good luck, Eusebio!"

"May your luck continue, man!"

"Well I'm damned! What a hunter!"

The owner of the *Bulevar* now put up a round of drinks on the house, and the waiters and even the customers called out "*¡mucha suerte, don* Eusebio!" Very good luck.

Don Eusebio modestly acknowledged their good wishes, called for a round of drinks for all and proudly collected his Winchester from the Colonel's hands. The owner ordered a waiter to carry the sack with his trophy.

"I must be off now, amigos. I've got to get the head mounted on a plaque before I go to the printer's. *¡Muchísimas gracias* for your good wishes, *amigos!* Very many thanks, my friends!"

When he reached the door the Colonel called out "Beware of those horns! Ha! Ha! Ha!"

And to a hearty round of guffaws, with a "See you this evening" Eusebio made off to the Volvo and the taxidermist.

"I want it mounted today" he told the artisan. And having

selected the wood he wanted and given detailed instructions as to how it was to be done, he said he would send Celestino to collect it in the late afternoon.

In the afternoon, because that evening there was a gala event at the *Liceo*. No less than Verdi's *Othello,* with Plácido Domingo. Elvira had bought a new outfit and had spent half an afternoon in this pose and that before the huge *salón* mirror.

"Mirror, mirror, on the wall" she intoned with a smile. But there wasn't much doubt who would be the most beautiful woman at the *Liceo*.

Celestino managed to fix the plaque with the goat's head above the vast stone fire-place just before it was time for *don* Eusebio and *doña* Elvira to leave for the opera. Eusebio had been fidgeting impatiently and getting in Celestino's way, but the old man ignored his meddling and with good humour turned to him for a moment.

"*Don* Eusebio, you did the great thing in hunting the animal. Allow me to carry on with the menial work, the collocation of your triumph. And hadn't you better get going for the *Liceo*?"

Celestino had been with *don* Eusebio and his wife for many years, and well knew how to handle and to humour his master, as most long-serving servants do.

Their arrival at the opera was perfectly timed. The First Act had ended and the audience was almost all seated after the interval. The orchestra was tuning up when *doña* Elvira, resplendent in a black silk dress studded with gold sequins, five strings of exquisite pearls round her slender neck, and a dazzling diamond tiara adorning her queenly head entered her box and stood for some moments at its balcony. A spontaneous cheer arose from several hundred male throats and *doña* Elvira fluttered her ivory fan in acknowledgement. The curtains rose, and *don* Eusebio, standing just behind her and handsome in his 'smoking', smiled at his good fortune.

Elivra's parents, the *Marqués* and *Marquesa,* had joined their daughter and son-in-law in the box, which had been in the name of the *Marqués* for more than fifty years. They formed a truly convivial small family gathering. The orchestra played perfectly, the action of the opera was gripping, and of course Plácido Domingo's performance was magnificent.

At the end of the next Act, as the lights went up and *doña* Elvira leaned over the balcony to exchange greetings with friends, a figure in the front stalls stood up and waved his arms wildly, gesticulating at *doña* Elvira herself, and shouted something of which the only audible words were "Elvira" and "Ronda". This untoward behaviour caused quite a commotion, astonished faces turning from that person to *doña* Elvira, necks craning from the other boxes to see what it was all about. And still the foreigner gesticulated and shouted. A mirthful murmur arose as the men got up to go to the bar. *Doña* Elvira realized with horror that it was Henry, his flushed face radiant, and his two young companions grinning broadly. Elvira blushed a deep crimson, hastily waving her fan in a somewhat peremptory manner and withdrawing to the back of the box.

Don Eusebio had already made off to the bar the instant the Act ended. But the *Marqués*, who had observed the incident, looked troubled.

"Elvira, my dear, who is that individual who waved to you as though he was drunk?"

For once *doña* Elvira was discomfited and ill at ease, but she managed to say, quite casually as it were

"I think, if I am not mistaken, he is an art student who came to one of my exhibitions and had a brief chat with me."

"Oh, an arty fellow" chuckled the *Marqués*, "That explains everything. Bound to be drunk I'll warrant."

But he wondered. The *Marquesa* looked pensively at her daughter, yet decided to say nothing.

What had happened was that Henry had met a couple of his friends from the British Council Institute and invited them to farewell drinks. He had indeed landed the job in Ronda – what he had been trying to communicate to Elvira – and he and his pals had got very drunk to celebrate. His erstwhile colleagues had persuaded him to join them for champagne cocktails and all at the *Liceo* for a last fling before he left for Ronda next morning. Although Henry despised what he called 'the opera antics' he had been too merry to refuse.

Meanwhile, *don* Eusebio had been enjoying a solitary whisky in the bar when the Colonel, Serafín and Manolo came boisterously over to where he stood with the usual backslapping and ribald repartee.

"By the way, old boy, who was that young man waving and shouting drunkenly at your wife like a madman from the front stalls?" giggled *don* Serafín.

"Young man? Waving to my wife?" *don* Eusebio asked, flabbergasted. "You must be mistaken. She doesn't know any young men of that sort."

The three winked at each other, swallowed their whiskies, and let the matter drop.

"Incidentally…" Serafín began, but was interrupted by the Colonel who said softly but sharply "I say! There he is."

"There is who?" asked *don* Eusebio.

"The drunken young man who was gesticulating at your wife" the Colonel replied. "Look, over there in the corner with a pair of drunken pals by the look of it. The tall one with blond hair."

Don Eusebio followed his gaze, and shrugged indifferently.

"Impossible" he said casually, "she couldn't know anyone like that."

The three young men had got hold of a bottle of champagne, and the tall blond fellow was shaking it violently. Suddenly the cork exploded, narrowly missing a woolly-haired Professor of philosophy. Amid the commotion, with inane laughter the youth began spraying the opera aficionados in their elegant 'smoking'. His companions guffawed like louts of the Oxford Bullingdon club, before the ushers grabbed them by the scruff of the neck and frog-marched them to the exit. The tall blond one turned for a moment at the door to make an obscene gesture at the opera buffs, apoplectic in their reaction. And as he turned Eusebio saw, unmistakably, his own check scarf hanging out of the lout's pocket.

"It's him, of course it's him" expostulated the Colonel, buttonholing the disconcerted Eusebio. "And wasn't that your scarf?"

"I don't believe it!" Eusebio spluttered, "it's impossible!"

The drunken English youths had by this time been sent packing into the street, and the bell for the beginning of the last Act had sounded.

"Come on, let's get back" gurgled Manolo, knocking back his third whisky.

"At least we've had a bit of comic opera in the interval" sniggered *don* Serafín. Laughing he turned to Eusebio and said

"Why bother yourself about such a whipper-snapper?" Observing Eusebio's perplexed expression he clapped him on the back, adding, "I'm sure there's a perfectly innocent explanation, old boy."

"Let's go" growled the Colonel with a twinkle in his eye, "forget it Eusebio. It's nothing. Time to join the ladies."

But Eusebio stood there dumbfounded, gulping whisky, and muttering "My own scarf, dammit! Who would believe it?"

"What's that?" *don* Serafín asked quizzically as he turned to join his squaw in the audience. "Did you say something, amigo?"

"Look alive, man!" the Colonel barked.

Yet Eusebio obstinately remained rooted to the bar as his cronies noisily burst through the doors of the auditorium. Eusebio could hear them guffawing, and he was sure he caught the stage-whispered

"It's the horns, old fruit! What did I tell you!"

The audience hissed as our heroes stumbled unsteadily to their seats, *don* Serafín's squaw cackling

"You naughty boy! How many whiskies have you had?"

But Manolo's 'dried up frump' as he affectionately called her, scolded that merry Chief of Police until their neighbours in the audience silenced her.

The *opera* was reaching its climax when Eusebio angrily barged into his box. As *Othello* was about to strangle the innocent *Desdemona*, amid gasps of horror from the elegant ladies of Barcelona, Eusebio abruptly ordered the disconcerted *doña* Elvira to leave.

The *Marqués* remonstrated with him and the *Marquesa* managed to plant a kiss on *Elvira's* velvet cheek, whispering "*No te preocupes, cariño.* Don't worry, darling. I'm sure there's nothing to it."

But Eusebio was obdurate. He opened the passenger door of his Volvo and roughly bundled *doña* Elvira inside. They drove to *Pedralbes* in silence.

It wasn't until they were in the *salón*, having dispatched the surprised Pepita, that *don* Eusebio gave vent to his feelings.

"What's the meaning of this, Elvira?" he demanded.

"The meaning of what, may I ask?" *doña* Elvira replied, inwardly uneasy but managing to appear calm and collected, as though she were offended.

"You know perfectly well" snarled Eusebio, raising his voice now. "You've made me the laughing stock of Barcelona society, that's what you've done."

"I don't know what you're talking about" Elvira persisted, with a note of scorn in her voice.

"Oh you don't, don't you. Well perhaps you'd explain why that drunken lout of an Englishman stood up shouting and waving to you like a madman from the front stalls. Don't deny it. The *Marqués* has told me all about it, and my friends from the *Bulevar* saw it too."

"What should I know!" Elvira sneered, "just because a drunk waves to me, it doesn't mean anything."

Don Eusebio and *doña* Elvira had never had a row like this before. Eusebio was maddened by her contemptuous responses. He now quite lost his temper.

"Then maybe you'd explain, if you'd be so kind, why I couldn't find my scarf and my map at the hotel."

Elvira blanched momentarily, but responded with apparent equanimity: "Why should I know why you couldn't find them. You're always losing things because you're so careless. You complain to me that the pair of one of your socks is missing, so that you have to wear one blue and one brown. Is that my fault? Is it?"

Doña Elvira was not without a little cunning, and hoped she could side-track her enraged husband in this way. But then came the thunderbolt.

"I'll tell you why you should know. Because you gave my scarf to that young rascal. You did, didn't you?"

"I know nothing about your silly scarf. Why don't you buy another and stop all this nonsense?"

"Nonsense! Nonsense is it?"

Don Eusebio advanced on *doña* Elvira, who stood beside the great gilt mirror near the French window. Thrusting his handsome face now contorted with rage and bewilderment close to her he bellowed like a stricken bull: "My scarf was hanging from that drunken bastard's pocket in the *Liceo* Bar. Eh! The Colonel saw it. So did Serafín and Manolo. You'd better account for it and do it quickly!"

Beside himself, Eusebio raised his fist to strike *doña* Elvira, who was overcome with fear and dizziness. Just in time she slipped into an armchair. But *don* Eusebio's fist, whether intentionally or not, smashed full onto the great mirror, which shattered into hundreds of shards. His hand was bleeding, but only superficially cut. He bound it in his handkerchief, horrified at his violent impulse, and got down on his knees beside *doña* Elvira's chair.

"Forgive me Elvira, *cariño"* he begged. "Are you alright, my dear?"

Elvira was trembling a little but she was able to disguise it and assured Eusebio that she was perfectly all right. Eusebio now got up, and his anger returned.

"Say it isn't true, Elvira!" he screamed.

"What isn't true, Eusebio? Elvira persisted with maddening tenacity.

"That you… that you… and that boy… He was in *Viñuela,* wasn't he? Didn't he shout something about Ronda? Isn't Ronda close by?"

"I refuse to be cross-examined in this way," *doña* Elvira replied coldly.

"Elvira, *cariño,* I must know! What will they all be thinking, those who were at the *Liceo*? What about my friends? How can I face them? You must help me, I beg you!"

"Nobody knows anything about nothing," *doña* Elvira answered, somewhat mollified by his supplicatory attitude. "Why do you torture yourself about tricks of your imagination?"

"But Elvira, my scarf! My check scarf! How is it that it was hanging out of that drunken lout's pocket?"

"Don't call…" Elvira broke off. "I can't tell you, Eusebio. No doubt he bought it himself."

"But you bought it for my saint's day! You don't think a penniless youth would be shopping there, do you? In *Loewe*! Do you? Oh, Elvira!"

Eusebio let out a howl like a wounded animal, and for the first time Elvira glanced at him with utter contempt. She had never seen

Eusebio like this. But once he saw her withering look he roared: "Damn you, woman! You've ruined my name. You've made me a figure of ridicule."

"That's what concerns you, Eusebio" she replied with a little smile, "it isn't me you are concerned about but your name. Just your name. I am merely an ornament, an appendage to your success."

It was that smile. Eusebio could stand no more. With something between a snort and a whimper he charged into his study, slamming the door.

It was now about midnight and the wind had got up, rattling the slatted shutters and moaning eerily. He could hear it as though soul-searching the cypresses outside the study windows. *Don* Eusebio poured himself a large whisky, his hand trembling, drowned it in water and drank it rapidly. Pacing up and down he went over and over *doña* Elvira's words.

"That damned woman is so self-possessed" he muttered. "What am I to make of it? That lout's waving to her in public! And shouting! My scarf! The *Marques's* reaction!"

He poured another whisky, without water this time. The fiery glow in his guts both reassured and inflamed him. He glanced at his Winchester, leaning against the wall in the chimney corner.

"What about the Colonel, what about Serafín, and Manolo? Do they know something? No, they couldn't know anything in the *Bulevar* this morning. How could they? It's just their joshing. They do it every day. But at the *Liceo* Bar? What did they blurt out as they barged into the auditorium? Of course they were half drunk.

What was it…? Something like 'It's those horns!' Eusebio felt the blood rush to his head. The back of his neck burnt unbearably. He looked up at the goat's head above the chimney-piece.

"Damn you! Damn you! Damn you! he growled, shaking violently his bandaged fist at it.

Then he remembered Serafín's words. 'Why bother yourself about a whippersnapper!' Didn't he say he was sure there was an innocent explanation?

"And yet, the scarf! But perhaps that brat had bought an identical one himself. Life is full of extraordinary coincidences. It's incredible that he should have been in *Viñuela*. How could he?"

24

But there was to be no peace of mind for *don* Eusebio. The more he rehearsed these accursed hypotheses, the less he could come to any comforting conclusion. Distraught, he gulped yet another whisky. "And even if there is an innocent explanation, there will always be suspicion. How will I ever live it down?"

Doña Elvira opened the *Mallorquínas* – those slatted doors – and stepped onto the balcony of the *salón.* The wind was seething in the pines, and the cypresses bent before it ominously. She looked up beyond them at Orion's Belt, boldly bright in the troubled sky. Henry's guide! She smiled sadly. Would he be sleeping now in his *pensión* in *Muntaner*? What a head he would have! But his youth would shrug if off and he would be sure to make an early start for Ronda in the morning.

It was true. She did think of him as son and lover. Her maternal instinct fretted for his future. He had all the carelessness of youth, which ignores reality. *¡Oh Dios mío!* She was suddenly overcome with longing, the aching anguish of a lover…

And then she heard a report. A sharp crack that must have come from the study. She ran to it, frantically pushed the door, which would not yield. Something obstructed it. She shoved with all her strength and gradually it opened wide enough to allow her to get through. It was obstructed by Eusebio's body, which lay on the floor. There was a small hole in his head from which blood oozed. He was completely still. His Winchester repeater lay by his side. One shot only. And that a dead shot.

The goat's head with its long curved horns seemed to be grinning from its plinth above the chimney-piece.

EPILOGUE
Spanish Proverb

Better to be a cuckold, no one knowing; than to be thought a cuckold, not being one.

Note: The Spanish for goat is *cabra;* and for cuckold is *cabrón.*

25

EL POLLETON

Isaías didn't particularly like working. He was foreman of the Town Hall plumbers in the village of *El Trujillo* and cut quite a fine figure as boss of the little troupe of workers. He never did any manual labour himself, preferring to stand still for hours at a time supervising the lowly peasants he employed, occasionally impressing them by clamping shut one nostril of his outsize aquiline nose with a finger and discharging the contents of the other to a distance of some three metres.

However the time came when the interminable delays in his attending to blocked pipes or the setting up of new water supplies to the outlying hamlets resulted in a rather pompous letter from the Town Hall. It was addressed to *señor don* Isaías Zapatero: they deliberately set out to ridicule him by using the equivalent of Isaías Zapatero Esquire on account of his somewhat gentlemanly approach to work. And of course it advised him that his service as foreman of plumbers was no longer required. Nevertheless there was a vacancy for a sanitary officer (that is to say a dustman) with the local refuse collection gang, and any application from him, complete with updated curriculum vitae, would be sympathetically considered.

Don Isaías was not especially concerned, in spite of the insulting tone, chucking the letter into the local refuse bin which they could collect for themselves.

It was about ten in the morning of an Andalusian summer day, and as was his custom Isaías dragged his bed onto the north-facing balcony and prolonged his slumbers there until midday.

Isaías had a small and ancient van – most rural labourers had to content themselves with a 125 c.c. 'moto' at best – and at two o'clock he regularly got into it and drove to his sister's house, although it was only a few hundred yards up the country road. There, in her cramped cottage, he would get his lunch with the family, which included his nephew who had done some two years' time for robbery. Isaías Zapatero did contribute leeks or tomatoes from the little garden at the back of his house, on the north side, that is. And he did make himself useful by holding down the pig when it came to slaughter time, with a cruel grin cutting its throat while it squealed and roared. His sister, dressed in widow's black weeds, a wizened figure though not much older than him, with an old woman's spindly legs, known to some locals as 'the witch', had cauldrons of steaming water to hand, and the dismemberment of the porker proceeded apace, the blood being carefully siphoned off to make black pudding.

But these were about all the contributions Isaías made to his sister's household of impoverished peasants, and they began to resent his somewhat lordly assumption of his rights to free meals. Inevitably, one day they quarrelled, and advising them that it was all the same to him whether he came or not, Isaías's visits terminated. He left in carefully concealed high dudgeon, having that pride of some Spaniards that is no more than obstinacy and self-regard.

Yet Isaías was left with a problem. Although he was forty-five, he had no wife. And like innumerable peasants in the district he was called *El polleton:* a bachelor without intention or inclination to get married. Isaías distrusted women, suspecting that all they wanted was to inveigle themselves into a man's house and get hold of his money and possessions. He didn't mind eyeing up pretty girls; but in the country there were practically none anyway, most of them having migrated to the towns with their families where they could earn much more and where there were more eligible young men. The women left behind were mostly either old crones, uncouth country wenches, or the half-wit products of incestuous encounters like *La Loca,* the crazy one, who lived nearby.

So the problem was, how was Isaías to get his meals? Like the typical Spanish male, Isaías would not deign to cook or do kitchen work. And like many others, he took a perverse pride in being unable to fry an egg. To demean himself in that way would be to put himself on a level with women. He well knew the Spanish proverb *"La mujer y la sardine, a la cocina."* Women and sardines, to the kitchen.

The upshot of it was that he began going every day to a little wayside bar-cum-restaurant much used by local lorry drivers and peasants from round about. Isaías knew them and they knew him, although he regarded himself as a cut above them. Hadn't he been foreman, after all, hadn't he got his own quite substantial little house, and what's more, his own transport? Besides, he could read, which was more than half of that riff-raff could do. He made a point of sitting on the small terrace at the front of the house that was next to the road with a book in his hands, even if most of the text was illustrated with pictures of one kind or another.

When Isaías had been coming for some time to the Bar *Picasso*, the name of the lorry driver who owned it, some peasant eyebrows and speculations were raised. One day one of the peasants, Pepe González, nudging his neighbours and exchanging winks with the owner, slyly asked "Had a little disagreement with María have you, eh? How is it you don't go to your sister's for lunch every day as you used to?"

"Why don't you mind your own business?" Isaías answered haughtily, wiping up the remains of his bean stew with a crust of bread.

"There's no need to take offence" retorted Pepe, a typically diminutive Andalusian peasant with sandals home-made from old tyres held in place by string that wound round his ankles and stretched between his big toes.

"And there's no need to give offence either" snarled Isaías, now fixing his beady eyes on one after another of the smirking company.

Well, after that no questions were asked for a week or two, though Isaías could feel eyes fixed on him curiously as he sat at a little table apart with his blood pudding, fried chicken or sprats, and a bottle of *vino tinto* mixed with *gaseosa*, sweetish fizzy water.

Then one day Pepe's cousin Paco turned to Isaías during the usually raucous conversation and asked "How did you ever get that strange name, Isaías? And how is it you're not married? You must be well over forty, aren't you?"

"What's it got to do with you?" Isaías answered abruptly. "Do you find married life so wonderful?"

Now it was well known to all that Paco's wife was a flirt and had gone off with a bus driver for a couple of weeks, so this reply unleashed a whole lot of rather ugly guffaws. Paco ground his teeth in embarrassment, but Isaías, sensing his victory, couldn't resist adding spitefully

"That's shut you up, anyway!"

But the day after, when Isaías entered the ramshackle pub there was ribald laughter. And he knew that it was directed at him as he sat down at his table, as usual, in the corner by the window. He was continually aware of sniggers and sidelong glances at him, particularly from Paco's table, with his cousin and two cronies. But Isaías decided to ignore them, ate his paella in his usual noisy way, turning over, nonchalantly as it were, the pages of El Sur newspaper taken by the bar owner.

When he was driving back to his house, dawdling along in his little van he began to reflect on his life. "I enjoy it" he said to himself, "and I don't need contact with anyone. But I don't like those sniggers in that bar. Maybe I'll go somewhere else. I could go to Puente don Manuel or to Trapiche. But both places are quite far away. I can just scrape by on the unemployment money I get, but if I start spending a lot on petrol…. Anyway, it would be cowardly to desert the Picasso, and they would laugh behind my back and say I had no cojones, no balls." And he knew that if he continued going to the Picasso it would never come to a fight. The Andalusians are not like the Basques, who are always ready to settle a dispute with fisticuffs. On the contrary, the Andalusians have long tongues, but it doesn't generally go further than that. So he decided to continue going to the Picasso every day.

And it was always the same: guffaws, sniggers, sidelong glances, knowing grins.

"So what is it all about?" he asked himself as he drove the three kilometres home. "What's so peculiar about me?"

He looked at himself in his make-shift shaving mirror next morning after his siesta on the balcony. The mirror was a broken pane of glass he had fixed to the dark green wall of his little salon where he had a bowl on a table for his ablutions.

"You know, I'm quite handsome" he thought to himself as he gazed abstractedly at his reflection. "Black hair slicked back with oil, a truly Roman nose and black eyes that may be rather small but are what you might call penetrating. So what's so odd about me? I've never had these sniggers and all that carry-on before, never in my forty-five years. Will it be that as I'm a solitary and used always to eat at my sister's I didn't notice other people's reactions?"

Isaías was of stocky build, quite a bit over the average height of Andalusians of his generation, which wasn't much, but he had a somewhat forbidding aspect that used to cow the plumbers he worked with, and even the customers. What was it then? Was it only those non-entities at the *Picasso,* those good-for-nothing illiterate peasants?

As he drove along the road Isaías began to notice that people in cars were giggling. He could see them behind in his mirror. Sometimes their eyes met and driver and passengers seemed to regard him knowingly with malevolent grins. As for passing cars, he took to avoiding glancing at their occupants, looking straight ahead. But once or twice he said to himself "This is cowardly" and stared straight at drivers. But always it was the same. They appeared either to burst out laughing when their gaze met or to make peculiar faces, smirking in a way that suggested he was an oddball.

As he sat in front of his house by the roadside ostentatiously perusing a large illustrated edition of *Don Quixote* he was fascinated by a picture of the knight taking wine through a straw inserted into the visor of his helmet, surrounded by the tarts he took to be noble damsels in a country inn. "That's just what I need" he reflected; "a helmet would keep the curious gaping of the hoi polloi off me."

Like many solitaries Isaías had developed the habit of talking to himself and he now became acutely conscious of this. "I'm becoming neurotic" he thought. "I must get away for a time. I've got no ties. I can do what I like."

So Isaías decided to go to Seville for a couple of days. He had heard it referred to as 'the pearl of Andalusia' and had always wanted to see that city. He took the bus to Málaga and from there the train, changing at *Bobadilla,* named after the ancient Arab ruler Boabdil. The people in his compartment from *Bobadilla* were mostly country folk going to market to sell their produce, women with children and bags with hens peering out of them, and elderly peasants with strings of onions and garlic. They passed round *empanadillas,* small pies filled with anchovy and liquefied tomato, oranges and a bottle of *tinto.* They were all friendly to Isaías, although he had nothing to offer, and he began to feel quite jolly in their company, joining in the general conversation. By the time the train reached Seville he felt a different man, as though the scales of his neurosis had fallen away.

One of the peasants had recommended a cheap *pension* in the *calle Vida* in *Santa Cruz,* so he crossed the *Murillo* gardens with his overnight bag. He was warmly welcomed by *don* Andrés, who gave him a bear hug, and by the gentle *doña* Ana. He took a cheap room with no outside window but looking onto the patio on the ground floor. He much enjoyed the dish of cuttle fish Maria brought him, no less than the *postre* of quince that followed at lunch time.

After a siesta, he decided in the evening to look round the town, marvelling at the *paseo,* when all the girls went walking round in one direction, and all the young men in the other. He was intrigued to observe how the young men pinched the bottoms of the girls, whispering lascivious messages into their ears, the girls attempting to maintain disdainful looks that almost invariably and involuntarily were betrayed into a smirk,

"How pretty the *sevillanas* are" thought Isaías, much prettier than the dowdy peasant wenches of our part of Málaga province. How they glide along! How proud they look!

After wandering round admiring the magnificent buildings, plazas and parks in the evening, he stopped at the restaurant *La Punta del Diamante,* the Point of the Diamond in the *Gran Via*, where he got into a friendly conversation with a *sevillano* drinking *coñac* at the brass-railed bar.

"Whose photograph is that in the frame above the bar?" Isaías asked.

"That is Alexander Fleming" his diminutive companion answered grinning. "It is said that the owner of the *Punta del Diamante* is also owner of the *Marina* Bar by the river, where the tarts go. He is said to be grateful to Fleming for curing their amatory infections with penicillin."

Isaías dutifully laughed as he asked "And who is the owner of the *Punta del Diamante*?"

His companion, after downing another brandy, reached up to incline his head confidentially to Isaías and in a stage whisper said "They say it is the Bishop."

Isaías laughed at this apocryphal anecdote but he didn't altogether believe it, though he had heard many tales about the supposed sexual prowess of celibate priests in convents.

However, when he had had his dinner and several *coñacs,* out of curiosity he wandered towards the river. It was getting late and it wasn't long before he noticed a large garish neon sign advertising the Bar Marina. Isaías went in and sat on a bar stool among a group of professional ladies and soon took a fancy to a slender olive-skinned woman by the name of Maruja. She seemed much younger and fresher than the rather haggard mien of some of her colleagues.

It wasn't long before they went upstairs, accompanied by an old crone who unlocked the door of a dingy bedroom. When Isaías asked where the W.C. was the old woman pointed to his trousers and then at the wash basin, cackling as she retreated downstairs clutching the duro he had given her. It was a much bigger tip than she habitually got.

After the usual performance Isaías asked Maruja who her regular customers were.

"Quite a few married men" Maruja laughed.

"Married men? Why would that be?"

"One said to me 'you can't be drinking the same old soup every day'"

It was Isaías's turn to laugh now.

"And d'you know?" Maruja continued, "some of them are sent by their wives. Cant be bothered with them, or tell them to learn some new tricks."

"D'you get any priests?"

"Couldn't tell you, dear, they don't come with their vestments on."

Isaías lit a cigarette. He really began to like Maruja. She seemed so sweet and innocent, unlike those hard-faced old whores sitting in a row in the bar. She told him that she lived in Santa Cruz with her little daughter. She said the father was an English sailor who had deserted her, so she had to earn money by prostitution to keep the little girl. Isaías began to feel sorry for the young Maruja – she couldn't have been more than thirty or so – and was much taken with her affectionate interest in him. Tweaking Isaías's nose she inquired sweetly.

"Would you like another go, love?"

"Later, later" Isaías said, rolling over to go to sleep. "We've got the whole night, you know." Isaías having indeed paid Maruja for the whole night.

"Listen, dear," said Maruja "I've gone and left a parcel in the bar. I knew there was something I'd forgotten. D'you mind if I run down and get it before someone takes it?"

"What's that?" said Isaías, half asleep. "Yes, yes, do that Maruja." And he rolled over again onto his other side.

"Wont be long, darling" said Maruja, giving him a little kiss. And off she went.

Isaías sank into a blissful slumber, waking some two hours later to find himself a little chilly, so he got under the sheet in his nakedness. Gradually waking into full consciousness he realized that Maruja was not there. And that she wasn't going to return, *"La sin vergüenza"* – the shameless slut – he said out loud. "She'll be sleeping with someone else by now."

But he didn't much care and he couldn't help a sheepish grin breaking out on his face as he thought of her ruse. It must have been about four in the morning when Isaías, feeling a little foolish, dressed and crept downstairs to the street.

Isaías walked across the deserted streets of Seville to the *Santa Cruz* quarter, where the gentle old *doña* Ana got up and pulled the inside chain to open the wrought iron grill for him, dressed as she was in her while night dress.

"Buenas noches, don Isaías" she whispered, carefully locking the *reja* again.

Isaías found that Maria had left his supper on a little table in that interior room on the ground floor, and although he had enjoyed a splendid dinner in *La Punta del Diamante,* Isaías ate the cold fish with relish and swallowed a glass of wine before settling down to sleep until after ten on a bright sunny morning. When he had had his coffee and a *magdalena* in the patio he took leave of *doña* Ana, *don* Andrés, María and the giggling Anita, who all cordially wished him "¡Buen viaje, don Isaías!"

Isaías made his way along the *Callejón del Agua* and down through the *Murillo* gardens to catch the train for *Bobadilla,* when he unexpectedly came across Maruja walking with her little girl.

"¡*Hola*!" said Isaías, "what happened last night?"

"Oh I am so sorry, *cariño*" Maruja smiled sweetly, "but I felt quite ill when I went back to the bar and found my little parcel gone, so I went home to bed. Will you forgive me? I can make it up to you another time."

"Of course, of course" grinned Isaías genially "let's have a little stroll through the gardens together. I've got half an hour until my train leaves."

They stopped at one of the many bars in the gardens where Isaías invited Maruja and the little girl, Marujita, to join him for coffee. He clapped his hands for the waiter, who gave him an old-fashioned look when he presented a till ticket on a little plate; but when he saw the size of the tip Isaías had left him he was all smiles and thanked him profusely. "*Muchisimas gracias, señor. Vaya usted con Dios.* Thank you very much sir. God be with you."

Isaías was very taken with the little girl, the English sailor's daughter, and felt quite indignant that poor Maruja had been left in such a predicament. They walked on a little and sat down on one of the benches with *azulejos,* coloured tiles, by a fountain enclosed by box hedges which gave off an enchanting aroma. Marujita, little Maruja, looked solemnly at Isaías with her big black eyes, so he playfully gave her a *peseta*, which produced a gap-toothed smile.

Isaías glanced at his watch. It was time to go. He noted Maruja's address in so far as she would give it to him: "I live in the *plaza*" she told him, and he promised to call on her when he was next in Seville, and he kissed them both goodbye as he reluctantly left for the station.

On the journey back to Málaga and *El Trujillo* Isaías found himself thinking more and more of Maruja. She was sweet and unaffected, and he had the picture of her well-groomed black hair, slightly sad eyes and the olive skin of her face which was like velvet to touch. Yes, she would be about thirty or thirty-five. Just the right age for him.

"That's it" Isaías decided. "There's no reason why I shouldn't move to Seville, where the people are so friendly, and marry Maruja. And take care of her little daughter. I can certainly make a living there as a plumber."

However, unknown to Isaías, who had had little acquaintance with women, Maruja was in fact living with an unemployed stevedore and had been for some years. The black-eyed daughter was his.

Nevertheless, Isaías felt a new man when he got home. Looking at his little house he saw it was only a hovel after the grand buildings of Seville. He would just put his tools and belongings into his van and move to the capital of Andalusia. What a surprise he would give Maruja! And Marujita too!

But he decided to make a last visit to the Bar Picasso at lunch time after the labours of his packing and engaging a *corredor* – literally a runner, an independent one-man house salesman at 5% commission, to sell his small house.

There was much ribaldry in the bar when he walked in. It was just the same as ever. But for a time they were inoffensive as the *catetos* – peasants – were curious to know where he had been for the past two days.

"Sevilla" he answered proudly. He felt quite different since his stay there. "And, *por Dios*, the girls are lovely there" he said, putting his fingers to his mouth in a gesture to indicate their succulence. "So elegant! So friendly!"

"And the boys?" asked Paco with a sly look round at his companions. "Yes, what were the boys like?" chimed in Pepe.

"I didn't notice them" retorted Isaías. "But that's what would interest you" he added, fixing his beady eyes on the assorted *polletones*.

"Tell us" gibed Pepe, "when are you going to get married, Isaías? You're getting on a bit, aren't you?"

"Him! He's going to marry a goat" giggled Paco, "like the wandering tribesmen."

This made everyone roar with laughter, even the owner's ugly wife and daughter behind the bar.

Isaías turned white and left without saying anything. He could hear the coarse laughter as he got into his van to drive back to his little house, where his chattels were ready to be loaded into the van for the journey to Seville.

But twenty minutes later, to the surprise of the customers at the Bar *Picasso*, they heard Isaías's van drive up again.

"Will he have forgotten something? Maybe his pride!" said Paco to much laughter. But Isaías didn't enter, though he kicked the door open.

"Come out, Paco, I've got something to show you" Isaías called out behind the open door.

Sniggering still at his own witticisms, Paco stepped out jauntily. To find himself looking down the twin barrels of Isaías's 12 bore shotgun. Isaías let him have both barrels at point blank range, got back into his van and drove like fury back to his house.

"What's up with Isaías? Never seen him drive fast in that old jalopy of his" commented the neighbours as he rushed back into his house and bolted the door. A few minutes later there was a sound of an explosion. The police soon came. They say the devastation was terrible.

"Blew his head off and blood splattered all over the walls and ceiling of his salon. It was a 12 bore, mind you."

EL PARAÍSO

El Marqués was one of the last in Vélez-Málaga to wear a broad-brimmed Córdoba sombrero such as one sees in the advertisements for Sandeman sherry. He habitually carried a smart little swagger stick of light knotty wood with a small knob of polished turquoise held in place by a gold band. Everyone said he gave himself airs, so they called him *El Marqués*.

But his father and mother had been poor peasants, scraping a precarious living in the country, beating olives off scraggy trees with long poles and then scratching them up from the ground. This forced splinters under their finger nails, so that their hands became like claws over the years in the muddy wet and the scorching heat. If they fell ill there was no question of going to a doctor. There was no money. They even went barefoot at times, dressed in rags, brewing a miserable pot of lentils as an occasional luxury besides the usual crust of unleavened bread from their crumbling kiln, fired by old olive branches piled beside their hovel from the time of pruning. Their well always dried up in summer, which meant taking the donkey with straw-covered flagons to the public fountain by the market in Vélez-Málaga: a good three hours there and back. No neighbours would let them draw from their jealously guarded wells, which might be down to half a metre of water; or less. There had been murders…

El Marqués had been the only survivor from their brood of three. The two girls, Jasmin and Marisol, had died of typhoid in infancy and the *Marqués* had only just survived. But now he was one of the most prosperous citizens of the busy country town of Vélez-Málaga. He owned three big ironmonger's stores, although he had started by selling a few implements tramping round the villages. Yet when he had managed to rent a small ground-floor shed in the town his business began to pick up. Vélez-Málaga was at the start of the building boom, and he got in just at the right time.

So here he was in the early nineteen-eighties, bald, with a sand-coloured face and a drooping paunch after forty years standing behind counters six days a week, even on Saturday afternoons. But by God he was proud of it. Having made a fortune, relatively speaking, he lived with his '*señora*' in a grand flat overlooking the *Plaza de Las Carmelitas* – the square of the Carmelita nuns – in the very centre of the town. What's more, below the flat there was a garage, a double one, where he kept his bronze-coloured *Ford Granada,* which, as he made a point of telling everyone, "Cost three million. Three million *pesetas,* no less" he invariably added.

And now, having installed his three sons, José, Juan and Antonio in the three grand emporiums that the stores were, he was about to retire. And what better than to retire to the country. He would build a great 'chalet', as the locals called a mansion, and cultivate tropical fruit, which was just then becoming the latest craze among the newly rich merchants of southern Andalusia.

Wild speculation was common as to the enormous fortunes to be made, with avocados actually selling for well over a hundred *pesetas* a kilo. When a hundred *pesetas,* or '*un billete*', a banknote, was real money. Local plantation owners were known as one thousand tree men, ten thousand tree men, or more modestly as five hundred tree men, which would still produce enough "*papa comer*": to live on, or literally, to eat. "How many trees has he got?" rivals would ask, rather as Stalin inquired the number of divisions the Pope could muster.

Even wilder hallucinations were indulged over planting mangoes, which at that time were making a thousand *pesetas* or even more a kilo, although they had to be sold as soon as ripe, unlike avocados which could be left on the trees for months, according to the vicissitudes of the market. It was like the gold rush with the feverish sale and purchase of land hitherto worthless. All kinds of lunacies were taking place. One plantation owner, completely ignorant of agriculture like most of those caught up in the scramble for undreamt of wealth, on hearing that these tropical trees needed iron as a constituent of their fertiliser but balking at the very high price, went round scrap iron yards buying up lorry loads from the astonished dealers. Old bedsteads, motor car parts, discarded washing-machines were carried off to be planted alongside the delicate tropical plants. In some cases fantastic quantities of nitrates were applied in the belief that the trees would grow apace. Which they did. But produced no fruit, all their energy being taken up with shooting into the sky.

The fever had entered the blood of *El Marqués*. He spent hours every evening pacing up and down the long balcony of his flat, contorting his brain with hypothetical figures of fruit production at three years, four years, five years, and translating these chimerical speculations into millions of *pesetas*, so that when he reached ten years he became dizzy contemplating the fortune he would make. Was he not *El Marqués*? He would enter on a new lease of life that would astound his neighbours.

To pacify his wife, who regarded his speculations with scepticism, he told her how they would drive to one of the new and fashionable restaurants in *Puente don Manuel* on Sundays, where the new rich went to show off their wealth, the women arrayed in rather vulgar garments festooned with garish ornaments, the men ostentatiously displaying their magnificent cars. All this against the background of rural poverty. One of these restaurants called itself *El Bocadiyo*, the owner unaware, like many of the customers, that *Bocadillo* is spelt with double *l* and not with Y. The Sandwich was, incidentally, a converted pigsty, not so very much converted, the sounds emanating from the greedy hordes of the new rich on Sundays not so very different from the restaurant's previous occupants.

But the wife of *El Marqués* remained dubious. "Will there be cultivated people in the country?" demanded Encarnación.

"Of course, of course" answered *El Marqués*. "Of course there will. The good simple peasants are the salt of the earth. They live in contact with Nature, uncontaminated by the tricks of the townees. Just think of the number of customers in Vélez-Málaga who cheated me; who if they were given credit never paid up, getting off with cement-mixers, aluminium ladders and all the rest. And pinching spanners and screwdrivers when we weren't looking. No, no, the country folk are quite different. You don't know, *Marquesa* as you've always lived in town."

"But life will be boring" Incarnation persisted, "what will I do? How will I meet my friends for a chat and a coffee? And what about 'el barato'? You know I never miss the cheap Thursday market with all those wonderful stalls set up by itinerant vendors, who sell at half the price of the shops."

"Listen, *Marquesa*" – he frequently called her by this title, for he had come to believe that he really was a *Marqués*. Especially as the locals referred to his sons as '*Los marquesitos*', the little marquesses, just as though the title was hereditary – "listen, *Marquesa*, there are buses to Vélez-Málaga at least twice a day from almost all the villages…"

"What are you thinking of? Do you think I'm going to get on a bus with those common people, those smelly peasants who've never had a bath in their life?"

"Listen, *Marquesa,* listen, I'll buy you your own car, a nice little Talbot is what I've been thinking of. Then you can run into town whenever you want and do whatever you like. So just keep calm and leave everything to me. I was the one who built up the business, wasn't I? And you…"

But he didn't go any further. He didn't need to. She knew he alluded to her background as a mere assistant in a fishmonger's while her parents had made their meagre living with a lottery ticket stall, even if it was the biggest in the town.

"I tell you what, Encarnación, I'll get up early on Sunday and look round to see what I can find."

"All right then" retorted Incarnation, "you look round. But don't dream of settling in that dump where you were born. Just a few hovels, all deserted now and the tiles stolen from the roofs. I tell you flat, *Marqués*, I won't live there even if you were to tie me to mules' tails and drag me there."

"Now don't start nagging, Encarna, as I told you, just leave it all to me."

El *Marqués* set out very early the following Sunday morning in his wife's new white Talbot. It wouldn't do to let the country folk see the big bronze Ford. He was looking for land to buy and he intended to get it cheap. He had a very good idea where he wanted that land. There was a village called *El Paraíso* about twenty-five minutes drive from Vélez-Málaga where he had long dreamed of building that 'chalet', having passed close by on his hunting expeditions on Sundays. But he never let on to anyone, not even to the Marquesa, just in case it got about that a man of his wealth was looking for a bargain there. He well knew that the way to get land cheap was to betray no interest in it until the last minute, generally belittling it and pointing out all its drawbacks. In fact he had decided to let it look as though he was out for an excursion to the countryside, taking with him his pointer, Sambo.

But of course the village folk were not deceived. They had all at one time or another bought rakes, sickles, picks and shovels, or household implements at one of the *Marqués*'s stores, and were not taken in by his appearance so early on a morning outside the hunting season. As for the pretence of going for a walk, well, no Andalusians go for walks, which seem to them a perfectly pointless pursuit.

El Marqués parked the *Talbot* outside the Bar *El Paraiso* in the centre of the village where the buses stopped, calling in for a quick coffee and an *aguardiente*.

"What brings you here at this hour, *Marqués*?" queried Paco, the astonished barman who was serving coñac to two or three peasants going to hoe the weeds between rows of lettuces and tomatoes. They were all agog to hear what the *Marqués* had to say.

"Out to train Sambo" the *Marqués* grunted nonchalantly, "he gets restless in the flat when the hunting's over and I want to keep him up to the mark. Cost twenty thousand *pesetas*, he did. Not a *peseta* less. So I can't afford to keep him idle in town, can I?"

The peasants left with their *bocadillos* slung in plastic bags from their belts with a friendly "*Hasta luego*" – see you later – and the *Marqués* turned to the barman and said "Good people they are in this village, a very good lot. It's a pleasure to be here."

"Good people!" countered the barman. "If you lived here, you'd soon find out. You don't know them."

"Of course they're good folk. All countrymen are" replied the *Marqués* undeterred, as he drained his *aguardiente*. "Be seeing you".

El Marqués made his way casually up the sloping dirt track that wound between the sleeping villagers' newly white-washed houses, gleaming ready for spring and Holy Week. So narrow was the main street that he could hear the slumberers' coughs and groans, and the occasional resounding fart. He walked right through to the highest point of the village where he knew there was uncultivated land, with only gnarled, neglected olive trees with blackened branches and scrawny limbs that would produce a measly crop. This land belonged to *El Lechuguero*; the lettuce man, so-called not because he grew lettuces but on account of his notoriously fresh daughters. The ground was gently sloping, in all about six hectares stretching just over the horizon and with a stream running through it.

El Marqués walked right past *El Lechuguero's* big but tumble-down house, jauntily swinging his swagger stick. He knew that *El Lechuguero* had got that house by surreptitiously turning up at the auction when his cousin had been dispossessed by the Banco Popular for not paying his mortgage. *El Lechuguero* had got it dirt cheap, leaving his cousin Antonio destitute.

El Lechuguero was already up and about, although it was only just after seven that Sunday morning. He espied *El Marqués* through a crack in the wooden shutters which were always closed at night.

"I'll bet he's on the lookout for something hereabouts" *El Lechuguero*, Gaspar González said to himself as he watched *El Marqués* stop half way up the hill at the grove of aspens by the stream, where the golden orioles were singing in the still morning air. "When he comes down again, I'll just appear casually, walking up and down in the shadows of my terrace, and see what he says."

El Marqués looked down over the little hamlet *El Paraíso*, and a paradise it was that beautiful spring morning. The little stream ran through the aspen grove and then went down just inside the boundary of the derelict land with the abandoned olive trees. As a hunter *El Marqués* could distinguish hoopoes, collar doves and a nightingale's trill as he surveyed the land below him.

"This is it!" he said out loud. He had already decided where he would build his 'chalet', that imposing mansion of his dreams. It would be half way up the hill, dominating *El Lechuguero's* pile and that of *El Enano*, the dwarf, and *El Tuerto* alongside.

"*Eso es un verdadero paraíso*" – it's a real paradise – he muttered, tilting his *sombrero de Córdoba* to keep the sunlight from dazzling his eyes and averting his gaze from *El Lechuguero*'s land, then turning off on the track that led eastward, as though he was intent on examining an abandoned cottage half a kilometre in that direction. Knowing he would be observed, he made a great show of calling his pointer, throwing a stick for it to fetch as though he was in fact training it for hunting. He then walked round the ruin, and even into it, where the beams had fallen with the bamboo canes that had supported the roof tiles onto a pile of rubble, stones whose adobe cement had long since given way with the winds and rain. A big rat contemplated *El Marqués* from a corner, until Sambo entered and it scuttled away.

El Marqués then deliberately walked round the remains of the hovel, as though examining it from every angle, before briskly strutting the half kilometre westward again to the dirt track leading down from the aspen grove. Several times he stopped and turned back to survey the ruin, as if to prove that he had a real interest in it, then sauntering nonchalantly past *El Lechuguero*'s olives without even glancing at those irregularly planted trees, growing as though at random, in contrast with the precisely aligned rows of the Jaén province. The natives of Southern Málaga had been too lazy to bother cultivating their olives in straight lines, wasting land and labour thereby. But he noted with approval, out of the corner of his eye, that the stream did run just inside the boundary marked with white-washed boulders from north east to south west. It would indeed be some six hectares, all in all. That would mean, he calculates, some two thousand avocados or three thousand mangoes could be planted. In spite of his age, *El Marqués* felt like dancing a jig of joy. But not a word would he let on about the avocados or mangoes. One mention of that and the price would shoot up. When it came to it, he would pretend he intended to plant olives.

As he came down near *El Lechuguero*'s house he became aware of something he hadn't noticed on his way up. A newly scraped track running from *El Lechuguero*'s dwelling across the corner of the boundary. "That's strange" he thought. "*El Lechuguero* must have rushed out and marked it out with a hoe while I was up the hill inspecting the ruined cottage. Now why would he have done that?"

"*Bueno dia, Marque*" called out *El Lechuguero*, in true Andalusian omitting the letters 'S'. "Out for a stroll, are we? That's a fine pointer you have."

"Yes, I'm keeping him in practice now the hunting season's over. Cost twenty thousand *pesetas*, you know."

"But how come you're visiting us at this time of year?" asked *El Lechuguero*, his dim black eyes focussed on *El Marqués* with a sardonic grin that revealed three or four jagged yellow teeth encrusted with the remains of several days' food.

"Just that, what I told you" *El Marqués* replied, closely observing *El Lechuguero*'s cunning countenance, shaded by a filthy soft felt hat, its headband darkened by sweat. "It's true I was having a squint at that ruined cottage up there, and wondering if it could be restored. It belongs to *El Enano*, the dwarf, doesn't it?"

El Enano had the small house almost nudging *El Lechuguero*'s so *El Lechuguero* lowered his voice to a whisper.

"Yes it does. But you know as well as I do it could never be restored. Like all old houses here it's got no proper foundations. Build a superstructure on it and it'd collapse, as has happened with more than one place bought by an outsider. Only thing to do would be to pull it down and start again. Still, the site will be worth a fair deal and no permit-required to build, as long as its 're-building', see what I mean?" He paused a moment while he spat on the ground. "Fancy a house here in the country then, do you?"

"No, no, I was just looking at it out of interest. Is *El Enano* selling it?"

"I've no idea. You'd better ask him. But he's not about yet. What would you give for it?" he asked behind his hand.

"Nothing, I'm not looking for anything. As you know, I've got a big new flat in Vélez-Málaga. *La Marquesa* wouldn't want to live in the country. You remember the old refrain about life in *el campo*. How does it go?

Empobrece.   It impoverishes.
Embrutece.   Brutalizes.
Envejece.   Makes you old before your time.

She keeps coming out with it, ha, ha, ha!"

"Well that's a pity. I've got a nice piece of land over the track there. As you can see, the stream runs though it."

"Ah, but the stream'll dry up in summer, that's certain."

"Where d'you get that idea from? It's never dried up in all the years I've lived here and it won't dry up ever. That land could all be re-planted with olive trees in neat rows, not in the haphazard, higgledy-piggledy way our ancestors planted. And you know what? The government's subsidizing new olive plantations."

"Well, that's funny, I'd heard they were paying people to uproot olive trees and plant something else. But if what you say is so, why don't you re-plant it yourself?"

"Ah, I'm getting on a bit and don't much fancy manual work myself. Besides which olives are slow growers and I might never recoup the expense. And these young fellows expect to get 2,000 *peseta* for a *jornal*, only a seven hour stint with half an hour off for '*el bocadillo*':, the mouth-filler as we call it. Anyway, I don't need money. I've got my own house and goats, and the girls bring home their earnings."

El Marqués couldn't prevent a sly grin breaking out on his face yellowed by those forty years behind the counter. It was rumoured that *El Lechuguero*'s four daughters earned quite a bit from after hours trade in the park near the big bar where they worked as barmaids in Vélez-Málaga. It was certainly true, *El Marqués* knew that they were all remarkably beautiful. 'How could that be, with such a wizened, ugly old father?' he thought to himself.

El Lechuguero noticed that sly grin, and knew what it meant. But he poked *El Marqués* jovially in the chest, adding "Besides, I make a fair bit on the side breeding pigeons in that there dove-cote. A stupid foreigner came up here the other day and paid over the odds for four of them. Within an hour they were all back here. The fool didn't realize they weren't young ones that had never been out. But it was he who chose them!"

They both laughed heartily.

"All foreigners are the same" agreed *El Marqués*, "so dead dumb they can't speak the language, but loaded with money, they are. But your goats'll bring in more than pigeons, I'll be bound. Making a new goat track from your house across the corner of that derelict land while I was up the hill, were you?"

"I wouldn't be making a goat track. The goats make them. Listen *Marqués*, that track's been there as long as I can remember. You must be imagining it. You can't have noticed it on your way up for the blinding early morning sunlight."

El Marqués said nothing. He knew now what *El Lechuguero*'s tactic was. Making out that the derelict land had a right of way over it. He must have guessed *El Marqués* wanted it. He didn't have to wait long.

"What about that land for a new house?" he said with a crafty flicker in those opaque eyes. "Then we could be neighbours, and Encarna and my woman, Rocio, would have company. 'What d'you say to five million *pesetas* for the six hectares?"

"No, no, that land wouldn't do. Specially if there's a right of way. And those olive trees are as good as dead, as you know."

"I tell you what, I could let you have it, right of way and all, for four and a half million. How about that?"

"Make it two and a half million and I might be interested."

"Four million, two hundred and fifty thousand. What d'you say?"

"No, I'm sorry" said *El Marqués*, straightening his *Córdoba sombrero*. Making ready to go down to the village, he lit a large *Havana*. "I cant go above two and a half."

They shook hands and *El Marqués*, twirling his swagger stick nonchalantly after whistling for Sambo, trotted down the hill. He hadn't gone fifty metres before *El Lechuguero* called out "¡Marqué! I'll let it go for four million, cash down."

I'll think about it" *El Marqués* shouted back. *Hasta la vista*".

And off he went jubilantly, for he knew *El Lechuguero* was going to yield. When he reached the Bar *El Paraiso* there was a small crowd of peasants admiring the gleaming new *Talbot* he had bought for Encarnación. When they saw him coming, they moved apart, as though they hadn't the least interest, those impoverished countrymen who had nothing better than a mule, a donkey, or at best an underpowered motor cycle. But when *El Marqués* got into the car and a voice called out "Fasten seat-belts", there was astonishment among the illiterate spectators.

46

"*Por Dios, ¡ese coche habla!*" – For God's sake, that car speaks!

El Marqués called at the Land Registry in Vélez-Málaga where he discovered that there was no record of any right of way over *El Lechuguero*'s land. But he decided to keep quiet about it. He got a contract typed out and a week later he got the land for three million, two hundred and fifty thousand *pesetas*. *El Marqués* paid over the money in cash, and got a receipt besides *El Lechuguero*'s signature on the contract, both effected with his thumb print. These were ratified by the Notary Public, who drew up the title deeds having consulted the Land Register; so that no reference to a right of way appeared in them.

Both parties were triumphant. *El Lechuguero* having actually got two hundred and fifty thousand more than he had thought possible and confident that he could enforce a traditional right of way, which could not be made over to any individual.

A peasant always likes to keep something back when he sells.

El Lechuguero had made his living in the past by horse trading, traversing the country from the north to the south, and was notorious for the crafty deals he had made with unsuspecting customers.

His face was burnt a very dark brown from his forays across the sierras, though some said it was from gipsy blood. However that may be, he knew he had pulled one over *El Marqués*. Who in turn was convinced he was the winner over their negotiations.

El Marqués was cock-a-hoop at getting land with water at three quarters of a million below market price. And of course he had no intention of planting olives, subsidy or no subsidy, which he had so cunningly allowed *El Lechuguero* to think was his plan. By the time the olives were productive he would be in his grave. His only problem now was to decide whether to plant avocados or mangoes. Though he couldn't tell a Tommy Atkins from a Hass.

In the end, after consulting his friends from the town who had gone in for the tropical fruit craze and who knew little more than he did, he settled for mangoes, beguiled by the astronomical price in the market. Like all the other speculators, the frenzy of the prospect of a quick and easy fortune got the better of him. He wasn't to know that by the time his would give fruit the price would drop to the level of avocados; or that mangoes are susceptible to frost, which may kill the trees, besides a variety of diseases and insect plagues. However, he was lucky in one important matter. Mangoes need a fraction of the water avocados require, and with a mere stream to supply thousands of trees to have planted avocados would have been a disaster.

Three months passed, *El Marqués* driving out from Vélez-Málaga, in his big bronze *Ford*, every day to supervise the tremendous works on his new property, which he had decided to call *El Paraíso*, in honour of the village. He had employed a building contractor known as *El Zorro*, the Fox, a diminutive gap-toothed and ever-grinning figure who everybody said was as astute as his nickname implied. This was perhaps just as well as *El Marqués* had decided to forgo the expense of an architect. Or perhaps…

The great day came when the three-storey building was completed. It was as vulgar and ostentatious as the *Marqués's* wife: a bulging lurid pink structure with absurd over-decoration, in the end appearing like an elaborately iced three-tier wedding cake. But for all the *Marqués's* impetuous hurry, there remained the plantation itself. The land had to be cleared and cut into banks in the hill-side by five colossal bulldozers, the daily roar deafening half the villagers. Then *El Marqués* gave *El Zorro* the additional job of constructing a huge concrete water deposit that could hold three million litres of water, to be diverted from the stream. This was built at the upper extremity of the land so that the water could be canalised in great pipes leading to 18 millimetre tributaries and finally in micro tubes to run down to the three thousand individual mango trees.

Once this had been completed, and the mangoes planted in their allotted terraces, it only remained to fence off the whole property, a major job in itself. But *El Marqués* was so impatient to show off the wonders of his 'chalet' and his 'estate' as he called it, that he hurried the reluctant *Marquesa*, accompanied by Spark, her little brown lap-dog, into moving to this paradise that he had created before fencing it off.

When extravagant quantities of extremely vulgar furniture had been installed and illuminations suspended on every colonnade, terrace and balustrade, *El Marqués* decided to invite the villagers to a *tertulia* – an evening party - at seven o'clock on a Saturday. This was a peculiarly auspicious date, the village fiesta when for the first time and in imitation of other Spanish villages, a sacrificial goat was to be flung off the church tower just after dusk as a fitting end to the day's celebrations. *El Lechuguero* was of course to supply the goat, and had inveigled the mayor into agreeing to it.

About seventy-five villagers turned up, partly out of curiosity to see the house, partly lured by the free wine and pinchos of roast pork. For omitting no ostentation, *El Marqués* had a whole pig turning on a spit. He was anxious to ingratiate himself with the locals, and to show his wife how well they would all get on.

The *tertulia* was an amazing success. The four young fresh 'lettuces' appeared in flamenco dresses, some of the young if rather uncouth village boys dancing with them in the open air. But to the annoyance of the locals they were upstaged by the three handsome sons of *El Marqués* whom the 'lettuces' all too obviously preferred, making up to and making eyes at them with alluring smiles. The dancing was accompanied by the dwarf's son, already bald at thirty, on his guitar, and an aged toothless villager who fancied himself as a *flamenco* singer, going into endless Moorish quavers and tearful protestations of eternal yearning love.

The older men of the village meanwhile all crowded round the spit and the trestle tables replete with mountains of tapas, wine bottles and glasses, most of them disdaining a glass, hoisting a bottle above their mouths and letting the cascades of wine gurgle down their gullets, as though the bottle was a *porrón*. All knocked back as much, and in most cases more than they could hold, as though fearing this free feast might be spirited away as gratuitously as it had appeared.

There was a group of three seated in the shadows of a lantern, *El Lechuguero*, the Dwarf and a crafty-faced man known as *El Tuerto*, the one-eyed, who seemed to be engaged in some kind of conspiracy. The Dwarf was continually nudging *El Lechuguero* and winking at *El Tuerto*. *El Enano* was known, like many a pygmy, to be of an extremely envious temperament, perhaps on account not only of his diminutive stature but the extreme ridiculousness of his appearance. His short stumpy legs, his head as bald as an egg

49

adorned with a would-be military moustache, and his habit of winking and nudging all gave him the appearance of an evil clown. Like so many in the country he drew unemployment pay as a parasite on the economy for countless years, while working as an odd-job builder and sidekick to the itinerant fishmonger, which allowed him to keep abreast of all the house-wives' gossip. Of which there was plenty.

The third of the trio – the one-eyed, *El Tuerto* – had in fact two sharply observant eyes. His nickname sprang from the fact that he was the local water inspector, an important minor functionary in a district notorious for droughts. He had earned this sobriquet from his consummate ability to turn a blind eye to the illegal drilling of new wells in desperate drought years. As a result of which he had been able to buy himself a brand new long-wheel-base *Land Rover* and install air-conditioning in his house, a luxury unknown to any peasant. Something he never could have done on his meagre pay of sixty thousand *pesetas* a month.

"Of course" *El Lechuguero* leered, pressing his mouth reeking of garlic close to *El Enano* and *El Tuerto*, "when I was in the north on my horse-trading expeditions, it was in Zamora that I saw a spectacular throwing of a goat from the church belfry. At *Manganases de la Polvorosa*, it was. All the villagers crowded round when the goat was hurled down onto a canvas held by four of them. Now I've got *Marcapasos* to agree our own goat-throwing off the church tower tonight, but as we haven't got any canvas we'll just use an old sheet Rocío's let me have. So the three of us and the mayor will each hold a corner. But Marcapasos insists it must be after dark, hugger mugger, in case any outsiders see what's going on."

"One of your own goats?" whispered *El Tuerto*.

"One of mine but not the good one I promised him" answered *El Lechuguero* with a wink. "It'll be an old beast that's already half dead. But the Town Hall's letting me have a thousand *pesetas* for it, thinking it's the good one, get it?"

El Enano gleefully nudged *El Lechuguero* while *El Tuerto* giggled and slurped half a bottle of the *Marqués's* wine.

"Did you see any other spectacles in the north?" asked *El Tuerto* patting his stomach as the warm glow of the wine made itself felt.

"Did I? I'll say I did. In the Basque country, at *San Bartolomé de Pinares* they drove horses through enormous bonfires."

"That must have been worth seeing" *El Tuerto* grinned, seizing yet another bottle of the *Marqués's* rioja.

"You're right. It was a wonderful spectacle. Never seen anything like it. The beasts were terrified, leaping in the air, they were, whinnying desperately."

"Anything more?" *El Enano* hopefully nudged *El Lechuguero*, "any really good gory spectacles?"

"You bet! When I was passing through those village fairs in the north I saw bulls stabbed to death with lances like the ones they use in corridas. In Tordesillas, near Valladolid that was. A hundred men on horseback cornered the terrified bull before killing it with demoniac frenzy. But the bloodiest of all was in Extremadura. They hang cocks up alive by their feet and bash their heads off with poles. Some villagers even bit their heads off. A grand performance that was!"

"Oh, I wish I could have been there" sniggered *El Tuerto*. "Still, we've got our goat for tonight, eh? ¡Qué bien!"

"¡*Dios mío*! I was forgetting" shouted *El Lechuguero*, thumping the table with his fist so hard that the bottles trembled, "How could I forget? The best spectacle of all was in Catalonia when they tied firebrands to bulls' horns and set them loose. You should have seen them roaring about like mad creatures from hell. Let's drink to that, boys! Ha, ha, ha!"

Wobbling a little on their legs, the trio stood up and drank a toast 'To the animals! To the blessed animals!', as they turned to stare at the assembly of the village elders.

Never perhaps, were so many wizened and cunning old faces congregated so close, red hooked noses dangling over wine bottles, watery eyes ogling succulent pieces of pig before they were crammed into black-toothed and toothless mouths.

Apart from these guzzlers and the merrily dancing youths, on one of the terraces the *Marquesa* was cornered by the *Lechuguero's* wife Rocío, whose name was Virgin of the Dew, said by some malevolent villagers to keep 'the lettuces' really fresh. On seeing them huddled together three other village wives ambled up and expressed admiration for Encarna's gaudy purple dress, adorned with expensive brooches and hanging on her with all the elegance of a sack. From which protruded surprisingly spindly old crone's legs. Although *La Marquesa* was in her sixties, her hair was dyed bright blonde, swept round to the back of her head and held there by an impressive outsize tortoiseshell comb. Her sallow and heavily lined face was enlivened by a gash of purple lipstick and patches of orange rouge liberally applied to her drooping cheeks, her new false teeth clacking slightly as she condescendingly addressed these peasants.

These older village women themselves turned up in faded black dresses, one with a curious green mould creeping over the nether regions, variously kept in cupboards for first communions or funerals but adaptable for either by means of 'accessories', though now wearing carpet slippers on their gnarled feet. Dozens of tongues were yapping, now spitefully, now interspersed with loud cackling at sallies of crude humour.

There was a momentary silence as the Mayor, '*Marcapasos*' or Pacemaker, rode up on his mule, beaming self-importantly under a new straw sombrero. *Marcapasos* had a good strong heart, dismounting and walking with the long determined steps demonstrating authority that led to his 'apodo'. He made a little speech, welcoming *El Marqués* and su *señora* to *El Paraíso*, intimating that he had been glad to grant permission for a fireworks display that evening. He didn't of course mention that this was at the expense of *El Marqués*, or that he had received a back-hander. He had done well out of building permits, civil weddings, funerals, fines for irregular use of water as the result of 'denuncias' by jealous neighbours, fictitious expenses and all the little tricks of a busy public functionary. All the villagers knew this, but received his speech with hearty, if a little drunken, cheers. After all, you never knew when you might have to ask a favour.

After the firework display, which amazed the villagers by its variety and profusion – rockets of the sun and moon, catherine wheels, fire-crackers, jumping jack-in-the-boxes – most of the throng dispersed, swaying and staggering down to the church for the ceremonial throwing of the goat from the belfry. All, in fact, except three of the fresh 'lettuces', who disappeared into the bushes where they did a brisk business with the sons of *El Marqués*; the fourth of those daughters of *El Lechuguero* having to make do in an outhouse with *El Enano's* bald son.

Before leaving a few of the crowd now going downhill had expressed their admiration of the magnificent house and thanks for the wonderful barbecue; but they now remarked to one another on the garish ostentation of the 'chalet' and even on Incarnation's rig-out. Why did they want a house of that size when there's only the two of them. And why does she get herself up like mutton dressed as lamb, I should like to know. It's not as if any of our men could be interested in that old bag.'

When the drunken crowd reached the church, the unfortunate goat had already been hauled unwillingly up the steep spiral steps to the belfry where it was put into the hands of the biggest youth in the village, knows as Goliath for his brawny torso. Gathering it up, having tied its legs together, he hurled it with all his tremendous might into the air. To a great cheer from the mob below it crashed to the ground through the rotten old bed sheet held at the corners by *El Lechuguero, El Tuerto, El Enano* and *Marcapasos*. Its legs had broken but it was still whimpering alive. One of the spectators, who could hardly stand from intoxication, nevertheless rushed forward and kicked it with all his force in the head. This produced another cheer, which reached a crescendo when *El Lechuguero* slit its throat, grinning broadly all the while.

Next day *El Marqués* trotted round his boundaries with a tape measure and a bundle of bamboo canes, sticking the canes in the ground at three metre intervals to mark the places where the heavy metal poles for the mesh wire would be erected by his workmen.

Meanwhile Incarnation invited her neighbour Rocío to have a look round the 'pink palace' as the neighbours already derisively called it, Spark barking angrily at Rocio as she stumbled in on her arthritic legs.

"Goodness me, Encarna, what a magnificent house!" drooled Rocío as they did the rounds of porches, terraces, dining-room, sitting rooms and bedrooms. "But where is the kitchen, let me see that" Rocío insisted in spite of her exhaustion from this guided tour. She had heard rumours of micro ovens, mixers and other apparatus unheard of in the village. "This way" said Incarnation as they passed an open bathroom.

"*Pero, ¿qué es eso?*" – What's that? – called, out the astonished Rocío, staring at the WC. "Is that a deposit for drinking water?"

When Incarnation clarified what it was for, Rocío crossed herself exclaiming "Mother of God! Then you keep excrement in the house?"

Incarnation hurried to enlighten Rocío that the WC flushed out its contents into a septic tank.

"A poisonous well!" burst out a horrified Rocío. "I never heard of anything so horrible! I hope it isn't anywhere near our house. Couldn't it explode?" Then something else caught her eye.

"What's that roll of paper beside the WC for?"

When Encarna had given her explanation Rocío let out a scream of laughter. "And you have to buy that roll of paper! What a waste of good money! We always use a stone. Fancy using paper to clean the filthiest part of your bodies! Hey, look out of the window there. Can't you see the dwarf's head amongst the leaves? He's doing his necessities under that great carob tree. That's where we always do that. It's much healthier than keeping excrement in the middle of a room."

A cloud of big black flies swarmed over the spot under the carob as the dwarf emerged from the foliage. But it was the bath that had Rocío speechless with giggles.

"And you immerse yourselves in that? You sit in your own dirty water! Well, I'm glad to tell you *mi señor* and I have never lowered ourselves to that!"

But at that moment there was an interruption. The dwarf's wife, Puredad – Purity – a toothless hag twice the size of her husband ambled in with a bag of lettuces and tomatoes for Incarnation. But it was an excuse to get into the house and see what Rocío was doing there.

"D'you know what?" she burst out. "Joselito, little Joseph my husband" she said glancing at Incarnation "has just discovered he's got *la culebrilla*. When he took down his trousers, it was."

"What?" screamed Rocío, "the creeping snake!"

Purity crossed herself and whispered "Never use that word. It brings bad luck. The long creature, we call it."

"Yes, but you yourself said Joselito had discovered the long creature in his trousers just now."

"No, I didn't. I said he's got la culebrilla. The wriggling serpentine lines round his… well, round his middle."

"Ugh! That's shingles!" said Incarnation, drawing herself apart in horror. "That's a disease dirty people get."

"Are you saying my little Joseph is dirty?" screeched Purity venomously.

"I didn't say he was dirty" answered Incarnation haughtily, "I said it comes from dirty people. He must have caught it from…"

"That's enough of that, you yammering Pharisee!" snapped Purity.

"That's right" echoed Rocío, "you keep excrement in your house and lie down in filthy water, and then start calling your neighbours dirty! *¡Vamos!* lets go, Purity, let's get out of here before we get contaminated by something much worse than la culebrilla."

El Marqués was furious when he returned sweating and exhausted from his labours marking the boundary with bamboo canes.

"What the devil did you start trouble with the neighbours for, Encarna? After all I've done to make a good impression, inviting the whole village to the *tertulia*. What with that and fireworks, not to mention the backhanders to the mayor, it cost me a fortune, a fortune, it did!" he fumed, rubbing his thumb and forefinger under Incarnation's nose. "Why don't you go and make it up with them?"

"Make it up with that scum! Go yourself and grovel before them, if that's your idea, that dwarf with the culebrilla and his toothless wife. Tell them you drink the water out of the WC and the dirty bath water to save money. I can quite believe you would," she said with a sharp clack, clack, from her false teeth.

That evening *El Marqués* and *La Marquesa* sat, once more in harmony, on their colonnaded terrace overlooking *El Lechuguero's* house, and the two contiguous dwellings of the dwarf and *El Tuerto*, one on either side. They heard Rocío calling "Joselito and Paquito, - little Paco was *El Tuerto's* name – come down for hot chocolate and dominoes. Come now, come."

After a few minutes *El Marqués* could make out the clattering of the dominoes and the very animated chatter of the trio below.

For a time their voices were lowered, followed by the sound of raucous laughter. Straining every nerve to hear, *El Marqués* could not make out what it was all about. Tired from his exertions setting up the bamboo canes, he poured himself a large coñac and retired to bed.

Next morning *El Marqués* still had some bamboos to place, but as he walked down with a bundle, a hammer and an iron spike to pierce the ground he was astonished to see all the canes he had stuck in the day before opposite *El Lechuguero's* house pulled out and flung away. He at once replaced them, muttering to himself that it might be the wind. Making sure the bamboos were tightly gripped by the ground, he continued his rounds with Sambo. Putting the canes in was a relatively simple, if tedious, job and he didn't want to waste money on lazy labourers when he could perfectly well do it himself. Besides, only he could be sure not to lose a centimetre of land he had paid for. Several times he moved the bamboos over just a little beyond what he knew the boundary was.

But the heavy metal poles, the wire mesh and the three strands of barbed wire to be stretched atop the whole boundary, north, south, east and west, would be done by his workmen. Then his 'estate' would be impregnable.

However, the following morning, once again the bamboo canes in the same place had not only been pulled out but snapped in pieces, the fragments scattered inside the boundary.

"Aha!" said *El Marqués* to himself, "so that's your game is it? Well, I think I know how to put a stop to that."

He got into his big Ford and drove to one of his ironmonger's, telling his son Juan to get him a big tin from the top shelf marked Rat Killer. This was not the conventional poisoned bait but tremendously powerful glue which was used to surround a scrap of cheese and which the unfortunate rat had to cross. It would then be held fast, unable to move.

That afternoon he finished his post markers, but meanwhile left the broken bamboos as they were, strewn over his side of the boundary. It wasn't until after dinner that evening, when darkness had fallen, that *El Marqués*, having lit a faria, nonchalantly told Encarnación that he was going out for a stroll. Encarna knew that he was up to something, but knowing it would be useless to ask, told him to be sure he didn't catch cold in the chill north breeze that was blowing strongly.

El Marqués chucked away his faria, a cheap, strong black cigar, selected half a dozen good canes, picked up his tin of rat glue and silently shuffled his way to the boundary close to *El Lechuguero's* house. A dog barked at his approach, so he stood still that windy night until it became quiet. He opened his big tin of glue and dipped the top part of each of the six canes into the tin so that the glue ran slowly down halfway. Stealthily, he then stuck them into the holes in the ground, gripping them by the lower parts free of glue. As he crept away he could hear ribald laughter from *El Lechuguero's* terrace, where he and his cronies *El Enano* and *El Tuerto* were at their usual game of dominoes, dimly illuminated by a lantern. He was sure he heard the words *El Marqués* and *el Tonto*, the fool, as he beat his nocturnal retreat.

He got up early next morning and looked down from his colonnaded porch.

"Ha! Ha!" Not one cane had been uprooted, although two or three were slightly off perpendicular and one was quite crooked. "They will have very painful blisters on their hands. How they will have howled!" he exulted, and went in to enjoy his breakfast of coffee and *torrijas* that Incarnation had prepared, delicious little rounds of bread soaked in milk and then lightly fried with egg coating.

Nevertheless, sensing the possibility of trouble from the way things were going he decided to drive into town and get himself a new shotgun. The one he had was getting rusty and possibly dangerous to himself. A rather old-fashioned double-barrelled model.

There were two or three unsavoury-looking customers in the *Armería* when he walked grandly in twirling his swagger stick, but they edged apart with sullen glances at him.

"Good morning, *Marqués*, what can I do for you?"

"A repeater's what I want" he told the eager arms dealer, "but nothing too expensive, mind."

After handling five or six guns *El Marqués* decided on a nine shot Fabarm repeater.

57

"Italian, isn't it? How much?"

"Sixty-five thousand *pesetas, señor Marqués*."

"What about a discount?"

"I'm afraid we can't do that, *señor*, but we could manage a free carrying case."

"Very well" said *El Marqués*, counting out thirteen notes of five thousand *pesetas* and depositing them in a neat pile on the counter.

"Would you like me to demonstrate it?" the dealer asked.

"Well, I've been hunting for forty years" *El Marqués* boasted, "but go ahead."

The dealer filled the magazine tube with nine cartridges and then manipulated the pump action, which sent the cartridges flying all over the floor.

"Excellent" said *El Marqués*, obligingly bending down to help collect the scattered cartridges. "Right, then just put the gun in its case and I'll be off."

"Excuse me, *señor Marqués*, but the price is 65,000 *pesetas*. There are only twelve five thousand *pesetas* notes here."

"God damnit!" exploded *El Marqués*, thumping the counter after extracting another five thousand note from his wallet. "I carefully counted the notes twice. You can't trust anybody nowadays" he fumed, glaring at the three other customers who shuffled uneasily. But what could he do? With a snort he marched out of the door held open by the obsequious dealer, who handed him a free box of cartridges, got into his big Ford and roared off to *El Paraíso*.

Next morning was a Sunday and *El Marqués* got up rather later than usual. While Incarnation was making his coffee, strolling up and down his colonnaded terrace, he suddenly became aware of an enormous yellow bulldozer approaching the boundary where the bamboos with glue were still in place. Behind the bulldozer he could make out a crowd of neighbours, including *El Lechuguero, El Tuerto* and *El Enano*. There must have been about seventeen of them altogether. When the bulldozer stopped just in front of those canes, *El Marqués* grabbed his new Fabarm repeater and strode down to the boundary.

"What's going on here?" he demanded.

"We've come to clear the right of way" called out a voice from the back of the crowd, some relation of *El Lechuguero*, "to give the track a good clean up."

"No one and no machine will cross my land" shouted *El Marqués* defiantly, his *Córdoba sombrero* tilted against the morning sunbeams. The bulldozer was just below the boundary, its motor roaring.

"Put the blade in" screamed *El Tuerto*. "Yes, get the blade in" echoed half a dozen voices all at once.

This was too much for *El Marqués*. In spite of his age he leapt onto the bulldozer and yelled at the driver "If you go one *centimetro* into my land you'll see what'll happen to you. One centimetre only" he bellowed in the cowed driver's ear, brandishing his shotgun in his right hand.

"All right, all right" conceded the driver shakily, "it can't be done." And as he began reversing the roaring monster *El Marqués* jumped off triumphantly.

El Lechuguero, *El Enano* and *El Tuerto* now came up to the boundary, taking care not to trespass over it.

"It's a right of way" *El Lechuguero* snarled, "It's a historic right of way, a goat track."

"Nothing of the kind" retorted *El Marqués*. "It doesn't appear in the title deeds, and you know as well as I do that you ceded any so-called right of way in our contract. There's your signature" he countered derisively, pulling out the scrap of paper from his pocket with *El Lechuguero's* thumb print at the bottom, and waving it in their faces.

"A historic right of way can never be extinguished" *El Lechuguero* sneered, an ugly leer breaking out showing his rotten teeth. "What about the ancient right of goats and sheep to pass across the centre of Madrid? Aren't they driven through the city once a year to maintain that right? I followed them myself with my posse of horses nine or ten years ago on my way south."

"This isn't Madrid, and your mangy goats won't be crossing my land unless they want to end up in the stew pot" *El Marqués* chortled, which infuriated the crowd more than any insult. *El Lechuguero's* son, who had an even darker complexion and more of a gipsy look than his father, called out in a threatening tone as the bulldozer rumbled away "*¡Quien gana, pierde!* Whoever wins, loses!" an ominous threat as the disgruntled mob dispersed, while *El Marqués* proudly made his way back to the pink palace, Sambo trotting at his side.

In the early afternoon *El Marqués* and *La Marquesa* drove off jubilantly to the restaurant *El Bocadiyo* in *Puente don Manual,* joining the horde of new rich of Vélez-Málaga, the women showing off their vulgar dresses and the men their swanky cars.

When they got back Incarnation went upstairs to have a siesta, while *El Marqués* parked the big Ford, and lighting a Havana settled contentedly to contemplate the events of the morning with a glass of *coñac* in the pillared *portico*. Suddenly he heard Encarna scream.

"*¡Marqués! ¡Marqués!* Come quickly. My little Spark, my little Spark, she's having a fit."

The little dog was overcome by convulsions. It did not occur to either Encarna or *El Marqués*, who came hurrying up, that the dog had been poisoned. If they had given her a little water with a heavy dose of salt to bring up the contents of her stomach they might have been in time to save her. So poor Spark's life gradually ebbed away, her eyes became glazed although she was still warm. Then *El Marqués* realized what must have happened and called the vet. Meanwhile Encarna held Spark in her arms, tears streaming down her face. In half an hour the vet came, but it was too late. Spark was stone dead, her limbs already stiffening.

El Marqués marched down to the trio of houses, accusing by turn *El Lechuguero*, the Dwarf and *El Tuerto*. They disclaimed any knowledge of the poisoning.

"She'll have eaten some poisonous plant" averred *El Lechuguero*.

"Of course it'll be that" echoed the Dwarf.

"And if it's not that it'll be the poison hunters leave about in the spring to get the foxes" said *El Tuerto* with a sidelong glance at *El Lechuguero*.

El Marqués got the vet to do an autopsia. The vet held up poor Spark's stomach that was no bigger than a tomato.

"Chicken it was" he said, "laced with what looks like some kind of weed-killer. But I'll send it to the official analyst."

A day later chlorine poisoning was confirmed.

"Poisoning each other's dogs is an endemic pastime of the country folk" said the vet bitterly.

"*La Marquesa* was distraught. "My little Spark" she cried, "how could they? how could anyone do such a thing? You and your good country people. We should never have come here."

"It was you yourself who set them against us, Encarna, accusing them of being dirty people. But it's no good recriminating. I'm going to see what can be done."

He went to the printer's in Vélez-Málaga and ordered a set of posters offering a reward of a million *pesetas* for information leading to a conviction. These he distributed in the neighbouring villages, including *El Bocadiyo* in *Puente don Manuel* and all the other bars. Besides the bar in *El Paraíso* and two posters fixed on his own gate pillars. Next morning he found these two torn off and flung into the refuse bin by the track. Replacing them, he surrounded his pillars with barbed wire.

It was of no avail. After a couple of weeks it was obvious that no one would testify. Omerta. A silence based on fear and hatred. And the local *guardia civil* being close friends of *El Lechuguero*, it was pointless to get in touch with them. They regularly called for a glass or two of gin at his house where Rocío kept a bottle ready exclusively for them.

Meanwhile *El Marqués* got his labourers to complete the plantation of mangoes and the fencing off of his 'estate'. And for a time nothing more happened. Though the trio watched them from behind the bushes every time they came in or out of the pink palace. *El Tuerto* even climbed the great carob tree and spied on them in their house through his telescope: part of his equipment as water guard.

"*Les vamos a hacer la vida imposible*": We'll make their life impossible, *El Lechuguero*, *El Enano* and *El Tuerto* put about the village, where *El Marqués* and *Marquesa* were not popular on account of their opulence. Envy being a leading characteristic of village life. But not only were the villagers against them.

One day later, at the height of summer, as *La Marquesa* was baking a fish pie in her kitchen a tremendous rumbling began to shake the walls of the house, holding her petrified.

"*¡Dios mío!* An earthquake!" she called out to her husband, who was not there. She crossed herself in terror as she became aware of colossal cascades of water running past the house and boulders bounding and crashing by, racing down towards the centre of the village. Encarna cried out again and again "*¡Marqués! ¡Marqués!* Where are you?*" and hid her face in her apron in terror. She then fled upstairs to a portico where she was just in time to see a huge boulder smash through the kitchen wall. The poor *Marquesa* became hysterical, not knowing what to do or where to go.

El Marqués was in fact just above the great three million litre concrete water deposit built by *El Zorro*, having gone to inspect a leak from the bottom of the structure. He had been standing in front of it just two minutes before it burst with a sound like thunder as the water from the stream reached the top of the rotund concrete reservoir. More than two hundred mango trees were uprooted and forty metal fence poles toppled as though they were matchwood in the roaring deluge. By the luck of the devil no one was injured, though a huge boulder bounced down in front of a crowded bus in the village square.

But this was by no means the end of the catastrophe. *El Tuerto*, the water inspector, now decreed that the stream in its course through *El Marqués's* land was a public danger, and persuaded the mayor, the redoubtable *Marcapasos*, to send a bevy of Town Hall labourers to divert the stream so that not even a rivulet reached the plantation of *El Marqués*. It was now mid-August, the hottest time of year, and the *Marqués's* remaining mango trees were left without water.

Being a resourceful man, *El Marqués* paid for a series of tankers to discharge water into his irrigation system, but the expense was prohibitive. He wrung his hands as he watched the first sign of drooping of his young trees. And as his bank balance diminished.

"But we're not going to be beaten *Marquesa*" he said, comforting Incarnation, still trembling from the fright she had. "The great thing is neither of us was injured. Or killed" he added, putting his arm round his weeping wife.

"We must get out of this accursed place, *Marqués*" Incarnation whimpered. "I always warned you we shouldn't settle in the country"

The kitchen was in a little extension from the main house and the boulder that had smashed through the wall had damaged the refrigerator and the washing-machine. *La Marquesa* protested that she would neither cook nor wash any more in that benighted place. "I can't and won't stand it any longer, Marqués; let's go, I beg you."

"What! And leave all the money I've put into this place, our palace and our plantation! Never! Don't worry, Encarna. I'll order a new washing-machine and a new fridge, even better than the old ones. And I'll get the wall repaired today. I can do that myself. Then I'll see *Marcapasos* and give him a backhander that will get the stream returned to its course through my land. It's all a question of who can give the biggest backhander, you'll see. Even if *El Lechuguero*, *El Enano* and *El Tuerto* club together, they'll never be able to outbid me. That's certain. Absolutely certain."

And it was certain. With his usual broad grin *Marcapasos* gave no sign of noticing the discreet offering of tightly-rolled notes which *El Marqués* transferred from one palm to another when they shook hands.

The decision of course enraged the trio. *El Tuerto* stamped his foot on the ground and swore he would get the decision reversed. *El Enano* nudged *El Lechuguero*, saying "We must think of another ruse. I've heard that pretentious wife of his is on the point of breaking down. Just a little shove and we'll have them out of here."

"Yes, yes," answered *El Lechuguero*, "and I could get my land back dirt cheap! But what is there we can do?"

"Just wait" said *El Enano* with a sly grin, "He's always boasting about that pointer of his, isn't he? Well…"

El Marqués was very conscious of the danger of Sambo being poisoned or abducted, so he never let him out of his sight except when he went to town. And then he locked Sambo up inside the house.

And this was just what he did one Thursday when Encarna had gone to 'el barato' market and was staying the night with the sons in the *Plaza de Las Carmelitas*. He went on a tour of the bars in all the known haunts of *El Zorro*. And there were many, from Periana to Almayate, to Torre del Mar, to Los Romanes where he finally came across him after looking in half a dozen bars. He was surrounded by dark, forbidding faces but the Fox greeted him with his ever-lasting gap-toothed grin. Yet behind that sly grin the Fox was taken aback to have been tracked down. He had heard all about the collapse of the reservoir and knew very well why it had given way. He had economised on cement and the steel framework to reinforce the concrete, saving himself a pretty packet. But he promised to come and begin repairs next day. Especially as *El Marqués* had hinted at legal action.

El Marqués drove back to *El Paraíso* just a little merry after all those coñacs in the various bars in his search for *El Zorro*; not to mention the two or three he and the Fox had pressed on each other and the crowd of curious cronies eager to hear what it was all about, amid all those wily smiles and slimy handshakes. So it was late when he reached *El Paraíso* and mounted the steps to the pink palace under the starlight.

It was then he saw a window had been smashed, the window of the room he called his 'den', where Sambo had been shut in for safety. He quickly unlocked the front door and ran to his den, dreading the worst. Before he had opened the door he could hear Sambo whimpering. But as soon as the door was open Sambo leapt up to his master and licked his face. *El Marqués* embraced him with tears in his eyes. And then he looked round. There, under the window was what he expected: a leg of chicken, without doubt poisoned. But Sambo being a well-trained gun dog would touch no food unless presented to him by his master.

The evil plot had failed. *El Marqués* hugged Sambo again and poured himself a big coñac, muttering "I'll get those bastards, that I will."

But his relief didn't last long. Walking round the house in the morning, before Encarna returned from Vélez-Málaga, he noticed ominous cracks in the walls. He had heard about settlement cracks in new houses but these were fundamental, stretching from floor to ceiling right round the building and almost everywhere it was the same.

"Wait till that Fox comes" he said aloud between clenched teeth, "just wait!"

But the fox didn't come. All those promises and all those

handshakes had meant nothing. Apart from the house, the mangoes desperately needed water. Although the stream had returned to its channel, it could not supply enough water to two thousand eight hundred trees without the forceful canalization provided by the ruined reservoir.

When Encarna came back and he showed her the cracks she became hysterical and screamed "We've got to get out of here, *Marqués*. This is a cursed place, as I told you. The people here are diabolical. Last night was the first night I've slept since we came here.

"Just hold on, *Marquesa*, everything will turn out alright, you'll see. I've already got the stream back in its channel and…"

"What! with my little Spark poisoned, the house about to fall down and the reservoir in ruins. Just how will everything turn out alright? And what about my fridge and washing-machine. When are those marvellous new ones coming, I'd like to know. And when is that Fox coming to do repairs? But this house can't be repaired, the damage is too fundamental."

La Marquesa was right. The land where the pink palace had been built so rapidly was clay, with water courses from the stream permeating under the surface. Foundations would have to be four or five metres deep with massive reinforced concrete. Whereas the Fox had got away with a mere metre. Like so many others anxious to save money and time by failing to employ an architect or at least a structural engineer *El Marqués*, having relied on a rascally builder, was to find that his house was an irreparable folly.

And like so many others, *El Marqués* obstinately believed his building could be saved by under-pinning. To do which was merely to throw good money after bad.

"I have ordered a new fridge and washing-machine" said *El Marqués*, desperate to find something positive amid the wreck of all his hopes, his paradise. "Far better models than your old ones" he insisted. "Cost a packet, they did. They should be coming later this morning."

"Yes *Marqués*, everything has cost a packet, and where are we? We'll soon be sinking into debt and what then?"

El Marqués was becoming concerned about his wife's mental

state. He dared not tell her about the attempt to poison Sambo. And he was becoming demoralised himself. But obstinacy was a strong part of his character, which had enabled him to build up his ironmongery empire against very adverse odds at the beginning. Yet this admirable obstinacy was now blinding him to reality. Obstinacy and pride. How could he give in to the evil that those neighbours were? How could he not force the Fox to repair what was now his ruin?

Feeling dispirited himself, *El Marqués* suddenly turned to *La Marquesa*, taking her in his arms. "*¡Dios mío!* It's your saint's day, Encarna. With all these tribulations I'd quite forgotten. Encarnación, *¡cariño!* Listen, Encarna, let's go out to that romantic restaurant in the province of Granada on the road beyond Ventas de Zafarráya. You remember, *La Alcaicería*, don't you, where I used to take you on Sundays when we were young? Why don't we go there now for lunch and then have a stroll in the woods as we used to. What about it? What d'you say to that?"

"Yes, alright *Marqués*. But listen, a van is coming up the track."

"Ah! That'll be the Fox come to do repairs at last. Don't despair, Encarna, we'll get it all put right, you'll see. Just trust me."

But it wasn't the Fox. It was the delivery van bringing the new refrigerator and washing-machine.

"There you are, Encarna, see? Things are beginning to go right, as I knew they would. And what better moment than on your Saint's day. I'll just go down and deal with them, while you get ready."

The prospect of the *excursion* had cheered Encarna, and she hurried upstairs to get into one of her smartest outfits, laying on lipstick and rouge until she was satisfied she was at her best. Meanwhile *El Marqués* had the washing-machine and refrigerator, still in their cardboard packaging, unloaded in the porch outside the kitchen. If they were to be in time for lunch, they would have to install them in the evening.

In a quarter of an hour *La Marquesa*, resplendent in all her vulgar finery, came down impressively, and when Sambo had jumped into the back of the big Ford, they set off for *La Alcaicería* that stifling hot afternoon. They had a delightful lunch in the dreamy old building, which brought back memories of days and years gone by; and then started off on a walk in the cool shade of the gigantic pine trees, Sambo eagerly fetching the sticks his master occasionally threw for him. Yet when they had walked two kilometres or so the atmosphere changed. The enormously tall pines began making an eerie swishing sound, their branches scything in semi-circles and shedding cones unnaturally. "I don't like this" the *Marquesa* said, shivering in spite of the heat of the late afternoon, "what can it mean?"

"It's strange" agreed *El Marqués*, "as though some evil spirits inhabits those sombre trees that seem like spectres."

But that seething in the tops of the great pines continued relentlessly. And what was strangest of all was that there was no wind.

Nevertheless they hurried on to where they remembered a beautiful glade surrounded by chestnut trees and walnuts, cherries and pears. But now there was no fruit nor even leaves on those trees, which were black except where they were covered in vile grey lichens which had strangled them to death. It was as though the place was cursed, blackly ominous.

When they returned to *El Paraíso*, shaken by their experience in the woods which seemed, on Encarna's saint's day, to presage evil to come, it was discovered that the new refrigerator and washing-machine had vanished from the porch.

"That's the end" screamed Incarnation. "Tomorrow I return to town and I'll never come back here."

"Ah, rats are always the first to leave a sinking ship" bellowed *El Marqués*, "go then, woman. But I'll stay here and put everything right. This ship isn't going to sink."

El Marqués called the *civil guard* who had to come from a distant village. They arrived after an hour in a battered *Land-Rover*, shrugged their shoulders and sidled in their three-cornered hats into *El Lechuguero's* house, where Rocío rushed to get out the gin bottle she always kept ready for their visits.

On their way out, two hours later, *El Marqués* was waiting by the track, stopped them and asked what they were going to do.

"Won't you search the neighbours' houses?"

"Can't do that without a search warrant. Needs a magistrate's signature. No chance of that on a Saturday."

"Well, what can I do?" demanded the exasperated Marqués.

"If you catch them, kill them. Only make sure the bodies can never be found," said the corporal out of the side of his mouth.

El Marqués decided to make his own search, training his binoculars from his portico on the houses of the trio below. But he could see no sign of the stolen goods. He decided then to walk up the hill past the aspen grove. Once there he turned half a kilometre eastward to the Dwarf's ruined house, so as to spy on those below from a different angle. When he got to the ruin he had the surprise of his life. There, behind the ruin was *El Tuerto's Land-Rover*, jacked up with a wheel missing. And in the *Land-Rover* the still packaged refrigerator and washing-machine, besides a lot of other electrical appliances: micro ovens, mixers, TV's and a new Hoover.

There was no spare wheel on the *Land-Rover's* back door nor any sign of one anywhere. *El Marqués* realized what must have happened. Having no spare, *El Tuerto* had gone to get the punctured wheel repaired. Which meant he had gone to Vélez-Málaga. There was nowhere nearer where it could be done. They must have decided to hide the *Land-Rover* there during the siesta hour when no one was about, and were waiting for dark to take the stolen goods to a fence, of whom there were several in the local town.

In the late evening light *El Marqués* walked back down the hill to his house, observed by several villagers. As it began to grow dark a plume of thick black smoke billowed into the sky from behind the Dwarf's ruin, just as the Dwarf, *El Lechuguero* and *El Tuerto* returned with the repaired wheel of the *Land-Rover*. The Dwarf's heavily laden Seat 600 somehow managed, after many a stop and start on the rough track, to get close to the ruin. Where the trio found the *Land-Rover* a blazing inferno.

When they came down they were soon told by neighbours that *El Marqués* had been seen going up and down from the ruin, only an hour or two before.

"It's him! He'll have set the *Land-Rover* on fire" said the Dwarf venomously.

El Tuerto was dancing a jig of rage on the track. "The *Land-Rover* has no insurance against fire. I'm ruined, ruined!" he screamed.

"Listen" whispered *El Lechuguero*. "we'll have to get him. Kill him."

"Yes, kill the bastard, kill him" *El Tuerto* screeched, unable to control his voice.

"Quiet" the dwarf interrupted. "I'll tell you what" hissed *El Tuerto,* "he keeps that new shotgun under his bed, I've seen him put it there through my telescope. We can climb up to his bedroom window and surprise him in his sleep before he has time to get the gun from under the bed. It'll be said it was burglars."

"That's right", whispered *El Lechuguero*, we'll sling our shotguns over our shoulders and let him have it all at once from the window."

"But what about Encarna?" protested *El Enano*.

"She sleeps in a separate bed at the back of the room" *El Tuerto* confided. "His is just under the window. I've watched them many a night through that telescope of mine. Climbed up the old carob tree. Got a perfect view from there."

They all chuckled, but it was decided to follow this plan immediately.

As it happened, *El Marqués* was not in the bedroom that airless night, having had yet another violent quarrel with *La Marquesa*. He was dozing on the sofa of his 'den', the room directly below, and had taken the precaution of having his 9-shot repeater by his side.

Poor Encarna was no more than half asleep, sobbing intermittently and lying on top of the *Marqués's* bed where she had removed to get some cool air, having left the window open that sultry moonlight night with the ceaseless buzz of the cicadas. Suddenly she became aware of three shadowy hats silhouetted half a metre from her against the starry sky. She let out a bloodcurdling shriek which so unnerved the trio perched precariously on a narrow ledge that they tumbled over backwards onto the ground. *El Tuerto's* shotgun discharging innocuously into the air, but narrowly missing *El Lechuguero* as the three took to their heels. Hearing the scream and the shot, in a flash *El Marqués* was at the window of his den, firing at the retreating posteriors. *El Marqués* was a good and practised shot and three times his hot lead scored a direct hit on each backside. Amid the screams of pain he let off another couple of volleys over their heads to speed them on their way as they fled as fast as their burning bums permitted.

It was said in the village that they could not sit down for three or four months, and only in great pain ever afterwards. But they dared not report to the police on account of their own criminal activities.

Next day *El Marqués* and *La Marquesa* returned to their grand flat overlooking the *plaza de Las Carmelitas*. Permanently.

PRIDE

"*Director* say 'Invite all best society'" wheezed *don* Juan, the words emanating bitterly from his post-box mouth in his rhomboid head, grey hair oiled immaculately back above steel spectacles and sharply clipped moustache. *Don* Juan, dapper in white linen jacket, black trousers and black and white aertex shoes. "He say invite all best society as he is come from South America and he no know best society. So I invite all best society. Then director he say 'No don't invite, Consool will do that'. So now I must go house of all best society and uninvite, say don't come. It is a DISGRACE for me. *Es una VERGÜENZA*."

There was a pause. Then, leaning over at an angle of maybe forty-five degrees he said "What nice shoe! Very, very nice! I no have see such fine shoe. It must be Eenglis."

Young Robin Ramsden was for a moment taken aback, for his shoes were the standard line from a British chain store. But he examined them now with an attention he had never given them before. Well, yes, they were rather well turned, he was beginning to concede, when *don* Juan took him by the arm, turned him aside, and leaning over now at maybe sixty-five degrees, breathed acrid in Robin Ramsden's ear "I soopose you can oblige me one thousan *pesetas*, only one month. My wife, you see, sir, she has a very rich taste."

Don Juan and Robin Ramsden, a very tall, slim Englishman of twenty-two, albino blond, pink-eyed and with an Oxford 4th in history, were both members of the motley crew of locally employed language teachers at the British Council Institute in Barcelona. Already established a couple of months but to have an official opening that evening.

It was not so very long after the Second World War, and the

British Government had thought it might be advantageous to have more cordial relations with Franco Spain and at the same time discreetly to increase trade with a country that was still the pariah of Europe.

So a palatial building was rented in the *Avenida del Generalisimo Franco*. Which name was of course ignored by the Catalans and continued to be known as *La Diagonal*. In that very grand building the usual British Council apparatus had been installed: a Bechstein grand had been imported for the concert hall that doubled as lecture room and stage for local expatriate would-be actors who stumbled across the boards, book in hand, mumbling The Mousetrap for the delectation of Catalán audiences, Twelve English language classrooms had been set up and every facet of British culture included, from reproductions of Hogarth, Constable and Turner to periodic exhibitions of sculpture by Henry Moore, Epstein or Chadwick, though the Chadwick exhibition arrived after its closing date. But no detail had been overlooked, from the magnificent portrait of King George VI and his Queen to the shiny brown lavatory paper stamped 'British Government Property. Use Both Sides'. Due to the acute post-war paper shortage, as an additional economy the Foreign Office had employed the same printing stamp as that used for overseas typing paper.

Hitherto almost everything had gone smoothly. The splendid hall had been decked out for the evening reception of the best society, and the official opening of the Institute promised to be a great success. The only blot on British-Spanish relations in the two months that the Institute had been functioning was that the unfortunate *don* Juan had got into trouble with the Spanish police.

One day he had asked a dimwit Spanish student in his English language class what the word for bus conductor was in Spanish, and predictably got the answer *el conductor*, the driver. *Don* Juan always made a special point of teaching his students to avoid this confusion, and being now rather harassed, he put the question another way. "Who take your money, *señor* Sánchez?"

The pupil scratched his head and repeated "Who take my money?"

"Yes, *señor* Sánchez, who take your money?"

The bashful student contorted his brow, worried for a further half minute, and then, blushing furiously, replied "*Generalísimo Franco*."

Which earned him a vicious kick on the ankle by the Government informer – a fixture of every class – sitting behind him. And when the whole class split their sides with laughter *don* Juan himself was unable to contain a bronchial guffaw from the post-box.

He was later summoned to the commissary of police, where he underwent an interrogation surrounded by five burly civil guards in patent leather three-cornered hats, bandoleers and swinging batons. Why, it was demanded, had he provoked disrespect for the Head of State? There would be consequences, he was grimly warned, as he was roughly propelled into the street.

Later that day two ancient motor-cycles spluttered into the forecourt of the British Institute. A civil guard with a patch on his boot saluted the porter at the top of the steps and delivered an ultimatum addressed to the Most Illustrious Director of the Institute to the effect that His Excellency the Civil Governor requested that *don* Juan Berenguer be immediately dismissed as a teacher on account of his subversive activities. So *señor don* Juan Berenguer, paragon of the upper crust of Barcelona society, was called to the Director's office and advised that his teaching activities were terminated.

When a flock of fellow teachers demanded an interview with the Director in solidarity with their colleague, the tall, suave Crispin Millington-Blenkinsop received them with a jaundiced eye, seated under the portrait of his King and Queen and the British Council motto "Truth Will Triumph".

Surveying the sheepish crew of low-paid, part-time supplicants anxious to maintain a façade of respectability through their jobs with the British Council, Crispin Millington-Blenkinsop's eyes ranged over an artistic Australian desperate to get the part of Iago in a play-reading; an arthritic and impoverished old lag who had married a *Catalán* squaw when neither of them spoke the other's language and now found life lonely; a fat, cackling one-eyed woman; a superannuated purple-nosed ex-army Pioneer Corps captain who insisted on being addressed by his rank; and various drifters and beachcombers including Robin Ramsden. After a moment's consideration Crispin Millington-Blenkinsop delivered his response to their plea that *don* Juan should be reinstated.

"I am deliberating what action, if any, it might in the circumstances be incumbent and appropriate to take, should it transpire that it were in my considered opinion feasible to respond in any positive, or for that matter, negative manner, notwithstanding the concomitant complications inherent in this not altogether precedented and problematical contretemps."

Crispin Millington-Blenkinsop, the newly appointed Director, had as a young man been destined for the Church; but had somehow been sidelined into the British Council, without quite knowing why. He was a tall, distinguished-looking personage, grey-haired, with a grey face who invariably wore grey suits. He had been appointed to this post after spending the hundred and ninety-three days' leave owing to him, but had been sent to Barcelona only because the previous appointee had mysteriously died after only one day in that august city. 'Mysteriously' was the official explanation, although those in the know were well aware that A.N. Snodgrass was a recidivist dipsomaniac who had been the inmate of many an alcoholics' clinic, and had more than once wet himself on the platform during public lectures in Madrid.

There was something about London appointees to General Service with the Council: they were like vagrant dogs with no desire for a settled home, as though the British Council was a repository for misfits. Yet although endowed with an extremely amateur notion of administration they comported themselves with the evident conviction that they were omniscient, consequently treating less fortunate mortals with a certain casual hauteur. Nevertheless, they in their turn were regarded with disdain by their more elegant cousins at the Foreign Office, who tended to see them as little more than jumped-up schoolmasters.

These General Service Officers, as they were officially designated, were graded from A to F, but Crispin Millington-Blenkinsop had never managed to rise above grade E, in spite of twenty-two years' service. At the British Council Personnel Headquarters in Baker Street they hadn't known what to do with him. If only he could somehow be kept permanently on leave. But the sudden unexpected vacancy in Barcelona had forced their hand.

Millington-Blenkinsop had announced that he would give an inaugural lecture, following the impressive welcoming reception, on Anthony Trollope. "Interesting for the Catholics, you see, don't you know, for them to see, I mean how the Church of England conducted its affairs in such an exemplary manner at a time when Spain was riven – it was, wasn't it, so I believe – by religious wars."

Before dismissing the supplicant teachers, all locally employed, Crispin Millington-Blenkinsop advised them that he expected their full co-operation at the opening ceremony shortly to take place, which they should attend in suitably formal attire and mingle with the distinguished guests.

"I trust your knowledge of Spanish will be up to the mark; something I always take into account when appointing local teachers is that they should be au fait, that is to say au courant with the indigenous tongue and customs of the country. Especially, d'you see, as London-appointed staff tend to arrive in Spanish-speaking countries bilingual in Chinese or Arabic, but without any cognizance of Castilian. I may say in all modesty that my welcoming discourse tonight will be in Spanish, having myself spent six months in Colombia, where I was posted having made a special study of Urdu on secondment to London University. However, I man say I succeeded in picking up sufficient Spanish to enable me to prepare my inaugural address unaided but for the guidance of Cuyas's splendid dictionary. You will know it, I am sure. It includes, mirabile dictu, useful phrases for the traveller, such as 'Waiter, bring me the writing service'. A complete compendium on which I rely in all fidelity."

The reception began with a *tertulia*, the Director and his lady standing at the head of the grand staircase to shake the hands of the *élite* of Barcelona: the Mayor, the Civil and Military Governors, the Rector of the University, the Deans, Professors and lecturers of the various faculties, distinguished artists, writers and musicians and even some of the leading businessmen of the city, including the *Marqués de Nousma*. Not to mention the Chief of Police and a sprinkling of Government spies introduced as functionaries of the Town Hall. And of course the foreign Consuls General.

The Head of the École Française, a strutting peacock who had graduated from the Sorbonne and whose school was already well established, French being the only foreign language the Spaniards learnt, was notwithstanding fearful English would usurp the world's diplomatic language and so sideline French "*Culture, littérature, sculpture, architecture*" as he so exquisitely accented it. However, he was good enough to compliment the Director and his wife on their "*bon goût*" on observing the serried ranks of champagne bottles, and intimated that he had left two magnums of special reserve champagne with the "*Concierge*" for the "*délectation de Monsieur et de sa jolie dame.*" Edna, the Director's wife, dressed in an outrageous blue and pink balloon dress from which protruded thick brown woollen stockings and wearing a little green hat that appeared to have *hors d'hoeuvre* decorating its crown, clasped his hand in appreciation of his little bow and burst out "Ow! But we 'ave champagne every day at 'ome, don't we luvvy!" familiarly nudging her embarrassed husband.

The Head of the École Française, however, did not notice the Cockney elision of Edna's h's, as, after all, his own nation, in spite of its pretensions to 'culture', accentuated English in precisely the same way, on the rare occasions when they deigned to speak it.

As a young man Crispin Millington-Blenkinsop had, for career reasons, been obliged to marry Edna Smith when it emerged that she was pregnant. She had warned Crispin that she would "create the 'ell of a stink" if he didn't face up to his responsibilities. So Crispin had hurried her down hugger mugger to Stepney Register Office. Although it transpired a short time later that Edna was not pregnant after all.

The Director was surprised to encounter, among the last guests to arrive, *don* Juan, who was accompanied by the wife with "a very rich taste", elegantly dressed in a black sequin dress with several rows of exquisite pearls. Millington-Blenkinsop whispered, as he confidentially took *Don* Juan's extended hand "Didn't I make clear to you that you were dismissed?"

"You did so" loudly proclaimed the wheezing postbox, "but I no come as teacher but member of best society, invited by Consool."

" 'oity-toity! Coo! 'ark at 'im" cackled Edna, "whatever is the dagos comin' to with them 'igh falutin' notions!"

Fortunately, once again, the situation was saved by her Cockney dialogue, incomprehensible to *don* Juan and his lady.

When all the guests had been welcomed by the Director, with piquant remarks by Edna, the penniless local teachers were huddled round the bar, the Australian 'Iago' mouthing sinister quotes from 'Othello' to Robin Ramsden, who he had taken a fancy to and was trying to persuade to take the title part in the next public play-reading.

Ramsden saw his escape in putting down his champagne and taking a plate of *tapas* round the assembly, which might have been divided into those anxious above all to be British, those grateful to be continental, but all took his wares without thanks, none more assiduously than the French Consul's wife. The French Consul himself, though he had never met him before, asked cordially after Ramsden's family, while the local Manager of the Bank of London & South America, a vociferous Scot who was engaged in seeing significance in people's ties, on observing the Pioneer Corps captain's military insignia, fled into the throng, gratuitously protesting that he had been in South America during the War through no fault of his own. The French Consul General too took the opportunity to disappear at this point, though he wore the insignia of the *Légiôn d'Honneur* in his button-hole.

When Ramsden came round to Edna, who was complaining to the Mayor's wife about "the 'eat", that lady made good her escape. Edna at once detained young Ramsden, waving her fan in his face while she informed him that she found Barcelona "ellish", having been knocked down by a donkey and cracked her femur.

"Do you know, Ramsbottom" she continued, "that in the 'ospital, when I asked for some water, to wash m'self, for I 'ad not 'ad a wash, they brought me a glass!"

And as if to make her point with emphasis, the Cockney grouser tumbled her champagne glass with a crash. Ramsden must have been to obsequiously attentive, bending down too readily to pick up the pieces, for while he was still somewhere about her ankles she enquired, raising her skirts

"'ave you any knowledge of femurs, young man? Do feel this. I 'ope it's only cracked."

And before he knew what he had done, Ramsden had hold of her thigh, warm and furry under woollen stocking and balloon, and was left in some doubt as to the correct moment to let it go. But he was saved by the British Consul, who had approached unheard on spongy suede shoes, a faded Old Etonian tie fastened to his shirt with an outsize safety pin, and as Ramsden surreptitiously slid his hand from under the lady's vestments, the Consul insisted on him meeting his secretary, a pale-eyed spinster who wanly related, while the Consul disappeared, tales of her days in Athens, in Cairo, and half the capitals of the globe.

Meanwhile, Crispin Millington-Blenkinsop was surrounded by a group of Spanish intellectuals eagerly hanging on his every word as he stood towering above them, the dazzling sheen of his richly cultured poll superbly set off by the fountain in the vestibule, as though symbolizing exquisite taste allied to flashing wit.

"What wonderful religious poets there were in 17th and 19th century English literature" enthused the *Catedrático de Literatura Inglesa*, whose doctoral thesis was on Wm. Blake.

"Nineteenth century? queried Millington-Blenkinsop. "There were no great religious poems in the nineteenth century."

"What about Blake?" persisted the Professor deferentially, "And Hopkins."

"Blake eighteenth century, Hopkins twentieth" the British cultural emissary effortlessly corrected him with a condescending smile.

"But wasn't 'Jerusalem' published in 1805?"

"That may be, but it must have been written a good deal earlier, mustn't it?" countered Millington-Blenkinsop, glancing at his watch. "Oh my goodness, it's time for my welcoming discourse. You must excuse me." And with a patronising pat on the Professor's back he made his elegant way to the platform.

The audience of multitudinous representatives of the best Barcelona society looked up expectantly as a flock to their pastor as Crispin Millington-Blenkinsop gave a little cough, patted his notes for his speech in Spanish which he arranged neatly on the lectern and gazed, slightly abstracted, above the spectators' heads as though deep in thought.

"Your Excellency the Mayor, your Excellencies the Civil and Military Governors, The Most Excellent and Magnificent Rector of the University, Illustrious Professors and distinguished artists, writers, musicians and citizens of the noble city of Barcelona" (the audience now nodded in approval at each encomium) "it is with great pleasure that I have the honour to welcome you to this British Cultural Institute. I must say it is a shame that I cannot welcome you in English as it is not yet widely spoken in your magnificent city, but with the opening of the British Institute…"

But as Millington-Blenkinsop looked up momentarily from his notes in Spanish he was astonished to find himself looking at the backs of his audience as they marched rapidly out of the portals of British culture declaring in highly indignant terms that they would never return.

"*Pero señores, señores distinguidos*" bleated Millington-Blenkinsop to the rapidly emptying hall.

Alas! Crispin Millington-Blenkinsop had looked up the word for shame, meaning a pity, in his lexicon and found only

VERGÜENZA: A DISGRACE.

In the dismal silent aftermath a prolonged bronchial guffaw echoed from the doorway.

LIFE'S A LOTTERY

"Life's a lottery" muttered *don Ciego*, the blind old man crouching over the circular table in the patio of No 4 Life Street with *don* Andrés, the *dueño* of the *pensión*. Their legs were warm, thrust under the blanket draped round the *brasero* of smouldering olive branches below the table, where the house tabby and Penny the Pekingese nudged each other.

"Yes, that's right," grunted *don* Andrés, "some win and some lose."

There was a long silence while they contemplated these profundities that chilly December morning in *Santa Cruz*, Seville.

"Has this little square always been called 'Life'?", *don Ciego*, whose real name was *don* Diego, enquired.

"You should know that, *don Ciego*", *don* Andrés replied, shifting his colossal bulk in the wicker chair and kicking the cat. "You've lived here more than twenty years. Of course it's always been called Life" he asserted, lifting the clay *botijo* from the table high above his head and letting a jet of water pour down his gullet.

Once again there was silence, except for *doña* Ana's humming in her small sitting room off the *patio*. *Don* Andrés's little pig eyes fixed on the shrimp-like *don Ciego's* dark yellow-framed glasses. Andrés's hooked nose was red from the cold, and maybe from the *aguardiente* he had drunk as his breakfast. That nose seemed incongruously stuck onto the bullet head that had only a few wisps of white hair and two or three jagged teeth.

"Yes, but you've only live here twenty years yourself," said *don Ciego*. "I was your first lodger, remember, that day I took refuge here in the Civil War."

"Yes, that's so" *don* Andrés answered after a pause. "But I've lived in Seville all my life. I was never a vagabond."

"Yes, I know, I know that. You lived in Death Street, a few hundred yards from here, going down Water Lane. I helped you move some belongings, don't you remember?"

"Right you are, but it isn't called Death Street now, as you know, is it? The people who lived there were frightened by the name, and it was changed to Susona Street."

After a long interval, *don Ciego* ventured in his low rasping voice "Well I don't suppose you'll be moving again, *don* Andrés."

"Yes, I will. We'll be moving to San Fernando" said Andrés triumphantly. "To San Fernando, that'll be our next move."

Again there was silence, until a naïve young student lodger from Córdoba having his coffee and a *magdalena* at the table by the stairs called out "Where's that, *don* Andrés?"

Don Andrés glared at the student incredulously, gave a tremendous howk in his throat, spat on the tiled floor and snorted "The cemetery, of course."

When the student had gone out there was silence again for a while.

"What's that creaking noise?" asked *don Ciego*, lifting the blanket covering the *brasero* and inclining his ear.

"It's my new shoes. Devilish uncomfortable they are" grumbled *don* Andrés. "Ready made, can't afford the cobbler any more. But they'll see me through" he added with satisfaction.

A few minutes later Anita noisily burst through the wrought iron outer door with a *"Buenos días don* Andrés, *Buenos días don Ciego, Buenos día doña* Ana", and after going into the kitchen she emerged with a mop and pail of water, jammed the inner door of the patio open with a chair and sent a river of water racing round their ankles and a cascade of song into their ears.

"Let's get going" said Andrés, moving to the stairs. "Coming up?"

"No, I'm going out to buy a lottery ticket, the Christmas one that comes up tomorrow" answered *don Ciego*, fumbling for his white stick propped up in the corner.

Both *don* Andrés and *don Ciego* lived in separate hutches on the flat roof. *Don Ciego* because it was the cheapest 'room' in the establishment; and *don* Andrés because when he had returned, tail between his legs after an adventure in Madrid some eighteen years ago, *doña* Ana banished him from their *cama de matrimonio*, their wedding bed, to the roof. To support his temporary paramour *don* Andrés had worked as a waiter in a Madrid restaurant, the only job he had ever had. Or so the neighbours alleged. That's as may be. One shouldn't believe gossip. But the fact remains that Andrés occupied a hutch on the roof.

"Mind you get the *'Gordo'*, the fat prize of millions of *pesetas*" expostulated *don* Andrés with a bronchial guffaw as *don Ciego* made his escape from Anita's ablutions.

Don Ciego tottered towards the *plaza Doña Elvira*, but as he reached the narrow passage connecting it with Life Street he became aware of a tremendous commotion. A donkey cart had got stuck in the passage and the diminutive carter was kicking its testicles and beating it ferociously with a bamboo cane, striking it again and again on the muzzle with the butt end of the cane, causing the terrified creature to panic. Instead of getting the overloaded cart free the frenzied beating and the shouts of encouragement from the little crowd of onlookers had driven the donkey deeper into an alcove.

"What's going on here?" demanded *don Ciego*.

"However much I beat it, the stubborn brute won't move out," the carter screamed.

"Come, give me your stick" said *don Ciego*.

Expecting some very clever manoeuvre from *don Ciego*, who in spite of his blindness was thought by the locals to very wise, the carter handed over his cane. *Don Ciego* took hold of it and with one surprisingly vigorous movement snapped it over his spindly thigh. Throwing aside the remaining fragments he caressed the trembling donkey's muzzle and with a few words in its ear succeeded in turning it round and freeing the cart. The carter raged at the breaking of his cane but the little crowd called out "¡Olé!, *don Ciego, usted ve cómo solucionar los problemas. ¡Usted ve mejor que nadie!* Better than anyone, *don Ciego*, you see how to resolve a problem."

Without a word, *don Ciego* proceeded on his way to the Bar *Giralda*, though he had another *plaza* and a short street still to negotiate, feeling his way along the walls. When he came to a corner he was passed by a smartly dressed *caballero* who chucked away his cigar end. On turning to see how the blind man would negotiate the gap between walls the *caballero* observed that *don Ciego's* nose was more acute than his enfeebled eyes. He bent down, picked up the stinking butt, and stuck it in his mouth.

The lottery ticket vendor, leaning against the wall of the Bar *Giralda* was also half-blind, the concession of selling tickets being very frequently in their hands. But old José had also had his legs sawn off in the Civil War, so he walked on two wooden blocks just where the knees would have been.

"*Ay* Diego!" he said, (of course he wouldn't call him *don Ciego*) "¿Qué tal, hombre? How are you, man? I've got some lovely numbers for tomorrow. Which would you like?" And he fiddled with the many tickets attached with clips to his ragged jersey, reading off numbers with a thick and grubby magnifying glass.

"Stop!" called *don Ciego*. "That's the one. Repeat the numbers to me" he said as he handed over a coin. The vendor called them out, *don Ciego* repeating the numbers three times, committing them to memory.

"Are you sure it's a winner?"

"Quite certain that'll be the number of the 'Gordo', the big fat prize" José chortled, clapping *don Ciego* on the back as he went into the bar.

Don Ciego never had meals at no. 4 Life Street. He couldn't afford it, and he had hoarded the lottery coin, 50 *pesetas*, for weeks.

The owner of the Bar *Giralda* gave him a few stale crusts of bread and some rind of *Serrano* ham besides some cheese parings, and treated *don Ciego* to a glass of cheap *vino blanco*.

Next day, as *don* Ciego came back from his usual frugal repast and went through the patio where lodgers were being brought smoking plates of chick peas by Maria, the cook, she called out laughing "Listen, *don Ciego*, the N.O.D.O. – the news – is just coming on the radio. Let's hear if any of us have won *El Gordo*."

With the usual crackling and shrill whistles the national anthem wheezed from the loud speaker, and the voices of young boys began to sing out the winning tickets and the sums of money won in the national lottery.

3691483 Five million *pesetas* called a boy.

"Incredible! Incredible! That's my number." croaked *don Ciego*,

"Let's see. *Vamos a ver.*" Growled *don* Andrés, and all the lodgers crowded round *don Ciego*.

"Let's see your ticket!" they all called out.

"*¡Ni hablar!* Don't even think of it" answered *don* Ciego, defensively putting his arm across his ragged jacket and holding onto the collar. "I know the number by heart, and I'm not risking losing my ticket."

"What's the number, then?" several voices demanded as the boys sang out the numbers of other winners.

"3691483" rasped *don Ciego* breathlessly.

"*¡Por Dios!* By God! He's right!" shouted *don* Andrés hoarsely amid cheers and cries of amazement. "That's the number. They've just repeated it. He's won five million on *El Gordo!*"

Five minion *pesetas*! At a time when a barman at the *Giralda* earned 35 *pesetas* for a day and half the night, was an enormous sum, unbelievable wealth to the inmates of 4 Life Street.

"Come on, we must celebrate!" was the general concensus as curious neighbours pried in from the doorway.

"*¡Don Ciego ha ganado El Gordo!* He's won the fat prize!" sang *doña* Ana in a soft Moorish quaver as she unlocked a cupboard and taking out a bottle of *coñac* poured little glasses for everyone.

"For being good boys!" said the young lodger from Córdoba ecstatically, a cry taken up by all.

"We must celebrate, tonight and tomorrow and the day after: *¡La Noche Buena!* The Good Night! Christmas Eve! *¡Olé! ¡Olé! ¡Olé!*"

"*¡Venga!* called out *don* Andrés to the neighbours in the *plazuela*, the little square that Life Street was. "*Pasen ustedes,* come right in and join us. We're celebrating *don Ciego's* win." So in came the grey haired, bespectacled tailor, abandoning his sewing machine and his shrewish wife; the dairy girl with rosy cheeks, followed by the Mexican family opposite: dapper father with well oiled hair and black and white shoes, simpering mother, pretty dark daughter and baby.

"*¡Ay Que chiquirritin!*" crooned the women, planting smacking kisses on the baby's cheeks, his bare bottom and peering at his private parts.

To everyone's surprise the long-bearded herbal doctor with his bare feet in outsize green leather shoes came flapping in to take *don Ciego's* hand. *Don Herbalista* was a shy solitary but when things got bad and the local doctor failed *Don Herbalista* was always called in.

"Remember how he cured Merceditas, the little Mexican girl when she had a temperature of 104 and the doctor couldn't save her!"

"Yes, that's right. She was at death's door. *¡Hola Don Herbalista, ¿qué tal?* How are you?"

But *don Herbalista* soon slipped away to his quite grand house with a roof terrace in the corner. No one could guess where he got the money, for he charged his few patients very little.

"*¡Don Ciego!*" María called out above the general hubbub, "what about your daughters. Aren't you going to invite them?"

"As you know, they're in Barcelona and have never been to see me." answered *don Ciego* unenthusiastically.

"Telephone!" screamed Anita, "book a long distance call and tell them to come."

"A long distance call to Barcelona" snorted *don* Andrés. "Why, think what that'll cost. I don't like it. It'll go down on our bill. I'm telling you, I don't like it."

"Yes, but *don Ciego* is a millionaire. It'll be nothing to him."

"Well all right, but I don't like it" muttered *don* Andrés grudgingly, "I don't like it at all."

However, *don Ciego* was encouraged by all to telephone the daughters who had never come to see him in his poverty, and after a lot of shouting down the phone fixed to the wall on the stair landing above the patio the call was booked for that evening.

Meanwhile stupendous preparations were made for the 3-day celebrations. Whole legs of *serrano* and York hams were ordered, huge jars of black and stuffed green olives, *kilos* of crayfish to be kept on ice besides prawns, almonds, pistachios and walnuts by the sack, and all kinds of crystallized fruits, as well as the almond and honey sweet meats known as *turrones*. And of course copious quantities of Spanish champagne were laid in, not to mention *coñacs, riojas* and *manzanillas* from *Sanlucar de Barrameda*. As well as the coarse dark *Farias*, other Canary Island cigars were procured and even a couple of boxes of *Havanas*. Maria had already got busy with Spanish omelettes, a pot of cuttle fish in their black ink, and a cauldron of fish soup as rich as any Bouillabaisse.

Gradually the whole family of *don* Andrés and *doña* Ana began to arrive. Their magnificent daughter, Isabel, tall, robust and imposing, with jet black hair, bright red lips and flashing eyes above her armour-plated bosom. Her voice was hoarse and boisterous and her deep laugh infectious. It was said that the cook was in love with her husband, Fernando, who had the disorientating habit of clawing the wall and letting out shrieks of laughter in mid-conversation. However that may be, María doted on Fernandito, their little son, whom she allowed to piss in pails in the kitchen when the only W.C. off the stairs by the phone was occupied. Which it often was as the ABC newspaper was used as toilet paper, so giving some of the poorer lodgers a chance to keep up with the news whilst otherwise engaged. Some even left with the imprint of *Generalisimo Franco's* photo on their underwear.

That very evening things got into full swing when the solemn gangling Count Alonso, the Count of No Account as he was known by his fellow lodgers, got out his guitar and began strumming. *Don* Andrés and his daughter Isabel began dancing *flamenco* in the centre of the patio, the floor and walls trembling with the tremendous fervour of their performance, Isabel's eyes glinting proudly under the snake-like movement of her arms and hands, a cruel smile on her lips, her whole expression as if suffering demonic pain while the old man resembling a baited bear stamped round with snorts and grunts.

¡Olé! ¡Olé! ¡Olé! called the clapping spectators, already heart-warmed with copious quantities of alcohol. Then the telephone rang.

"Quickly, *don Ciego*, it'll be your long distance call" yelled Anita, and as silence descended over all, *don Ciego* felt his way up, holding onto the wrought iron balustrade, while Anita rushed up to help him take the call.

"¡Barcelona! ¡Barcelona!" called the operator, "the call booked for *don* Diego is through now."

But then the voice faded, and Andrés shouted "Wind the handle,

Anita, wind it quickly and keep at it or there won't be enough electricity."

So Anita would that handle feverishly while *don Ciego's* low voice could be heard telling his daughters the good news. "They'll catch the *Rápido*", *don Ciego* announced to the throng listening with bated breath below in the patio and rather hesitatingly stepped down to sit with *don* Andrés at their usual table with the *brasero*, the only source of heat in the house.

"*Don Ciego*" whispered *don* Andrés in his ear, "when are you going to collect your winnings?"

"There's plenty of time, *don* Andrés, the ticket is valid for two weeks after the draw, and it's only two days now. I'll collect it when the celebrations are over. I couldn't keep that money in the house."

"You're keeping the ticket carefully, aren't you?" Andrés inquired with a look of concern, for all the food, drinks, sweet meats and cigars had been ordered in the name of the pensión.

"Don't you worry" said *don Ciego*, guessing what was troubling Andrés, "there'll be plenty of time to pay for all these celebrations, a mere fraction of the winnings. And I can assure you I keep the ticket concealed on me". He put his right hand through his ragged coat and felt his shirt pocket. "I won't let anyone see or touch it. You never know. And I'll have to arrange for a bank account when the banks are open again on the twenty-sixth. A bank account is something I've never had."

"Nor me either" whispered *don* Andrés, "though I am the master of the house. Ana keeps all the money locked in her cupboard. Never lets me near it. She only gives me a *duro* – a five *pesetas* coin – every day so I can play dominoes with the Moorish barber at the Bar *Giralda* and treat my friends to an occasional *vino blanco*."

Don Ciego didn't particularly take to all these boisterous celebrations, and when the *zambomba* got going after an orgy of food and drink on *La Noche Buena* – Christmas Eve – he retired to his hutch on the roof. But just as he was passing the telephone on the little landing half-way up it rang raucously.

"Answer it, *don Ciego*, it may be for you" called *doña* Ana emerging from her sitting-room where *don* Andrés had his meals with her.

"Hullo, hullo" answered *don Ciego*. "Wait a minute" said the operator abruptly, "a call is coming through from Barcelona for *don* Diego del Campo."

"Yes, that's me" said *don Ciego*, "I'm holding on." After a series of buzzes and wheezing the voice of his elder daughter announced that they hadn't been able to get tickets for the *Rápido* until the night of the twenty-fifth. So they wouldn't arrive until the morning of the twenty-sixth. *Don Ciego* gave a non-committal reply and rang off. He seemed relieved they would be delayed. Perhaps even hoping they wouldn't come after all.

Even in his tiny bedroom on the roof the infernal noise of the *zambomba* kept *don Ciego* awake all night. "Umpah, umpah, umpah" it went on and on to a back-ground of shrieks of laughter, Sevillanas sung and danced to the guitar of the lugubrious *Conde* Alonso, the Count of No Account, who dreamily told anyone interested through the tangle of his long black hair that he had taken up the guitar because his life had been very sad.

But *don Ciego* managed to sleep through the morning of Christmas day before the uproar began again with children sliding down the tiled stairs on tin trays as a prelude to the festive lunch at half past three in the afternoon. *Don Ciego* was invited – after all he was paying for it – but he ate frugally and left early to sit in the sun in the *Murillo* Gardens. He wanted to think out quietly what he would do with all that money. He stayed out until sunset and then, in spite of all the protests of the revellers, climbed the stairs slowly to his hutch with a cigarette in his yellow holder.

Next morning he hadn't yet come down when his two daughters noisily arrived. They were tall and spindly like two daddy-long-legs and looked round disdainfully with their yellow faces as they settled themselves in wicker chairs in the patio.

"Where is *don* Diego?" they demanded impatiently.

"Anita, run upstairs, girl, and tell *don Ciego* his daughters have arrived and are waiting for him in the patio" said *doña* Anan turning her gentle smile warily on the ladies from the north.

All the lodgers emerged from their rooms to observe *don Ciego's* daughters, all except *don* Antonio who had got so drunk the night before that he had a terrible headache, but even he swung open the window onto the patio from his interior room with his toes and gazed at these superior beings from his pillow. Maria offered to make them a coffee, but this they grandly refused, saying they would take a glass of *fino* a the Hotel Alfonso XIII where they would be staying.

But just then came a scream from the *azotea*.

"*Doña* Ana, *don Ciego* is lying on his back and doesn't move. He doesn't even answer. The door was unlocked and when he didn't answer…"

"Come down, Anita, and run over to *don Herbalista* and tell him to come quickly."

In a couple of minutes the diffident herbalist appeared holding a little brown bag and lolloped upstairs in his outsize green shoes, followed by the two daddy-long-legs, their yellow faces expressionless.

"One moment please" said the herbalist to the daughters entering and closing the bedroom door.

"*Don Ciego*" he said, "what's the meaning of this? Get up, man. Is there anything wrong? Sit up then and let me examine you."

Don Ciego always went to bed in his only suit of clothes. He hadn't the money or inclination for pyjamas. On getting no response *don Herbalista* gently rolled *don Ciego* over. Below his back was an empty bottle of coñac. *Don Ciego* was dead.

As soon as the herbalist opened the door the two daddy-long-legs rushed in, paying no heed to his remonstrances. They shook the body violently, and realizing it was lifeless feverishly undid his clothes to search for the lottery ticket. Having pulled off his ragged jacket and found only a packet of cigarettes, they stripped him of his shirt and trousers going frantically through the pockets. Eventually they found the little plastic wallet with the ticket intact. It was in the shirt pocket over his heart.

"Quick" the younger sister demanded in the patio, "Where did *don Diego* buy this ticket?"

"From the lottery seller at the Bar *Giralda*" spluttered *don* Andrés in astonishment and horror.

The elder sister clutching the ticket, they made off to the bar without a word, as fast as their elegant high heels could carry them.

Arriving at the *Giralda*, they accosted old José with great abruptness, demanding to know where the winnings would be paid.

"Let me see the ticket a moment" said old José, "just to check."

The elder sister refused to let go of the ticket but rudely thrust it down to the part-blind man's face, saying "There you are. You can see it, can't you? Let's not waste any more time."

Old José swivelled his grubby magnifying glass from the string round his neck, gazed at the number for a moment and, his face turning white, cried out "*¡Oh Dios mío!* Oh my God! This is not the winning ticket. The last number should be 3, not 2. 3691483 it should be. Can my friend Diego have misremembered? I sold the winning ticket to a rich gentleman *don* Jerónimo of Sierpes Street. I remember perfectly. He came just after *don* Diego had gone into the *Giralda*, smoking a big *Havana* cigar. His second that morning, he told me. He had just bought it at the tobacconist's over there."

DON JOAQUÍN, POET,
& THE CHIMERICAL TOWER

El *Conde* Alonso, the Count of No Account, was sitting huddled in his voluminous black overcoat that morning, puffing a Canary island cigar in an effort to keep warm and desultorily reading Unamuno's *El Sentido Trágico de la Vida*. Like everyone else, perhaps including the author, he didn't understand much of it.

The Count had the best room in the house, the long one on the first floor overlooking the little square that is Life Street. This room was in a perpetual state of disorder, with books lying pell mell all over the place, some open, others covered in dust, besides a profusion of notebooks in the count's microscopic writing. In a far corner was an assemblage of empty wine bottles, some of the labels obscured by cobwebs. For the Count would only allow Anita to make his bed and mop that part of the tiled floor that was uncluttered. Which wasn't much.

Gloomily smoking his cigar while pondering Unamuno's opaque prose, the Count imagined he could see damp creeping up the whitewashed wall by the door. Then slowly and irresistibly a pool of liquid rolled towards his chair. He sat mesmerised by the frothing hiss of the flood, until something familiar about the flat, salty tang and the ochre tincture of the waters made him leap-frog to the door, in time to help the huge house tabby downstairs with a kick in the bum.

As the night's condensation cleared from the window across the passage he found himself gazing through a curtain of shower drops at a Moorish tower high on the Alcazar wall behind the house, its whitewash flaking, its windows broken. Wondering at that pointed castellation, that splendid isolation he felt a longing for that refuge from the tribulations of Life Street.

"Oh my poetic soul!" he gasped, "if only I could live there."

He went down to the *patio*, where the cat had taken refuge under the green baize cloth overhanging the table where *don* Andrés was sitting disconsolate, and at once began grumbling about the bills for the wild celebrations of *don Ciego's* supposed lottery win.

"You'll pay part, *señor Conde*?" asked *don* Andrés, fixing an eye on the Count intently

The Count Alonso, who had a small private income, gave an indefinite reply in his high piping voice as he absent-mindedly made some obscure notes on a scrap of paper, and then querulously mentioned Félix's misdemeanour.

"I've got a cure for it" grunted Andrés menacingly, and the Taby shot out of the door.

It was quickly followed by the Count who set off moodily in quest of his tower. Thinking that he might find consolation by enticing there the buxom, chubby-cheeked English girl he had met while strumming for the gipsies at *El Guajiro*, he made a detour to see if she would come with him. Honour was a teacher at the British Institute, and English girls were regarded by Spaniards as an easy conquest.

But when one day he had invited Honour to 4 Life Street, all the women in the patio had hissed her out of the house. Equally, when the gangling long-faced Count had called at the *plaza Santa Marta* where she lodged with two strictly religious spinster sisters, the amorous Count was refused entrance, permitted to speak to Honour only through a window grill. As was the custom of the time.

But now, the two spinster sisters having gone to Mass, he was shown in by a giggling maid. The Count found Honour established, with a huge white napkin round her neck, at an oval table with in front of her a dish of two full-sized pheasants which she was in state consuming. When she saw him she paused blushingly, cleaver suspended over a juicy leg, to explain that a senior pupil at the Institute had presented her with the birds yesterday. But this morning, *requiescat in pace*, she had heard that her provisioner died in the night, "at seventy-two, I think" she said. "And he was to have gone shooting again only next week."

Commiserating with her the Count of No Account asked her, after a pause, what she thought of joining him in that tower. As he sat watching legs and wings and breasts slide down her throat she eyed him warily over a wish-bone, conceding coyly that she did need a man but she would co-habit only in matrimony. Otherwise, why should she give up the comfort and security of her home with the virtuous ladies of the *Plaza Santa Marta*? Anyway, she couldn't marry a man ten years older.

The Count looked so crestfallen that staring straight at him now, suspicious as she was of his motives, she determined that she would help him in his search for a tower. Strictly for himself alone.

When they asked at the *portería* of the *Alcázar* for the director, an old rascal in a rumpled grey uniform gave them a gap-toothed grin as he came out from behind the *Correo Andaluz* and put on his outsize official peaked cap.

"Ah, *señores,* you want to see *don* Joaquín, its *don* Joaquín you want to see."

They agreed that they did, though it was the first time they had heard the name, and would have been just as glad to see *don* Alfonso, *don* Pepe or any other *don* whatsoever. The veteran shuffled of in carpet slippers down the cobblestones of the passage way, telling them, over his shoulder, to follow him.

They were shown into a dark, old-fashioned study, where a quaint figure with bushy eyebrows sat behind an ebony desk, writing with a quill pen clenched in slender talons, and scrutinizing them with black hooded eyes sunk on either side of a hooked beak. There was friendliness in the gaze, as well as something of mocking irony, which just perceptibly increased when the Count announced, with a certain sense of the ridiculousness of the proposition, that he wanted to live in one of the *Alcázar* towers.

"Ah, the young," smiled *don* Joaquín, waving them into highbacked chairs, "you are incurable romantics. But you have come just at the right time, for here I am writing an article on the unicorn, about which I know nothing. You of course," he said turning to Honour, "as it is in your Britannic coat of arms, will be able to help me. Tell me what it signifies."

Honour blushed brightly, for all she could tell their quizzical acquaintance was that for some reason King James VI had transferred one of his two Scotch unicorns to the British arms on becoming king of the united kingdom of Scotland and England. Where it has remained ever since, cavorting before an English lion.

"I have it!" cried *don* Joaquín jubilantly, "as the unicorn symbolizes virginity it represents the impossibility of the union of Scotland and England, an eternally virgin unicorn bedded with a rampant lion." Honour glanced significantly at the Count.

"But have you ever" he asked after a pause, "have you ever seen horses in the sky? Ay! The poet Pedro Salinas, when he first lived in Seville… He had a flat below the level of the street, and looking up one day from his desk to the firmament reflected in the high window, he saw the hoofs of horses prancing amongst the clouds."

There was a log fire crackling in the far corner of *don* Joaquín's study and having sent the toothless old porter out for a bottle of *rioja* and *serrano* ham Joaquín invited them to sit by the fire, above which were two large portraits.

"Who is the man in diplomatic uniform?" asked the Count, gazing with curiosity at the picture on the left.

"That is Stendhal, my literary hero. You know his wonderful novel *Le Rouge et le Noir* was hardly recognized in his life time, so he eked out an existence as a French consul in Italy. It is a novel of the very first rank, on a par with the great Russians."

"Damnation!" exploded the County angrily, "one can only keep apart from a society that is so fickle in its judgements. It was Dickens, wasn't it, who said 'The law is an ass? But he might have said the same about the mass of humanity."

"Disdain for one's society does not necessarily imply superiority" responded *don* Joaquín with an ironic twinkle in his eye. "But I am sure you, my friend, will find your 'forte' and become a distinguished figure in whatever sphere you choose."

The unhappy Count groaned inwardly. The problem was that he had not found his 'forte'. But he was roused to defend his misanthropy by the scornful countenance of the figure in the other picture.

"Wasn't that the attitude of Lord Byron, despising society and preferring to be hated by it?"

"Well," answered *don* Joaquín ruminatively, "there are two Byrons in the poet, as different as could be. The solemn, self-dramatizing Byron of '*Childe Harold*' was the figure that captured the imagination of all Europe at the time, instantly becoming a best-seller. Byron adopted the role of world-weary sinner, damned by a dastardly past. Which led to the extraordinary phenomenon of thousands of ordinary young men imitating their idol, attitudinising, dressing, speaking and attempting to act as the Byronic hero. But there was no outlet for their romantic aspirations in contemporary life. As Lermontov wrote, in *A Hero Of Our Time*

'Many young men begin life with the idea of becoming an Alexander the Great or a Lord Byron, but never become anything more than a low grade civil servant." The Count's heart missed a beat.

"And what about the other Byron?"

"The anti-hero *don* Juan, progenitor of nihilism, leading to Dostoyevsky's Stavrogin. *Don* Juan appeals to our faithless time, while we find the posturing of Childe Harold ridiculous."

Again the Count began to feel uneasy, recognizing something of Childe Harold in his own adopted role of 'he who had a crushed youth'.

"*Don* Juan of course was a native of our city," smiled *don* Joaquín, eyeing Honour.

'In Seville was he born, a pleasant city
Famous for oranges and women –
He who has not seen it will be much to pity'.

After drinking a toast to *don* Juan and Seville, Joaquín rose saying "Come, la Torre! I was forgetting. I know just the tower for you."

This caused the Count's heart to leap in joyful expectation of that splendid isolation his soul longed for.

Don Joaquín paused a moment to inscribe his own '*Lejos y en la Mano*' to the Count as they left.

'To my friend Alonso,
Dreamer of dreams
And lover of towers.
With affection,
Joaquín Romero.'

"The streets of Seville were not made for hurrying" said *don* Joaquín as they wind-wandered in his little black car through serpentine alleys while pedestrians flattened themselves against walls to let them pass. "Seville is a coquettish woman, you never know where she'll lead you. But she is brainless too, and she dresses in the newest fashion. So we are getting straight streets now instead of the old labyrinth of mystery, fumes instead of scent, and mechanical roar instead of songs. And once a woman has lost her mystery, who wants to explore her more?"

Honour gave a surreptitious downward tug at her mini-skirt, and from the back seat it seemed to the Count that *don* Joaquín flashed his ironic eye on the white expanse of disappearing thigh as the car pulled in beside a high white and yellow wall over which leaned giant eucalyptus.

They pushed an ornate gate into a garden and passed through bowers of pale unearthy green, where golden orioles whistled from the branches, squawking like flying cats in the deep leafy glades. As they made their way to the door of a tower surrounded by creeping foliage, Joaquín produced a massive key from his pocket, and after two turns to the right and two to the left, led them wonderingly up a spiral stair which seemed unending. At length they emerged on a belvedere and found themselves a hundred feet above the trees looking out over the flat Andalusian campo.

"You know", said *don* Joaquín, as they gazed at the meandering undulations of the *Guadalquivir* in the distance, the *torres* de campo, the spires of the *plaza de España*, the *Torre de Oro*, the *Giralda*, and the myriad Moorish towers of the town, "what is the most succulent dish in the world?"

"Oh, do tell us" pleaded Honour eagerly, fluttering her eyelashes ecstatically, "do *don* Joaquín, oh do tell us."

"Ah" answered *don* Joaquín, "it is chicken with walnuts. But only three people in the world know the recipe. It was sold for a valuable stamp in Paris by the Shah of Persia's cook and was communicated to me under pledge of secrecy."

When they got back to the *Patio Banderas*, the great enclosed square at the old entrance to the *Alcázar*, the sounds of a woman's singing echoed round the white court as the sun sparkled on the oranges fresh with the night's rain in their greenery; the haunting Moorish quaver of the song carrying up into the air beyond the *Giralda*, rearing clear against the eternal sky.

Joaquín led them through his study into the silent *Alcázar* gardens, past pools replete with whirling fish, through groves of orange trees and grapefruit, up avenues of palms and cypresses and lemons, by splashing fountains, planes and cedars all exuding an aroma that mixed into a blend of yearning sadness with the red and yellow sands.

Entranced, they followed this strange figure, who plucked a leaf in passing and crushed it in his talons, thrusting it under their nostrils, demanding, as though Creator, which sense they found most poignant.

They followed between pomegranate trees and marble, through galleries and colonnades, up staircases to balustrades where they looked down on Life Street, where they heard the noises faint, where they saw the figures small, where they smelt the smells uprising as though God.

"Taste" said Honour, "like chicken with walnuts."

"Sound" intoned the Count, "like…"

"Smell" said Joaquín, "in every dreaming garden anguish, love and beauty can be felt, can be touched; the past is physically present."

By the entrance to the *Alcázar* in Seville there is now a street named Joaquín Romero y Murube.

THE COUNT OF NO ACCOUNT
AND CANON VILLALOBOS

The Count couldn't sleep that night. His mind, like his tangled long black locks, was in turmoil.

"Ah, failure" the Count dreamily reflected, "failure is intoxicating. In this purposeless life it is a defence and defiance against vulgar activity and what humans call success. He recalled the funeral of *don Ciego*, the coffin brought to San Fernando in a high, glass-sided hearse drawn by two huge horses with black plumes. The lodgers of 4 Life Street had followed on foot, led by *don* Andrés and *don* Herbalista. They had all contributed to the expenses of the undertaker, *don* Andrés wringing his hands. What was it the little girl, Isabel's daughter, had asked as the earth drummed on the coffin lid? 'What do we live for?' Holding her mother's hand, she had looked round at the small circle of mourners. But there was no answer.

The Count was perplexed. There was neither purpose nor meaning in his life. And he could find none. Though he half wanted to. When daylight came he did some desultory practice on his battered guitar, going over and over the same notes and phrases ad nauseam. Then he fell asleep and did not get up until shortly before lunch time, when he established himself at a table in the patio, making endless entries in his note-book.

Oblivious of his surroundings he recited aloud in a near falsetto tone "Yes, philosophy is like a plaything compared with theology. Yes, yes, theology is far in advance of philosophy. For while the philosopher is perennially concerned with things as they are, with what he calls ultimate reality, the theologian is concerned with things as they should be. So you see that the philosopher is only a recorder of his own notion of reality, which is of interest only to himself, and which has already ceased to exist at the moment he conceives it. But the theologian is struggling to bring the universe into the focus of God's vision. And it's no good your objecting that there are 'idealist' philosophers, for those men are only artists, trying in their conceit to copy God. What they forget is that all men are born myopic. It's all a question of focus, you understand."

Glancing up over his note-book the Count became aware that his new friend Antonio, renegade priest and now *Coca-Cola* salesman, was sitting at the next table regarding him with a cynical grin.

"Why don't you buy a colossal telescope" he jeered, "you could set it up in the *Murillo* gardens and make a living by inviting passers-by to focus on the great vision at 5 *pesetas* a time?"

The Count of No Account stared at Antonio in astonishment. "By God Almighty, what a wonderful idea! But how could I get such a telescope?"

You'd need to go to Austria or wherever the Zeiss laboratories are, or possibly to Great Britain where they have a wonderful telescope that scans the universe. Jodrell Bank, I think it's called."

"But what would such a telescope cost?"

"Oh, hundreds of millions of *pesetas*."

The Count's face fell. For a moment it had seemed that he had found a true vocation.

"Listen, Alonso" Antonio said, black squid's ink running down his chin, "let's be practical. Let's deal with real possibilities. Couldn't you convince people of your vision by explaining how to synchronize their focus with that of God? Spiritually, I mean, without any technology. God doesn't employ telescopes or astronomers, does he? What you need to do is convince the masses to see as God sees."

"That sounds like Bishop Berkeley's idealism."

"Yes, of course it does. But Berkeley's creed is a wonderful fusion of the philosophical and the religious. Isn't that just the dichotomy you want to resolve?"

"By God it is! This is wonderful, Antonio! Could you suggest a succinct message readily, immediately, comprehensible to the multitudes, making clear that all reality is in the eye of the beholder?"

Don Antonio scratched his head for a moment, and then he jumped up, throwing his arms wide as though in a pulpit, to the amazement of the lodgers consuming their octopus in the patio, and shouted "I've got it, I've got it. The very thing. A limerick, no less. Everyone likes a limerick. Listen, Count.

'There was a young man who said 'God
Must think it exceedingly odd
If he finds that his tree
Continues to be
When there's no one about in the Quad'.

And then comes the reply. You can proclaim that you are God himself speaking.

'Dear Sir: Your astonishment's odd!
I am always about in the Quad.
And that's why the tree
Will continue to be
Since observed by,
Yours faithfully,
God'."

"Magnificent! Wonderful!" called out the Count in exaltation, "That's it! That's what I've been looking for. Philosophy and religion reconciled. Now I don't need to go to Salamanca, as I intended, to spend years in lonely study of *Luis de León, De Soto* and *Jaime Balmes*. I've seen the light! Eureka! *¡Qué alegria!* my friend *don* Antonio, *¡Qué maravilla!* Write the limerick down in my notebook."

"Yes, *señor Conde*" responded Antonio, "but as I say, we must be practical. Let's think how you can get in a position to convey your new vision to the masses. How old are you, Alonso?"

"How old? Oh dear! I'm 32 and I've never done anything."

"Yes, it's that private income of yours that has stifled, has inhibited the flourishing of your genius, Count."

"Wait a moment", interrupted the Count of No Account. "Christ was 33, wasn't he? So there's still time. I tell you what. I'll consult my friend Rufino Villalobos, Canon of Seville cathedral. D'you know what? I'll become a priest myself, *don* Antonio, proclaim my message of how to synchronize focus with God. I'll go and visit the Canon this very afternoon. I'll call myself 'THE INTERMEDIARY', the man through whom God speaks."

"What about HIS MASTER'S VOICE?" sneered *don* Antonio, "*¡Me cago en Dios!* he rejoined in that phrase characteristic of the Spanish unbelieving believer. "I shit on God! I thought you were going to abjure simple religion for something higher."

After his *siesta* the Count betook himself to the Cathedral, which was empty and silent. When he had passed under the grinning stuffed crocodile in the porch he wondered at the gloom beneath the great Gothic arches, at the pungent smell of incense lingering, the priceless gold of the altar.

"Yes, yes, this is my true home" he mumbled to himself, to the surprise of an aged crone in black *mantilla* who had entered noiselessly to pray.

"Yes, yes, I have found it." repeated the Count, louder now as he gained confidence in his new mission. The old lady nervously moved herself several rows back behind the ecstatic Count. However the ecstasy of his vision was interrupted by a horde of schoolboys. The Count was kneeling. When he turned his head, his long black locks covering his face so that only two brown glinting eyes were visible, three or four boys stopped in the aisle to stare. "He's in a coma" stage-whispered a ten-year-old, causing them all to titter.

The Count was considerably vexed by this intrusion on the greatest moment of his life. He got up abruptly, the great illusion befogged, and made his way out, blinking blindly in the bright sunlight on the Cathedral steps. As his sight was restored, he gazed conspiratorially at the Gothic gremlins crowding the architectural monster, the second greatest Gothic cathedral in Christendom. "Ah, my friends, we shall work together very, very soon, very shortly indeed."

The Count then crossed the *Gran Via*, narrowly avoiding being run over by a Leyland Royal Tiger bus, which honked at him mercilessly but of which he was oblivious.

It was just after five when the Count climbed the stairs of the *Residencia de los Venerables Sacerdotes* on the other side of the *Gran Via,* opposite the Cathedral. He was ushered in by Father Villalobos to a dark room where they sat formally at a small circular table under which a bowl of charcoal was smouldering. The Count was introduced to the Canon's eighty-one year old mother, who sat beside them beaming benignly but apparently understanding nothing. The Canon's sister then appeared and brought in the tea: a bottle of dark sweet wine, sausages, cheese, olives, anchovies, salted biscuits and what the priest called pig-meat, hard little squares of smoked *Serrano* ham.

"All from my parishioners," Villalobos expanded his arms as though to embrace them, "and I have many, many more bottles of delicious wines."

But before they set to on the spoils of priesthood, Villalobos determined on their having some monstrous cigarettes, long hollow tubes of cardboard half-filled with loose shreds of tobacco, which they both lit but neither smoked. Then they ate and drank while the priest, as promised, told the Count of No Account about his life and work, the scraggy sister and the old crone otherwise ignored but apparently happy to be ordered in and out of the room at Villalobos's pleasure.

"Ah, Count, my dear, it is a hard life, that of a priest" explained the canon, who was much younger than his face, which had suffered the toll of his arduous calling. "Be prepared, my dear Count, for a 9 year novitiate and to hand over all your worldly wealth and possessions to the service of Our Lord. Once that novitiate is over you will embark on a life of strict discipline and never-ending labour. I myself never go to bed before midnight and am always up on my feet by 5:45 in the morning." The Count looked aghast.

Villalobos now left the room, his mother continuously smiling at the crestfallen Count, who was called into the priest's study to be shown his books, as he explained how he organized every day of his life. He produced a note-book in which he had written everything he had done in all his life since he took holy orders: the number of confessions he had heard, the total of sermons preached, the tally of his hours of meditation, prayer, the number of visits he had made to parishioners, where he had lived, for what period of time, and so on. His whole life was a rigid routine of study, prayer, sermons, confessions, and the compilation of statistical tables.

The Count's heart fell. Was this to be his new life? How and when was the messianic vision to be fulfilled?

"And I am a writer" the Canon proclaimed proudly, beckoning the Count to come nearer to his closely mown head, breathing sour breath in the Count's ear as he exultantly showed him piles of books and pamphlets on religious and quasi-religious topics, ranging from 'Celibates Without Irony', and 'Single Women Without A Vocation', to 'The Bible and the Telephone' and 'Is it a Sin to Dance?' The latter he presented to the Count.

"And is it?" the Count was temerarious enough to ask, thinking with some qualms of his guitar accompaniment to the delirious rapture of the gipsy flamenco dancing.

Which provoked the priest to reply by opening his book at the sixth chapter and placing an expository finger at the paragraph beginning.

"The dances into whose morality we are enquiring are not classical dances. Nor solo dances, as Cecilia did with a broom handle to release the ecstasy of her heart at having realized her dream of becoming a nun. Nor are we concerned with regional dances, nor gymnastics. Nor is it even our intention to deal with dances between persons of the same sex."

Once assured that the Count had understood the vague generality and perhaps even frivolity of his question, he was then referred to the facing page, where under the admonitory eye of his preceptor he dutifully read:

The dances we are concerned with are those and only those in which persons of flesh, blood and bone participate, generally youths, and who dance close together or intertwined, him and her, to the sound of light music.

And in case there should still, after the conning of this paragraph, be doubt as to what was intended, the precisian had annotated each phrase below:

Those and only those dances waltz, mazurka, gallop, polka, schottische, tango, fox-trot, turkey-trot, camel-trot, shimmy, cheko-cheko, one-step, two-step, boogie-boogie.

Persons of flesh and bone that is to say, not angels, but descendants of Adam and Eve and, therefore, with the corresponding passions, and the concupiscence that is the consequence of original sin. Remember what was said in Chapter Four.

Generally young although sometimes a spinster of fortyish may dance or even a girl of twelve, they must be considered exceptions. We mean those between the ages of 15 and 35.

Who dance Intertwined held close in each other's arms, or going even further, and not only with their hands. This is a detail and circumstance of the greatest importance, which we should bear constantly in mind.

To the sound of light music tunes such as The Milking Cow, The Shorn Woman, The Paper House, and He's Gone to the Crocodile.

At this point the lugubrious Count was overcome by a choking fit of coughing, letting the volume fall on the desk, where it lay open, as though by divine ordinance, at the final page where the peroration proclaimed between triple exclamation marks.

¡¡¡DEATH BEFORE DANCE!!!

"But there were, is that not so, there are dances in the very cathedral before the *altar* by young boys?" spluttered the choking Count.

"Well, my dear, these dances were forbidden by His Holiness the Pope, it is true. However he decreed that they might continue for so long as the altar boys' dancing costumes lasted. We have got round that by stitching patches of the old costumes onto new ones."

The Canon giggled conspiratorially.

Villalobos clapped the Count briskly on the back, saying "Come, my son, for some Spanish coffee" and while the silent sister served *Nescafé* they sat for a short time in the glow of the old lady's smile.

"Do you know" enquired the Canon, "that the Pope has given permission for half of tomorrow's prayer to be undertaken today? This makes our time-table so much more flexible, allowing much more activity to be included with careful planning."

Abruptly getting up, as though reminded of the necessity for activity, the Canon in some agitation insisted that they should go out for a walk.

"I have something important to ask you and to tell you" he said as they made their way along the *avenida*. Short figure though he was he set off at an astonishingly brisk pace, so that in no time they were in narrow *Tetuan* street. Stopping suddenly he asked "Do you believe in miracles, Count?" looking sharply up into Alonso's dreamy face.

"Well, yes and no. But all those amazing happenings in the New Testament strain credibility."

"Then your faith is weak, my son. Do you know that I am to preside next week at the ecclesiastical court to consider a new candidate for canonization?"

They had now reached the street Jesus of Great Power. Villalobos kept stopping every few metres and the Count was obliged to halt opposite him, bumping into irate *sevillanos* out for the evening *paseo*, while the Canon narrated a further point in his ardent discourse.

"And who is the candidate?" the Count dutifully enquired.

"Cardinal *Spinola*, who lived in Seville fifty years ago. The tribunal will meet" he said, standing on tiptoe and catching at the lapel of the Count's great coat, fixing him with his fanatical eyes. "The tribunal will meet and then go to disinter the Cardinal's body. I observe your scepticism but we shall take with us a famous bone specialist. Nevertheless I am certain we shall find the body in pristine condition. And that will be a sign from God that the Cardinal is to become a saint."

The Count in turn stared at the Canon with incredulity. "Unless he has been mummified" he stammered, "his body is bound to have decayed."

"That is just where you are wrong" countered Villalobos with a freezing smile, taking three abrupt paces and then stopping again. "Do you not know that King Ferdinand, who liberated Seville, was buried in a metal coffin and has not decomposed after seven centuries? Do you not know, my friend, that that coffin is now preserved high up in the cathedral and that every May people come to see it and the coffin is opened?"

The Count was nonplussed. "But maybe the coffin is airtight, hermetically sealed."

"How could it be, if it is opened to the air every May, and yet the body remains intact?"

"But surely the body will be under glass" the Count protested.

The Canon made no audible reply. They were now at the end of Jesus of Great Power and the Canon breathlessly turned back towards the Cathedral in the gathering dusk.

"Forgive me, my dear Count," said Villalobos, again catching at his lapel, "I must prepare myself for Mass in the Cathedral, if you will excuse me. Pray for me, dear Count, I am in frail health" he said by way of farewell. And with that he threaded his way rapidly through *Tetuan* and back along the *avenida* to the Cathedral. The Count at first was inclined to follow him but then felt the need of a solitary walk to think over his encounter with the Canon of the Cathedral. He was dejected and dispirited by the mechanical practicality of the priest's life. And bewildered by his confident recitation of fantastic miracles. What was he to do? He wandered the streets until he found himself by the *Isabel II* bridge, crossing over into *Triana*. There always seemed to be a river in Spanish towns to divide the rich from the poor, he reflected.

The Count made his desultory way past old crones squatting coughing outside long passages leading to their ramshackle hovels, old pirates glaring hostility at this intruder, spitting contemptuously on the ground. A middle-aged hag, with enormous breasts bursting out of her blouse, wild hennaed hair and tattoo marks on her arms staggered about in the twilight of a cul-de-sac by the railway, shouting and drawling with the bass voice of a man, roaring out

"¡Maricón! ¡Maricón!" as she did a grotesque drunken dance. Nearby an old man and a child indifferently scraped up cement from a spilt pail. Ragged urchins swarmed the streets, tugging the Count's sleeve and begging for "una pesetita". Two of them, pissing from the gutter, with great care arranged the pennant of a parked 'moto' so as to drench it. The atmosphere was undoubtedly saltier than in Seville across the Guadalquivir, which flowed placidly and pungently by, and as he made way for sheep, donkeys, pigs and cows roaming the streets at random, the Count inhaled an aroma of urine and excrement, human, bovine, asinine, sheepish and swinish. As he approached the lower bridge a small brown pig, in colour more like a dog, ran across the road and into a dwelling, while the tongue of a great church bell swung up in the dusk to call to this truly catholic community.

The Count's dejection had now turned to despair. And the conviction that the life of a priest could not be his. He was overcome by the sense of the utter futility of his life. As he trudged back along the bridge towards Seville, quite suddenly he launched himself over the parapet into the river twenty metres below.

But like everything in the Count's life, this escapade ended in failure. He was ignominiously fished out of the murky waters with a boathook by three stalwarts on a barge passing under the arches of the bridge, which he had just missed landing on in the encroaching darkness.

THE COUNT OF NO ACCOUNT'S ESCAPE

The Count banged into a *caballero* with a bag, tripped over a child, steering hopelessly through the helter-skelter for Valencia, Córdoba, Madrid. Málaga train, gleaming aluminium automotor, 9.35. No time for a ticket – let me through damn you, after all my train's… "Excuse me, *señor*, ticket please. No *señor*, can't let you on without a ticket. Next one's in three and a half hours."

"Watch my case, I'll be back in a…"

"Yes, that's right" the peasant woman panted through the tiny aperture in the window, "I want nine third class for Córdoba, yes nine, *si*, seven children, my grandchildren, *coño*, you can see I'm long past bearing, can't you."

The Count zig-zagged back, ready to jump, to pay double, to stand, to see the automotor slide slowly out of the station. Platform now deserted, bare, was it possible, without his case? "Porter, have you seen that inspector? Have you seen my case?"

"The inspector goes with the train, *señor*, and as for the case, well what did it look like? No, *señor*, we haven't seen a case like that. Someone on the Málaga train…"

Walking dazed away, upbraided by a braided hat: stationmaster, stern. "Your Honour should not leave a case unattended. I know, I know, I have watched you. It must not be done, *señor*. We're still honest in Seville, you know, but don't you tempt us. You will find it in my office.

Well, one o'clock train, it's all the same. The Count wandered lugubriously through the *Murillo* gardens and round the walls of the *Alcázar*, returning at length to join the already long queue for the next Malaga train.

"¡Hola! Señor Conde. How are you? Don't you remember me? I'm a friend of *don* Pepe, the owner of *El Guajiro*, where I've often seen you play your guitar so well. It's a very long queue – Christmas and New Year holidays, always the same. As I'm a RENFE agent, if you like to give me the money I'll get your ticket right away and save you waiting. For Malaga, did you say? By the way, return, did you say? Yes, yes, much cheaper."

The Count gladly proffered the fare with profuse expressions of gratitude, and stood aside, gazing with pity at the wretched throng queuing with bulging cases, bundles tied in table cloths, screaming children and tottering ancients jostled as the queue moved slowly but inexorably forward. Five minutes, ten, twenty. The Count glanced at his watch. Half an hour. *¡Maldito sea!* The 'agent' was not coming back. With that curse the distraught Count rejoined the end of the queue, having lost fifty places and a hundred and fifty *pesetas*. But he must escape from Seville after the ignominy of being fished out of the *Guadalquivir*.

An hour and a half late, the Málaga *Exprés*, wooden, creaked companionably southwards to *Bobadilla*. Where a further grandmother, bulky in black, struggled aboard, taking delivery of massive bags, four-foot potted plants and a sack of walnuts, to be dragged to the Count's compartment, for this is, isn't it, the Málaga train, *señores*? And they crouch with their legs held by holdalls, peering between fronds, walnuts plopping from the rack, while the old crone smiling placidly knits, multi-pinned.

A Japanese student now shared their compartment, cameraed, light-metered, mapped, strictly enveloped in apparatus, speaking pidgin American to a stupefied Spanish counterpart, population of Tokyo, figures of production, astonishing reserves of the Bank of Japan. Prising himself free the Count found himself in the corridor next to Pepe Rosas, trilling, toe-tapping, actor, producer, operatic extra.

And on with a lurch, and on with a groan to a gorge, grand canyon, chasm of green water, red cleavage of the sky, glimpsed as they twist out of tunnels, wailing train in eerie light: *La Garganta del Chorro.*

O wonder! Here descend. Never mind Málaga. The Count struggled to free his case, trapped by a creeper.

"You won't find anything in *El Chorro*" protested Pepe, "come on down to Álora."

But abandoning his case to a platform bench, the Count sprinted downhill into the chasm, squinting at bored trout hanging aimlessly in shoals in the grey-green water, purple light suffusing the circling crags and up past the hum of a grotesque transformer dumped in the middle of the grotto for drinks at the station bar.

"*No pensión, señor*, but in Álora, *si*. The last train's in half an hour." *No coñac* either. The Count fumbled in his voluminous damp great-coat pocket and found a quarter bottle of Scotch whisky, duty free from a tramp steamer and slipped into that pocket by one of the bargees after his ducking. Poured by the station-master and Pablo into their *copas* of white wine and pronounced perfection.

"*¡Por Escocia!* To Scotland! Here comes the train, *señor*, steady does it, mind the step. *Hasta la vista, señor*."

When the train coasted into a pueblo on a mountain reaching chaste white into the sky, a halo of orange trees under the stars, there was a familiar humming in the twilight as the Count got down, wondering whether he would find anywhere to spend the night.

"Didn't I tell you" said Pepe Rosas, taking his case and prancing towards the street, leaping round the Count like a jolly dog, "didn't I tell you you'd come to Álora? Why, there's nothing in *El Chorro* but a gloomy grotto. Dead as a dodo. But Álora! Now you have arrived my friend!"

The Count allowed himself to be taken up the steep, winding hill, passing shadowy figures in the lantern light, a soft winter wind filling the air with the scent of oranges as Pepe led him, tripping lightly in his duotone shoes, a comradely arm round his shoulders, the Count feeling like a virgin on her first night out.

"*¡Hola Pepe!*" voices called out from doorways as they rose up amongst the stars, "and who's this you've got with you?"

"Back again, Pepe. But where have you been all these days, *hombre*?"

"London, London" called back Pepe Rosas, "for the new production."

And he trilled an aria as he dodged into a *bodega*, a cavernous cellar obscure down a corridor but splendid in antique decoration, where the intelligentsia of Álora sipped Spanish champagne.

"¡Pepe! ¡Pepe!"

"Ah, Mari Carmen, ah, ah," sighed Pepe, throwing his arms round the yellowing neck of a middle aged admirer, kissing both eager cheeks, and then disengaging, calling to the barman "¡Champan! ¡Champan, Manalo! ¡Champan *para todos*, Manolo!"

"But was it a success, Pepe?" clamoured his *amigos*, "how did it go, Pepe?"

"¡*Magnifico!*" triumphed Pepe, "but let me present my friend.

"Is he from the production?" curious voices insisted, avid glances turned from all sides on the gangling Count's long black locks.

"No, no, he's an artist, an intellectual come to stay among us. He paints, he writes books, I could see it at a glance. He's a composer."

It was no use the Count's muttering bashfully that he was merely a traveller, arrived by accident, for there was an English writer at *El Chorro*, and so of course he was an artist, for who else would come from *El Chorro* to Álora?

Ten minutes of celebrity, until the Count reminded Pepe that he had nowhere to stay.

"Take him to *doña* Isabel."

"No, no, better to *doña* Eusebia."

"Sí, sí, to *doña* Eusebia."

And so it was settled. With an "*Hasta pronto*" they turned up the passage and out into the dark street once more.

Eusebia too, sad-eyed and fading, but beautiful still, was kissed by Pepe. In the dim light of the *entrada*, jammed with chairs, with slow-ticking clocks and innumerable relics of long ago. She led them to inspect the room, through a damp passage like a cave to a dormitory with vast bed, image of the Virgin, jug and chamber pot. 25 *pesetas*.

"Must rejoin my fellow artists, will you come?" beseeched Pepe. "Not tonight? Well tomorrow, then" Pepe called out as he trotted through the *patio*, "tomorrow at twelve I'll call for you."

The Count sat for a while in the dim light with Eusebia, until a quartet of ancient Aloranos ambled in and established themselves at the table, getting out the dominoes with grunts of satisfaction and settling to a game of dark cunning in the shadows.

111

"It's my father" whispered Eusebia outside by the balustrade. "he wont have more money spent on light."

"Then he's not your husband?" the Count ingenuously remarked.

"¡No! *Por Dios, ¡hombre!* I keep house for my father."

"Eusebia, *guapita*, you bonny lass," grinned a couple of passing *campesinos*, ogling her over the balustrade in the streetlight, "what's this, have you got a boyfriend?"

"Well, he'd be better-looking than you" retorted Eusebia to Paco and Joselito, smelling of the land and *coñac* in the balmy night air.

"Join us for a *copa*" they implored, "just one, Eusebia, and bring along the *señor*. You'll see we'll behave ourselves."

"Well, said Eusebia doubtfully, as it's New Year, but only one, mind you. I'll just go in and tell papa."

And just one it was, with Eusebia, that is. For when the Count dutifully returned with Eusebia, Paco and Joselito swore to call for him later. "We'll show you" said Joselito, "for it's New Year's Eve and we'll show you how to drink. *Hasta pronto.* See you soon."

Meanwhile the Count sat with *doña* Eusebia in the dingy light of the domino parlour, where trouble was smouldering. Someone had cheated. And someone had not. Someone was right, and others were wrong. And these things were not done. Or said. And with a truculent rattling of the box papa stowed away the dominoes, for with certain people one cannot continue. He said.

Recriminations interminable, mutterings endless, over and over again. "That's what I told you!"

"And you with your sevens!"

"Well, we can't play again, that's clear."

Party broken up, shuffling, rumbling out of doors, Eusebia crooning softly "*Es el ultimo día del año. ¡Ay de mi!*" It's the last day of the year. Oh dear!

Then they all drank *coñac* on the Count's account until the quarter reassembled, pacified, and Paco and Joselito returned.

The Count left with Paco and Joselito for their deadly assignment, though who won will never be known, under the stars of Álora. They toured the bars making outrageous bets about how much they could drink, whether they could smell the orange trees from the bar with the half-wit barman, whom Joselito beguiled with a trick rubber spider that jumped on the counter and the barman tried to feed. "¡*Mal asunto!*" said Paco, a bad business, you mustn't take advantage, ¡*mal asunto*!

The Count was woken in the night by spitting and grunting, and the sense that the ceiling was falling in. Then he slept heavily to wake to a concerto of donkeys, one striking up where another ended, blending unharmoniously into motion perpetual of ha-hum, ha-hum, ha-hums, beginning in agony, bursting into buoyant joy and ending in dismal despair, mimicking the human experience.

The Count came out to the tunnel leading from his room and found *doña* Eusebia padding in carpet slippers about his door. She stood back with a start when she saw him, and then said she would bring him his coffee, only did he know where to…? Well, did he know where…? He followed Eusebia to the lavatory, where he found the familiar waste-paper basket crammed with strips of crumpled newspaper stirring with cockroaches as he tried to do his duty by Eusebia, holding his breath in the stench.

Eusebia brought him his coffee in a bowl in the porch and the Count looked at her apprehensively, with the certainty that he would have proposed matrimony on his return from the bars with Paco and Joselito. For she gazed at the Count long and slowly, a last blush lighting up her fading beauty. And the Count lowered his eyes and stared shamefully at the floor. It was the first day of the year. The Count knew he would have to go. He bolted from the house when he was sure Eusebia was in the kitchen, leaving twenty-five *pesetas* on the table and another fifty for the *coñacs*.

Silence in Álora, even in the shabby bar where the station bus waited. Civil guard and two *campesinos* slurping *café solos* and *aguardiente*. Silence broken only by spitting on the floor. What had he, what had he done? Oh shame! Had she accepted…?

As the automotor for Seville cruised northwards without stopping through *El Chorro*, the Count leaning our of the window, the station-master stood to attention, flag furled, giving then a wag of recognition, an imaginary *copa* thrust up in his left hand "¡*Por Escocia*!"

★

113

But the Count didn't reach Seville, where he was never seen again. He got off at *Bobadilla*, and took the train to Jerez de la Frontera, where he wandered round the bodegas tasting all sherry from *solera* to *seco*, and doing some murky deals over casks. He later took a taxi from Jerez de la Frontera to Sanlúcar de Barrameda. In that small Atlantic harbour he haggled with the owner of a sea-going fishing smack, loaded it up with barrels of sherry, *manzanilla* and *coñac*, and set sail unsteadily for the Bristol Channel. With the certainty that he would make a fortune in his new career as smuggler.

DON ANDRÉS TRIUMPHANT

It was a week after *don* Ciego's pauper's funeral.

The inhabitants of Life Street were cowering in their doorways and porches. The dairy maid at the foot of the African tower exchanged shrieks of terror with the Mexicans peering fearfully out of their portico. Cascades of planks hurled from on high were landing with tremendous crashes in the little square, scattering the few pedestrians unwise enough to risk crossing from one side to the other.

"¡*Don* Andrés! What are you doing? Stop or you will kill someone. Stop at once! You cant do this!"

"Can't I just!" came the bellow from the heights, "this is my own house and I can do what I like."

This was followed up at once by the hurling of further planks, landing in the square with a resounding crash and sending up a cloud of blinding dust.

Even the tailor next door left off quarrelling with his wife and half opened the boxed window in front of his sewing machine, remonstrating impotently at the figure looming over them, outlined against the sky.

"¡*Don* Andrés! ¡*don* Andrés!" he called out in his weak, hoarse voice, "tell us, what is it you're doing?"

"I'm demolishing *don* Ciego's residence, if you want to know, though it's no business of yours."

With that he hurled an enormous joist over the parapet of the flat roof.

The terrified neighbours consulted one another in smothered calls across the square and it was decided to call the police.

After about a quarter of an hour two civil guards in patent leather three-cornered sombreros came trotting into the square. They stopped at the entrance to number 4, the corporal calling out "¡Don Andrés! ¡Don Andrés! Desist, ¡hombre! There are children about. They might be injured or even killed!"

But all they got for answer was a series of rafters flung down which forced them to take refuge in the porch.

"It's no good" protested a neighbour, "he won't stop. You'll have to arrest him."

But don Andrés had locked the iron grill that prevented entrance to the patio. It was decided to call for reinforcements. As the corporal telephoned from a neighbour's house to the comisaría to report what was happening, the other civil guard cordoned off the entrances and exits of Life Street. Very soon a posse of three further guards under the command of a sergeant marched into the square, neighbours applauding, only to scatter as more roofing came hurtling down.

"We shall have to arrest you, don Andrés. Come down and give yourself up" shouted the sergeant, warily looking out from the porch of the house opposite.

"Give myself up! You must be crazy! I am master of my own house and the pavement adjoining it belongs to me."

"You must come with us to the comisaría, don Andrés" the sergeant repeated.

This time don Andrés re-appeared at the parapet and roared "Down with the civil guard! Up with Andrés!"

All the inhabitants of the square were astonished at this effrontery, even from don Andrés, who was famous in Santa Cruz for his outrageous and domineering behaviour.

"Arrest him! You must arrest him now" shouted several voices.

As a well-known supporter of Franco – didn't he take the ABC newspaper – the authorities generally humoured him. But this was going too far. Nevertheless the sergeant ordered his men to disperse, and strutting into the centre of the little square called up

"Don Andrés, usted es un caballero. You are a gentleman. If I ask you kindly to come down and join me for a little chat, would you be so kind?"

The sergeant of course knew the psychology of the Spaniard. Order him to do something and he will refuse. But appeal to his nobility and he will respond.

So the *patio* grill was unlocked and *don* Andrés and the sergeant sat down together in the corner of the *patio*.

"May I ask" the sergeant began, "why you said 'Down with the civil guard!'?"

"It's obvious" retorted *don* Andrés, "I was up there and you were down below."

The black-moustached sergeant gaped at *don* Andrés for a moment, and then suddenly burst out laughing in that gravel tone of those used to plentiful red wine and *aguardiente*.

"Ana, two *coñacs*!" ordered *don* Andrés

When these had been downed in one gulp, the sergeant shook hands with *don* Andrés, begged him as a personal favour to desist from endangering fellow *sevillanos*, saluted, and left. Leaving *don* Andrés master of the morning. Much to the chagrin of his neighbours.

THE TRAGEDY OF DEATH STREET

In the early evening that very same day *don* Andrés was sitting at the corner table in the patio with *don* Antonio, the renegade priest turned *Coca-Cola* salesman. Just beside them were stacked four crates of *Coca-Cola* bottles.

"How much should I charge for them *don* Antonio?" whispered Andrés.

"You can sell them for five *pesetas* each, and keep one *peseta* for yourself" Antonio replied in an undertone, for *doña* Ana was within earshot in her shadowy little sitting-room, the door ajar.

"What time is it?" Antonio asked. I'll have to be getting off to the warehouse. The *patio* clock's stopped hasn't it?"

"Yes, it has" grumbled Andrés. "Ana says we'll have to get a new one, but that clock was given to me by the members of my club, as well as the big picture of Franco on the wall of my bedroom. It's a very good clock, even if it's a bit old. It goes very well when it goes" he added with a snort before spitting with a smack on the tiled floor.

"Yes, when it goes! When it goes!" came the gently ironic retort from *doña* Ana's room.

Don Andrés spread his hands out palms upward with a shrug of his massive shoulders and a jagged-mouthed grimace at Antonio.

Getting up and putting on a navy blue beret to cover his tonsure, Antonio paused a moment at the doorway.

"By the way, *don* Andrés, what's happened to the cat? I haven't seen it for days."

"I threw it into the dry moat surrounding the old tobacco factory" *don* Andrés whispered. "Dozens of cats there are in it. But a lot of crazy foreign women, English they say they are, feed them with scraps they throw over the parapet. 20 metre sheer walls the moat has, so the brutes can't get out" he chortled.

"*Hasta luego, don* Andrés. See you later."

"*Adiós don* Antonio."

An hour or so before dinner Andrés was holding forth about the history of *Santa Cruz* as the lodgers began congregating from their various activities in the town. Leaning forward on his wicker chair and fixing his small eyes on any casual listener, the knob on his left cheek protruding as his chin wagged, he was momentarily interrupted by Anita, who looked out of the kitchen and said "*Santa Cruz* is an enchanted quarter."

"Yes, girl it is" said *don* Andrés gravely nodding his head, "but you don't know its terrible past."

Suddenly there was a raised voice as though someone was declaiming in the little square. Andrés swung his left leg up and down to strike his right shoe and with a grunt shot out to Life Street.

An elderly guide was addressing a small group of Spanish tourists. No foreign hordes had yet descended on Seville. *Don* Andrés stood listening for some time with his head cocked on one side, and then advanced his bulky figure to confront the huddled group.

"Don't listen to a word he says" remonstrated Andrés to the astounded tourists, "he doesn't speak a word of the truth and makes it all up so that it is more interesting, or so he thinks."

The unfortunate guide had turned his flock towards the floodlit cathedral tower looming over the city two hundred yards away, buzzards circling slowly round it.

"The *Giralda* tower was not built in two stages. That's his first error. It was in three stages. The upright stones at the base were the foundation laid by the Romans, long before the Moors and then the Christians centuries later completed it."

The tourists shuffled uneasily.

"As for what your guide said about Water Lane having been a stream in the past, that is also nonsense." he fumed, turning to the *Callejón del Agua* at the south side of Life Street. "It was a Roman aqueduct" added *don* Andrés, "and never was anything else. A Roman aqueduct it was and that's how the street got its name."

The tourist flock looked sheepishly towards their guide, who stood sulkily apart with an absent-minded mien, as though he was indifferent to the scandalous behaviour of *don* Andrés.

"But his greatest mistake has been to say that Life Street used to be called Death Street. Life Street was never Death Street. Death Street, which is only fifty metres from here is now called Susona, after the young Jewish woman who betrayed her father to the Christians. Susona's skull was hung over her doorway. That is why it was called Death Street."

The women among the tourists gasped, Andrés now enjoying the rapt attention of his listeners.

"You must know that this is the old Jewish quarter of Seville, 'Juderia'. You can see it emblazoned on the wall over there, 'Jewry'. Now the Jews had a long and dangerous history in this town. Before the Arabs came they had been persecuted in Visigothic Spain and the Jews had planned a general rising with the support of African Jews. For the Jews had many trading outposts on the North African coast. But when they got wind of the proposed Arab invasion, they acted as spies and emissaries for the Arabs, facilitating their conquest. So the Arabs allowed the Jews to survive in ghettoes for more than five hundred years.

But then came the Christian reconquest. By the middle of the thirteenth century, in 1248 it was, Seville was re-captured from the Arabs, long before they were expelled from Granada. The Christian king Fernando III, the heroic leader known as San Fernando, allowed the Jews to coexist with the Christians, particularly in this part of the city: and under his son, Alfonso X, Alfonso the Wise, the Jews were given three mosques which they converted to synagogues. One of these was in the *plaza Santa Cruz*, just at the end of the *Callejón del Agua* over there.

The Jews were good businessmen and with their banks and other enterprises helped to make Seville prosperous. But the Jews were always suspect, living their life apart, and were regarded by many Christians with suspicion, who felt they were not loyal to their country but to their own race and Jewish interests.

And so it happened that the Christian archdeacon of Écija came to Seville in 1391 and stirred up anti-Jewish riots. Christians, many of them jealous of Jewish prosperity, came in hundreds to this quarter of Seville and ransacked and plundered their businesses and houses. Then the archdeacon inflamed the Christians even more by his preaching and urged the mobs to kill the Jews. In no time they returned to *Santa Cruz*, to this very quarter, and slaughtered Jews in hundreds. Many Jews tried to escape from *Santa Cruz* but the Christian mobs were waiting for them at the two entrances to the ghetto: one at *Mateos Gago* street just over there by the *Giralda*" exclaimed *don* Andrés gesticulating in that direction, "and the other at the *Puerta de la Carne,* both not far from here. When the fleeing Jews reached the gates in terror the Christians hacked them to death with knives, swords, axes, anything they could lay hands on. This was known as *La Matanza*, the infamous, terrible massacre."

Some of the women tourists were now in tears and there were mutterings from the men of "*¡Qué vergüenza!*" "*¡Qué horrible!*" "*¡Ay, Dios mío!*"

"After that dreadful slaughter" continued *don* Andrés, now absolutely sure of his audience, "the Jews who remained gradually built up their businesses again, but of course they were always uneasy and the Christians remained suspicious of them.

And then, almost a century later, the rich Jewish banker, Diego Suson, who lived in what became known as Death Street, led a conspiracy of leading Jews in Seville with the aim of overthrowing the Christian government of the city. He held clandestine meetings in his house – only two streets from here – in the evenings after business with the most prosperous Jews of Seville.

And now we come to the climax of the story. It happened that his beautiful young daughter, Susona, was the secret concubine of one of the aristocratic Christians of Seville. She used to slip out of the house at night, when her father had gone to bed, passing out of Judería by the *Mateos Gago* gate and spending the night in the young Christian's palace, returning to her father's house just before dawn.

But one night her father had a very late meeting with the Jewish conspirators, finalising their plans. Susona was impatient to go to her lover's house, so she put her ear to the door of the room where the Jews were in conclave to see if the meeting was coming to an end. And this is what she heard.

'We'll kill all the upper class Christians so they have no leaders. Then we'll free the prisoners from the jails and give them arms.

Likewise the galley slaves at the port, and the ordinary slaves too, besides the *moriscos. ¡Mañana!'*

Susona was breathless with terror when she heard these terrible plans. Her lover, as an aristocrat, would be one of the first to be murdered in his palace. She waited impatiently for the end of the meeting and when the plotters had gone home and her father to bed, she flitted like a shadow in the night out of Judería by the *Mateos Gago* gate to her lover's house.

There she threw herself into his arms and tearfully told him all she had heard. Her Christian lover immediately alerted the authorities and in no time the Jewish conspirators were arrested and imprisoned. Three days later they were executed, including Susona's father."

"And what happened to Susona?" called out one of the tourists.

"What happened to her? She was overcome with remorse for what she had done. She went to the cathedral, where she confessed and was received into the Christian faith. She then went to a nunnery and lived there in penitence for several years. But when she emerged she was reviled by Jewry for her treachery and lived the rest of her life in anguish. Susona made a will stipulating that her skull should be fixed to the wall outside her house on her death as a token of penitence and a warning to others of the imminence of death. And so that street was known as Death Street and a mosaic to this day commemorates that skull on the wall of her house. But the inhabitants of the street took fright and the name was changed to Susona. And that is the name of the street to this day."

The congregation of tourists applauded *don* Andrés for his masterly telling of the tragic tale, while their guide made himself as shamefacedly inconspicuous as possible.

"How well you narrated that tragic history, *don* Andrés" they said over and over again. "*Usted sabe, don* Andrés. You know it all."

"*¡Hay que ir con la gente que sabe!*" retorted *don* Andrés with a scornful glance at the wretched guide. "One must keep company with people who know what they're talking about! Now then, would you like to have a look at a typical Andalusian *patio*? You would? Well just take two steps, pass this way into the entrance to my house."

Don Andrés's patio was in fact quite ordinary and without any particular distinction, roofed over by a glass dome. But the tourists flocked in with exaggerated encomiums of admiration. Once they were inside *don* Andrés inquired, cocking his head on one side "How about a *Coca-Cola*? Only five *pesetas* each."

WISDON IS FOR SALE AT UNIVERSITY

Hasta la sabiduría vende la Universidad;
verdad – Góngora

There was a carnival atmosphere in the dreary old University of Deusto, looking in the semi-perpetual drizzle over the filthy river *Nervion* and derelict shipyards. It was degree examination day for the repeat students of English Philology and two stray French remnants. Tomorrow the hysterical females would be uncaged. Those who passed, that is.

It was in the nineteen-sixties, when Spanish Faculties of Philosophy and Letters were still more or less finishing schools for girls, with a sprinkling of somewhat odd males among them, particularly in private universities. The young ladies of this Jesuit enclave were generally the daughters of wealthy fathers such as the high state functionary who dispatched his rebellious offspring in the chauffeur-driven car of his office.

As the students thronged the dingy brown corridor outside the examination hall with yelps, giggles and exclamations of "¡*Qué falda llevas, chica!*" What a wonderful skirt you've got on, girl! and with that peculiar feminine Basque exclamatition "¡*OOUUUEEE!* "¡*QUÉ GUAPA ERES!*" How pretty you look! All shrieking now abated as the examiners loomed at the far end of the corridor; except for the high state functionary's daughter, who screamed "I hate books" just as those august personages drew near.

With considerable self-importance the examiners drafted in from State universities to legitimise the Jesuit curriculum were approaching in a crooked crocodile. With much hugging, planting of kisses on either cheek and loud "¿*Qué tal?*" greetings as acquaintance with colleagues after the summer is renewed this chilly

October morning. One or two of the Professors condescendingly greeted the awed gaggle of girls crowding the passage with an "¡*Hola, chicas*!" but passed on pompously into the examination hall, shepherded ceremoniously by the Jesuitically black-robed Dean of the Faculty.

At the head of the crocodile were two remarkable figures, one resembling a cross between Al Capone and Frank Sinatra with his jaunty-angled trilby at the back of his head as he made loud chirpy comments from his monkey-like mouth. His companion, solemn and soft-spoken in a brushed black Homburg and heavy black fur-collared overcoat epitomised the successful undertaker. These distinguished Professors were followed by *doña* Inés, a rotund cackling one-eyed lady known as *La Tuerta*, and the extremely elegant *doña* Lucía, dressed in furs and emeralds, who had a small quizzical smile on her exquisitely painted lips as she nodded at the caustic humour of *La Tuerta*. These *damas* were escorted by the rubicund, moustachioed Professor of French literature, *señor* Bocanegra, who had travelled from Castile especially to examine the two left-overs of French philology. Just then, *el Catedrático* Bocanegra, who never minced words, explained in his wine-soaked voice to the two lady Professors "I don't speak French. But my wife does, you know. After all, she's French, ha! ha! ha!"

All these dignitaries had arrived by plane or *Talgo*, (first class, of course) from the centre and the four quarters of Spain and were lodged in luxury hotels, besides being paid a huge honorarium for their academic acumen. It was of great importance to humour, flatter and appease these representatives of the highest academic prestige, in whose hands and judgement the fate of the students and the good name of the University of Deusto rested.

But when the Dean had adroitly ushered the Professors into the examination hall he revealed to them a serious hitch: one of the external examiners had failed to arrive, having sent an express letter to the effect that she had to attend a wedding on that day. And without her, the required quorum for the official convocation of the Ministry of Education would be invalid.

The super-subtle Jesuit Dean displayed the letter from the

absent lady Professor from Seville and approached the elegant *profesora* in furs and emeralds, saying with a significant leer:

"Her writing is very like yours, *doña* Lucía."

"What do you mean, Father?" the demure *dama* replied with a quizzical half-smile.

"Well, *doña* Lucía, couldn't you copy her writing and sign her name on the official convocation, so that we may proceed?"

"Reverend Father, I absolutely refuse" gasped the lady, "it would be quite against my principles to commit a forgery."

Nothing taken aback, the Dean fixed her with a slightly sardonic smile and with a twinkle in his eye jocundly mimicked her, repeating "I absolutely refuse! I absolutely refuse!" which he did at intervals throughout the day.

"What's this? What's the trouble, Father?" asked the undertaker in his suave, grey voice, gently nudging the Dean with his elbow. "A signature, no more? Give me the convocation sheet, please."

And in a moment, with effortless aplomb, the undertaker had inscribed such a perfect copy of the absent examiner's signature on the Ministry of Education convocation document that she herself wouldn't have known it to be fake.

This problem resolved, the doors of the examination hall were flung open by the beadle and the female hordes rushed in with many exclamations of "¡*Suerte, chica!*" Good luck, girl! And "¡*Qué miedo tengo!*" How scared I am! And so forth.

Capone-Sinatra called one of the front row girls up to put her hand into the little velvet bag with wooden discs numbered from 1 to 35, the total lottery numbers of examination questions. She withdrew number 1, to a chorus of OOOOUUUUEEEES from the feminine scholars. It was Chaucer. Then another very pretty girl was espied by Capone-Sinatra and called up with a wink to repeat the operation. She drew number 23, the modern novel. Again OOOOUUUUEEEEs. And the girls set to on the regurgitation of their memorised screeds, all questions having been in their possession for a month, in accordance with the idiosyncrasies of the Spanish university system. They had three hours for the task.

Meanwhile, some of the *Catedráticos* began walking about the hall, exchanging loud comments on their summer holidays, their journeys, and the situation in their various universities; not neglecting to criticise colleagues and absent rivals.

With these conversations in full swing, the undertaker slipped out of the hall on some pretext and made his way to the office of the Dean's secretary, a buxom woman of forty with flaming red cheeks, brought up in a convent where she had been in charge of the nuns' market garden. In contrast with her complexion her name was Virgin of the Snows.

"Good morning, *señorita*" said the undertaker in his smoothest tones, "you remember me, I think."

"Oh yes, we remember you alright" said the secretary with a glacial appraising glance, as if to deduce what it could be that brought him to her office.

"You know, as a pensioner I have the Gold Card that gives a discount on the railway. Now if you kindly arrange it with the University administration office they could give me credit for my return ticket, and of course the University would benefit by getting the discount."

"¡*Vaya tomate que nos ha traído!*" "What a tomato you've landed us with" the red-faced secretary exclaimed with a side-long look at the Professor. "Your hotel is paid for by the University, and the stipend you are paid for the examination more than covers all expenses, including the rail ticket. But if you like, I can get hold of the Dean and ask him about it."

"Oh, no. Please don't trouble to do that" hastily murmured the undertaker. "It's quite all right. Just a little misunderstanding, you know. Thank you so much for enlightening me" he said, making a dignified but rapid exit from the office, just in case the Dean should appear.

However, the undertaker was a man of considerable resource, and not likely to be deflected so easily from his purpose. Quickly he slipped down the back stairs to the Institute of Languages, where he knew the Dean had another secretary, a timid young girl with pigtails. Assured that the Dean was in the Faculty itself, he sidled into her little office with many a flowery compliment, and repeated his tale about the Golden Card and the favour he would be doing the University by letting them use it to get him a cut price ticket for the *Talgo*.

The obliging secretary, a little overawed but anxious to do well by such an important personage, hurried to the Administration offices, still open though it was a Saturday morning; where with a nod and a wink the matter was opportunistically settled. With a gracious little bow, the *Catedrático* accepted the blushing girl's discreet white envelope. Which of course meant that he had been paid twice for that journey.

When the undertaker returned to the examination hall he was astounded to see a figure standing on its head in front of the scribbling students. It was the portly Dr. Bocanegra, Professor of French literature, whose face was an apoplectic purple. But the undertaker having observed him north to south he rebounded to his feet, grunting with satisfaction that something must be done to relieve the boredom of invigilating, and pocketing the '*duro*' that Capone-Sinatra had thrown on the floor in appreciation of his bravura performance. The ladies laughed and there were predictable OOOOUUUUEEEEs from the students, as Bocanegra exclaimed "That'll pay for a couple of *tintos*." Judging by his complexion, that would be a small adjunct to his daily intake.

When the three hours came to an end, the Dean re-appeared to escort the examiners to the waiting University car and a taxi; having carefully closed the self-locking door of the examination hall where the students' screeds lay secure on their desks.

The *Catedráticos* were ferried to the best restaurant in Bilbao where they had a sumptuous lunch accompanied by the best wines, *coñacs* and liqueurs. Which brought forth multitudinous anecdotes by Capone-Sinatra and the boisterous Professor of French. One or two of which brought blushes to *doña* Lucía's velvet cheeks. So that when the time came for the oral examination of the students, they were all on top form.

¡*Caramba*! When the Professors passed through the throng of students clamouring at the locked door of the examination hall – having predictably arrived half an hour late – there was an unforeseen impediment. It being a Saturday afternoon, the beadle had gone off duty. With the key of the hall.

Amid loud complaints of "¿*Qué pasa?*" and "¿*Qué es esto?*" by some of the more rebellious students the Professors looked at one another in consternation. What was to be done?

It was then that the undertaker beckoned to the bejewelled *doña* Lucía, who obligingly came up to him. With assured sleight of hand the undertaker plucked a hairpin from that lady's elegant coiffure and in a trice, as though well practised in the art, picked the lock of the offending self-locking door. Clearly a man of many parts, in those days when university pay was paltry, and many professors had two or three outside occupations to help make ends meet.

Now proceeded, one by one, the reading out of their *temas* by the students, the Professors yawning and intermittently chatting to each other. But just occasionally, a Professor would pounce on a point, particularly if it was one that gave an opportunity for the display of esoteric learning by the illustrious *Catedrático*.

"Your paper on the modern novel" commented Capone-Sinatra with his monkey-faced grin at the one male student, "mentions Kingsley Amis. Now can you tell us, what did Amis have to say about actors?"

"About actors?" said the confused student, who could see no relevance in such a question, and had to confess that he didn't know.

"Acting is the only profession you can get to the top of without having any intelligence" Capone-Sinatra gleefully enlightened the bashful student, having saved up this gem to impress the other examiners. The *Catedráticos* dutifully laughed. But Capone-Sinatra wasn't satisfied with that.

"And do you know when Amis said that, and where?" the self-preening Professor persisted.

"I'm afraid I can't tell you" the student stammered. And then, as an afterthought he added "But I suppose it was before he joined the academic world."

There were shrieks of laughter from the assembled students, until they were reprimanded by the undertaker in most solemn tones for their frivolous behaviour.

Then there was a whispered confabulation between the Professors in which it was mooted that the offending male student should be failed for disrespect. But the bejewelled lady Professor took the part of the handsome lad, to whom she had taken quite a fancy, single lady as she was, and so he was saved by his good looks.

He was followed by a bespectacled girl who read out three or four pages on Chaucer – the first of the lottery questions – in perfect English; so perfect that the cackling one-eyed crone demanded that the student show her the dissertation. *La Tuerta* held the individual pages up to the light, screwing them round clockwise, anti-clockwise and back again until she could focus that eye on their content.

"I can recognize" she screeched, "the author of your script perfectly. You have copied, word for word, an essay in the Pelican Guide to English Literature, isn't that so?"

"Yes, that's true, *señora*."

"What excuse have you?"

"Well, he knows so much more than I do and he expresses it so perfectly."

Even some of the students could not constrain themselves from laughing, until the undertaker informed the girl that she would be failed for plagiarism. At which the girl burst into tears; only to be reprimanded by *La Tuerta* for childishness and lack of dignity.

When the following candidate claimed "Virginia Woolf is great writer" the bejewelled lady was able to admonish her "Mind with your English" and when asked who the influence on Woolf was the student replied that there were several possible influences, including James Joyce.

"Wrong!" the lady professor upbraided her, "Haven't you read the critical works? If you had" she said, pulling a little card from her handbag as she put on her jewelled glasses, "you would know that Woolf described Ulysses as 'an illiterate, underbred book … the book of a self-taught working man'." And with that trump she glanced along the row of Professors, who acknowledged with nods of approval her distinguished acumen.

"Well, but…" the student stutteringly protested, "who then was the influence?"

"Dickens" la *profesora* responded tartly.

"Dickens!" incredulously exclaimed the valiant student.

"Yes, Dickens" intervened the undertaker, "if the lady professor tell you it was Dickens, then Dickens it was. There can be no gainsaying that; you must not argue, girl."

And so concluded the hearing of the students' papers. There remained only the final conclave of the Professors to award grades of pass, fail or distinction. But before that, after a long morning, afternoon and now evening, they repaired to the University bar for refreshments, leaving Capone-Sinatra to enjoy a quiet smoke at the top of the steps looking over the yellow brown river illuminated by a blast furnace. Capone-Sinatra had procured a Partaga on his University expense account at the nearby Hotel *Conde Duque*, a few hundred yards up the river bank, and relished the smoothness of the Cuban cigar.

As he was about to rejoin his colleagues at the bar, a figure rushed up to him in the shadows. It was a little peasant woman, mother of the girl failed for plagiarism.

"Excuse me, sir" she said, "you know my daughter worked very hard to memorise thirty pages word for word. I hope you may feel able to pass her for diligence, at least. I am a poor widow and I cannot pay for another year's tuition for my daughter. And by the way," she added, adopting a subservient stoop, "may I present you with a box of cigars. I had found out that you are a cigar smoker, you see."

Capone-Sinatra took hold of the box of 'Capote' Canary island cigars and hurled it over the parapet into the swirling waters of the Nervion. "Good riddance to those lousy cigars!" he said turning angrily on his heel into the building.

"Lousy cigars?" said the dejected widow to herself. Just then she noticed the band of Capone-Sinatra's cigar on the top step. "Partaga! Will it be that the Canary island Capotes were not good enough?"

She hurried along to the Hotel *Conde Duque*, where she knew the examiners resided, and asked the barman for a box of Partagas.

"Haven't got a full box left, *señora*" he said, "but if you don't mind taking a box with one missing, I can let you have it. You see, one of the Professors for the examinations at Deusto asked for a Partaga this morning before going to the University."

The poor woman took the box, paying an outrageous price for it, and rushed back to Deusto, just in time to meet Capone-Sinatra leaving the bar with his colleagues for the examination hall. Creeping up on him timorously in the corridor, she managed to get him aside for a moment. "I've discovered your favourite smoke" she said, humbly abasing herself. "I could leave these in your hotel and no one would know."

"Begone, woman! I told you before I don't accept lousy bribes." And he noticed that the box was of Partagas.

The Dean joined the august Professors for the final assessment. The examiners were for failing the girl who had shouted "I hate books" in the corridor just as they arrived. But the Dean asked them to "*abrir la manga*" – to open their sleeves – and let her through. To fail the rebellious and not very academic student daughter of a high state official, might have unpleasant repercussions. The astute Dean knew all about the undertaker's manoeuvres with his secretaries, which he did not let on. But he laid a hand on his shoulder, of which the significance was not lost.

"I propose she be awarded the maximum grade" the undertaker proclaimed in his suave voice. And so she was. *Sobresaliente cum Laude.*

As for the plagiarist, Capone-Sinatra felt considerable compassion after his rude treatment of the widow – and after all, she had offered his favourites. So after a tussle with *La Tuerta*, he insisted that the widow's daughter be passed for diligence.

The girls were called in, the results read out, and with whoops and shrieks of joy, the young lady licenciates raced out of the University for ever.

DR LEAVIS IN SPAIN

6 March 1972

There was an air of rare expectancy. Dr Leavis's lectures, the star event of the British Cultural Week at the University of Deusto, were imminent. An audience of some 300 from all over Spain, including a busload of students and lecturers from the University of Zaragoza, was converging on Bilbao.

Dr Leavis had been due to arrive the day before, but IBERIA overbooked their plane with a party of Dutch businessmen, bundled him off and dumped him in a London hotel for the plane next day. 'He will arrive in time', IBERIA glibly assured us. About to go again to Bilbao airport to meet him today, a telegram ominously arrived.

STRARK DISASTROUS WAIT BLIZZARD VOICE
GONE PONTLESS PROCEED MISERABLE
WRITING LEAVIS

The ominous turned to the horrible with a cryptic telex, apparently from IBERIA via British Embassy shortly before the first lecture was to begin: pax leavis now canx ns 55 I/date pse pass fol message to ivar watson universidad de deusto pointless to proceed now voiceless due to wait for hotel bus have returned to Cambridge

One could hear the hordes pounding upstairs to the lecture hall. An urgent phone call to Cambridge produced the hoarse whisper:

'I protested to IBERIA that I was an important lecturer with a public function, something that my modesty naturally disinclined me to do, and showed them my passport indicating that I am 77 years old, but they wouldn't take me to Bilbao, although my ticket was in order. This morning I lost my voice waiting in the cold for the bus. Looking for IBERIA staff… I was looking for drains to clear my throat into.'

There was nothing for it but to take a stiff dram, face the audience, and announce that Dr Leavis wasn't coming either today or tomorrow. Groans, gasps and even incredulous laughter from those who had travelled from afar and booked hotels in Bilbao. A fiasco.

Mirabile dictu, after what he described as 'a nightmare', Dr Leavis determined to make another foray. By 27 March he let us know, and on 4 April telegraphed proposing 17 and 18 April for the lectures. The Managing Director of IBERIA gave me his guarantee.

Sunday 16 April 1972

The plane from London was half an hour late, so we had plenty of time to wonder, waiting behind the customs barrier, what he would be like. I had only realized from that phone call that he was as old as 77, and as the plane drew up on the tarmac before us I had anxious auguries of crutches, sticks, wheelchairs, or at best doddering with support from someone else's shoulder.

But there, with buoyant stride, overtaking disembarking passengers as though familiar with the airport, was that unmistakable figure, large brown dome gleaming in the twilight, a long fluffy collar of grey-white hair fluttering at the nape of the neck in the evening breeze. And then he was coming at us:

'Dr Leavis!'

'Ah! – Watson.' He seems severe and surprised

But we are interrupted by the attentions of two obsequious servants of IBERIA, avid to make amends with smiles, with hand-shakes and futile efforts to wrest the bulky Gladstone bag from that horny hand. We are ushered into a car with *bienvenidas*, and after a few cursory remarks on the fineness of the evening and saying, with a pleased smile 'They put me in the VIP lounge and sent a chauffeur-driven car to my house', Dr Leavis without more ado launches into a denunciation of Cambridge academics. I settle back against the car cushions with immeasurable relief: this is our man, unimpaired. And an enquiry whether he would prefer a small hotel on the coast or the grandeur of the Carlton in town is brushed aside with only the proviso that it should be one in which one can get up in the night and make tea.

FRL:

'You were at Peterhouse. Ah yes, you wouldn't get much help there – Kingsley Amis. Attended lectures by Graham Hough? A worthless non-entity.'

Watson:

'He had quite a following at his lectures, unlike T. R. Henn, who started with about 150 but dwindled to a dozen next time. All the women disappeared. He would say "Gentlemen, as you know from your military manuals…". Wasn't he a brigadier?'

FRL:

'Yes, typical of the military mind. It's not surprising that was as high as he got. That man must have suffered when he was young. That manly voice. But he is a quivering jelly inside, a bully, hated by the college staff. He keeps the porter's lodge of St Catharine's College like a guard –room. I could knock Henn down with my 8 and a half stone and 5ft 6 to Henn's 6ft 3 ins and God knows how many stone.'

Watson:

'A Cambridge don and writer I've never heard you mention: what do you think of E. M. Forster?'

FRL:

'Worthless, characteristic of Bloomsbury and the Cambridge of King's. One knows now from memoirs about the relations between the sexes, things one had only suspected. And then there was the odious Bertrand Russell. It makes me furious to have been likened to him in appearance. I have no desire to read *his* memoirs. And of course there was the revolting Lytton Strachey. The poets of the time were revolting too. Auden and his 'Spain'. He and 'the battle'. After all he had to say there, he took care to be in America when war broke out, and now creeps back with alleged reluctance, sneering at those who stayed. As for Spender, he reviewed *Revaluation* cattily as parasitic Eliot in Criterion. Eliot was a Bloomsbury man, a toady of the establishment, with no editorial integrity.'

Watson:

'What about a poet who did fight in the Spanish war, John Cornford?'

FRL:

'Cornford was ruthless, took advantage of his great family background. A tough.'

Watson:

'Talking of memoirs, as the only great critic in English literature who is not also a poet, would you consider a biography?'

FRL:

'No, I couldn't, there are things that would hurt my wife. Even if I were to write my one novel, however well disguised, she would understand.'

Watson:

'I wasn't thinking of autobiography. Would you accept a Boswell, if one emerged?'

FRL:

'No. Johnson was a virtuoso of conversation. Dozens of people have asked to write my biography.'

When we reach the seaside hotel it transpires that Dr Leavis has no money and no Spanish. We go up to his third-floor room; Leavis looks round, peers into the bathroom and comes back to the doorway with a tired smile, tottering slightly now against the doorpost.

FRL:
I'm willing to meet anyone, but I don't feel social tonight.
I'm disorientated by the plane journey.'

And in the light of a sunset over the sea we agree to meet at 2.0p.m. tomorrow. Thank God he's here.

Monday 17 April 1972

But today has been the day of days. A dismal wet morning, heavy clouds lowering grey over the water. I sent my secretary, María de los Angeles, to the hotel with an umbrella at 10.0, timorous to meet the maestro; to be told he had been in and out of the hotel since 7.0. 'Out,' as he later told me, 'for a walk this fine morning to the hanging bridge at Santurce.'

Six miles, there and back.

'I'm an old distance runner.' He intimated. 'Got the distance runner's perfect heart.' I wondered at the spectacle, 77 years of lean intensity splashing along the sea wall, coming suddenly on Basques agape in the mist.

Who's for lunch with Leavis? Little Fr. Fernando García de Cortázar pirouetting on tiptoe in the patio, planting piquant kisses on dowagers' cheeks at a cultural fiesta. Not the man for Leavis.

A glimpse of the super-subtle Father Santa María sidling close to the wall yet majestic in his movements along the corridor like a black shadow; with only a swish of skirted robes he turns the corner, and vanishes.

I had been earlier to visit the Secretary-General of the university, Fr Luís Reizabal, who has the flaming and knobbly face of one of Chaucer's (several of his) religious rascals but particularly him of whom children are afeared. Besides this, he has the girth and cruel cunning of Thos. Cromwell, acting as hatchet man for the Rector.

His office is wholly symbolic of that den. It has no windows. For air, there is a ventilator behind a picture, that emanates from the university library, where students plot their tactics for strikes. Reizábal is able to apprise the Rector of their next moves. On his desk (the goodly prelate can only accommodate his girth by having a semi-circle cut in front of his chair) there is the effigy of a saintly friar, like Ye Monks whisky bottle. And sure enough, inside the effigy, a whisky bottle there is. Reizábal has a little high voice like a eunuch's and little pig-like eyes that dart everywhere suspiciously, cunningly and sometimes fearfully. Pouring two whiskies from the half-empty bottle, he complains that the Rector had drunk most of it last night, describing how he had been wild-boar shooting with a smack of pursy lips. At the mention of lunch he fixed me with a slow stare, and said he would let me know later.

On the way back to my office, after making sure the lecture room was ready for Leavis, I met our Dean, the young Father Ramón de Areitio, striding along like a swashbuckling cowboy, thumbs in his cassock vents as though hovering over Wild West holsters. Flashing his smile, the handsome idol of all the female students stops to ask me how things are going, but is too busy for lunch. 'If Leavis is, as you say, as famous as Unamuno, make sure you go to the best restaurant,' he grins, 'and send me the bill.'

It is a little after midday when there is a tap on my office door, and Luís Reizábal waddles in with a surreptitious glance along the corridor as he enters, walks up to me, nudges me with his colossal bulk, and squeaks 'Have you got a sweetie?' Prompted, I get my whisky bottle out of my regulation steel filing-cabinet and we see off most of it in half an hour. 'What about lunch, Reizábal?' Evading the question, a film descending over his eyes, the priest recounts the delights of cat roasted in sherry, previously kept underground for a couple of days to get it tender, breathing heavily at the gorgeous memory. And then, proffering an enormous Havana cigar from beneath his vestments, he regales me with plans to prematurely retire his Jesuitical enemies. I tell him I can imagine him in hell assisting Satan in the roasting of those unfortunate enough to get into his power. An obsequious turning of the spit. He looks hard at me, a smile flickers momentarily as though it doesn't know whether to come or go. Abruptly: no, he can't join Leavis; got a summons from the Rector. Then a sudden glance at his watch: Jesús, it is lunch time, and he might miss the Jesuitical repast. So he shuffles off in his carpet slippers as fast as his bloated body will carry him.

Unable to bring a Jesuit for lunch and delayed by these attempts, my secretary, a female student friend of hers and I set off to find a taxi. None at the stance. Gone for lunch. The driver of a small car there stops a passing Fiat and asks him to drop his passenger and take us. The irate driver refuses. But he stops another, whose passenger gets out, and we get in, arriving at the seaside hotel at 2.20 p.m.

'I'm sorry to be late Dr Leavis.' 'Don't be apologetic' he drawls with half-closed eyes, lying back in his lounge chair; and then starts up, as though surprised at his own words and leaps to the door, dressed in some ragged outfit of yesteryear.

'No, I won't have lunch, thank you very much, I only eat breakfast, you know.'

What then shall we do? Having decided on a short motor tour of the Basque country, we rumble off in the diesel car, Dr Leavis and I in the back, the timorous Mary of the Angels between us, her friend with fixed wolverine grin beside the drive, stolid, silent.

'Ah, Wittgenstein', Leavis intones, leaning forward to fix me with his eye, 'ah, there was a man. A handsome genius. But I offered to knock him down, followed him outside after a lecture; bullying an undergraduate. There should be more study of philosophy, philosophers such as Blake's enemies. But not in those academic philosophy departments. I'm out to protect the intelligent student, you know, from the academic mind.'

'Of course it was T. S. Eliot who made the ugly remark that I was rotting undergraduates: in an essay on D. H. Lawrence, the inference was obvious. But he called at my house, and I knew why he had come. He sat for hours and deposited a mountain of ash on our carpet and tried to make his peace. But he got nowhere. I knew what he was: a toady of the establishment. No editorial integrity. He rejected an unfavourable review of – [I couldn't catch the name] in the *Criterion*. But there *was* rotting of undergraduates then, as there is *now*.'

Watson:

'But other than Eliot, there were also innovators, original thinkers among critics, such as I. A. Richards.'

FRL:

'Richards is and was a bogus pseudo-scientist. And practical criticism was not invented by him.'

Watson:

'But you had your own followers, such as L.C. Knights.'

FRL:

'Knights. Ah, yes. He ratted on me many years ago. Something might have been made of him.'

Watson:

'But Traversi, surely, was a devoted follower. I wrote to invite him to lecture this week too, but got no answer, in spite of telling him that you would be here.'

FRL:

'Yes, Traversi… one can tell a genuine man… I got Traversi's first book on Shakespeare published. Though it is sometimes naïve in arguing from imagery – take the claim that Lear is a play of wider, more inclusive range of human experience, evidenced by imagery ranging from slime to the ethereal. And his wife is admirable, as well as knowledgeable.'

Watson:

'I wonder why he didn't become a university teacher.'

FRL:

'Perhaps he was disgusted by the futility of the academic world. The world of C. P. Snow, the establishment creep. I met him in the thirties, the only occasion. In desperate days for me. He was lower-middle class. Gave avuncular, pompous advice of no use to anyone except Snows. Knew all ways and means to grants, and all the paraphernalia he used to advance himself.'

Watson:
'But what about Tillyard; wasn't he one of the better critics of the time?'

FRL:
'The worst type of academic.'

We were now passing the nineteenth-century neo-Gothic Castle of Butrón, once owned by the Dukes of Medinaceli, and the student in front turned excitedly on Leavis, giving him the full exposure of her ceaseless grin as she related some anecdote about its short history. Leavis gave a glance at the castle and went on:
'My son Ralph is a genius – could read all or most of Shakespeare at 5. Don't ask me what he made of it. But to read it he must have made something of it. He suffered fat-rejection disease; affects only the children of intellectuals. Had to be fed food with the fats broken down, and would only eat when distracted. He had difficulty with his mother, on account of early troubles over feeding. She had to feed him. At 16 or 17 he was sent to the organist at St John's. Asked to play a Mozart symphony score at sight on the piano. Which he did. And then he was asked to play it in a different key. He did it. He was told "You must find us very slow." I'm afraid for his future in the academic world. He's been told that if he would practice a bit more, he'd be a brilliant violinist.' We took the coast road round Baquio, up to the twelfth-century Romanesque church of Pelayo, and got out. Dr Leavis said he had never seen one so old or like that, and turning towards the hill showed concern for a donkey labouring downhill under a burden of grass and the stick of an old woman, but apart from remarking that he liked to see the waves come in, showed no interest whatsoever in town, village or country. On the return journey the flow is interrupted – we stop the car, for Dr Leavis is ill. We all get out again and he walks off alone up the road; helpless, we watch him retching afar off. I order the girls into the car, Leavis

comes back, and we put him beside the driver for the journey home. But between the twitter of the chicas, the grind of the diesel and the low drone of Leavis's voice directed straight ahead. I have to hold my breath to hear. I gather only that David Holbrook's motives for complaint against the permissive society were questionable; while John Holloway was disparaged, but for what reason was inaudible.

We reach my house at 4.30 and Dr. Leavis sits in a chair by the window overlooking the sea far below, while tea is brought. I retreat to the kitchen to stoke the central heating and my own reserves, returning to hear that he has revived with a solitary biscuit and a gigantic cup of tea.

'You see,' he intoned, 'I am so sensitive, I can't digest anything, I've had no digestion for thirty years. The trouble is I feel everything so strongly. Can't rest either; I don't really rest at night; if I'm spoken to while asleep, I always wake in time to hear the beginning of the first sentence. No, the only time I can relax is when I'm awake, as now in the sun or on the return motor drive.'

We walk down the hill to the hotel, and Leavis sprints upstairs to the third floor, disdaining the lift – 'I must get some exercise.' He took a long time, returning to say: 'I panicked for a moment. Couldn't find my tie. I wondered if someone had gone in and removed it.'

When we reached the university we had some time in hand, and I took him along to the English Department rooms, Leavis remarking, as we walked along the corridors, on Jesuit honesty. Original as always in his critical views. Observing a print of Blake's Newton he said: 'It is one of my favourites, though the colour is brighter in the original.'

We turned into the lecturers' common room, where there were paintings by the Basque Figueras on the walls, which provoked him to say: "There is a confusion of Seurat, Monet and himself: the result is nothing, really."

We sat at a table while Leavis ruminated on his lecture: 'Swinburne, Eliot & Yeats: the Revolution in English Poetry in the 1920s', fingering his first edition of Yeats, and remarking: 'I do sell my first editions, even with notes scribbled on them, in fact they give me a higher price for those with notes.'

I reminded him that we were due to meet the Rector before the lecture.

FRL:
'No, I don't object at all. I'm not difficult in that way.'

We found the bulky, black, goggling figure of the Rector hurrying along the corridor to meet us, and readily led us to what he called the secret entrance to his rectorate, ushering Dr Leavis in front of him and leaving me to follow his vast behind. As soon as we were seated in what had been a handsome oak-panelled study, converted by the busily modernising rector into a lurid pseudo-corporate magnate's office. Leavis embarked again on a panegyric of Wittgenstein, then mentioned that he was particularly interested at the moment in Polanyi: 'I discovered him for myself, an English philosopher.'

The rector eyeing him owlishly and claiming unconvincingly that he knew him too, Leavis ignored him and turning to me said: 'My favourite seventeenth-century poem is Marvell's "Dialogue Between the Soul and Body". It's my Puritan background coming out.'

Watson:
'I think Marvell's greatest poem is "The Garden", a poem that both defines, in the Coleridgean sense, the difference between Imagination and Fancy and is also imaginative in that sense.'

FRL:
'Yes, that is so.'

In his pidgin English the Rector now expressed the hope that Dr Leavis might come again.

FRL:
'In that case I hope I might talk on "The Idea of a University".'

The Rector riposted that he had written, by himself, a book, a book on university education, which he hoped to have published. With relief, we left for the lecture hall.

'A good man, but nothing more,' was Leavis's verdict. Mine was less generous.

When we got to the lecture room, I was taken aback by the paucity of people: only about a hundred. Leavis peered in, and I hoped he was not disappointed. He was received with loud applause, standing diffidently aside while introduced. The lecture ran on the expected line: Swinburne being a musical poet, but bogus; Yeats a lesser poet than T. S. Eliot, the two 'Byzantiums' illustrating his greatness and the speed of his decline. Eliot was the genius who changed expression in the twentieth century.

The lecture had included a good deal of reading out of poems, and Leavis stopped abruptly because, he said, he found his voice going. We shepherded him to the Jesuits' visiting room, where I left him discoursing to astounded Spanish profesores and profesoras, even the most garrulous hags among the latter struck into a reverent awed silence while I went to find the elusive Father Santa-María. He was at his desk in a small pool of light in the cavernous gloom of his ascetic study, the only sound the sharp ticking of the clock. He leaned back in his chair, eyes aglitter behind goldrimmed spectacles, turning over and over a small black rubber ball in his cancerous hand as though manipulating the world.

'You have invited the Rector?' he asked with a sardonic smile.
'No.'
'And Reizábal?'
'No.'
'Then I will come', he agreed, with a conspiratorial chuckle.

We were to go to my house in Algorta for dinner, and thinking Santa-María and Leavis would strike up a rapport on the way, I put them in a taxi with Mary of the Angels; who tells me they travelled in silence.

We settled in chairs in the long sitting-room over-looking the sea, Leavis established in his favourite place by the window, so that he was facing down the rows of keenly attentive guests as though it were a lecture hall. On one side of him sat Father Santa-María, on the other the genial doctora Luisa Grigera, expert on Quevedo and terror of the Hispánicas department. Eager young girls draped themselves on window-sills at his elbow, young men at his feet, absenting themselves only to collect plates of chicken and smoked hams, which they wolfed before, behind and beside the ascetic doctor, who contented himself with a brandy and soda, which he occasionally remembered he held clasped in a great glass, and then, with a start, swallowed with relish.

If his voice had been going in the lecture, the silence of the journey had revived it. For apart from these brief concessions to the body, not a moment was spared from matters intellectual, as though the record must be set straight, writers rightly placed, nonentities disposed of world-wide in the limited time at our disposal. Interruptions or uncongenial approaches were waved aside or ignored, according to their merit as the scourge of the academic world laid about him the ghosts of dead antagonists, trampling with fiendish glee on one or two who showed propensities to resurrection, re-enacting the death-rattle of the utterly vanquished, tolerating neither the naïve nor the repentant, sabring new 'scientific' critics and assaulting manfully the 'media' encampments of modern mediocrity.

But everyone wanted to know about his own life, and as was fitting, he began with the beginning. He was of Gascon origin, the family coming over into England before the Edict of Nantes.

'My father was an aristocrat. Though of course in the modern world that counts for nothing. There was a Cambridge lecturer who came speaking some lower-class dialect; and in two years he was speaking "diplomatic English". That made me feel ashamed of my origins.'

He now reiterated what he had earlier told me about his son, and his reminiscences then turned back to his earliest days: he remembered the Boer War, the emergence of the motor car, and from first-hand experience the horrors endured by the troops in the trenches in the First World War. He recalled his experience of travelling on the roofs of trains and the dangers inherent when entering tunnels, the use of the tank and the quick development of bombers.

But Cambridge was his life's struggle.

'It was Basil Willey, the pious Willey who got me a university lectureship, in my fifties. I had been an assistant lecturer till then. And it was only after a confrontation. I went to see Willey, the newly appointed Professor, and walked out when he said he doubted whether he could arrange it. But he did manage it. Joan Bennett and I were made lecturers together. And in my sixty-fifth year they made me Reader. But I had no say in the appointment of academic staff. I stood for Professor of Poetry at Oxford to keep Helen Gardner out. Auden got it. The only thing Oxford has over Cambridge is the High Street; but you can't see it for traffic.'

'I was urged to go to America in the difficult period. There were those who did, of course, like Auden, who got out in the war and now comes back with alleged reluctance, turning up his nose at those who stayed.

'But American universities, you know, are the end, with their "critical method", which comes back to Britain, helped along over there by I. A. Richards. Linguistics is a bogus science.

'My wife is the greatest modern critic of the novel, and yet an American could *tell her*' – he roared it out – "Nelly Dean is evil!"

His brandy glass lay alongside his thigh; if it, so thin, could be called that – and on being told, he picks it up, says he thought it was empty, and drains off the good deal that was left in it at one gulp. 'My wife reads widely and keeps an eye out for new development. We are practised, *ex-Scrutiny*, at keeping a look-out for new novelists likely to remain unheard-of, as reviewers review the works of their friends. The establishment is dominated by coteries. But we've won. Ours has been a collaborative achievement. *Ils ont peur*. I get my letters published in *The Times*, always, and very high up the page. But I have told *The Times Literary Supplement* I will never write for them again. *The New Statesman* and the Sunday papers are impossible. I won't take *The Observer* any more, and *The Sunday Times* is no better.

'The British Council excluded me from its pamphlet series: I heard it had been said "He's only a critic." My objection to the British Council is to Davies Street, not the men in the job. The Davies Street handling of a friend of mine who had been in Caracas during the war and was then offered a one-year contract in his fifties. My enquiries produced the answer "He's not one of us", though the man had been very successful.'

Asked what he thought of the new universities, Leavis replied: 'The standard is lower; it's inevitable. There is competition to get in, but the quality is down. And there is student indiscipline. And the giving in of staff. I kept order in my corridor. [University of York]. I have walked through a room of loafing students kicking legs aside. The behaviour is disgusting. Cigarette packets thrown on the floor, television all day. I get up early and go into the Common Room to read the papers, and meet the cleaning women faced with this. I have urged them to refuse to clean it – "You're irreplaceable – though I'm not inciting you" I have told them.'

Asked now if he got fed up with sycophancy by students in lectures, Leavis replied laconically 'Yes.' Questioner: 'Does anyone stand up to you in argument?'

FRL:

'Only stupid undergraduates. I can beat anyone, having superior knowledge, which helps, and practice in the use of weapons. I like to see my students for supervision two or three times a week. I did more than I was paid for.'

Q:

'Can you explain your apparent volte-face with regards to Dickens?'

Dr Leavis bypassed the question, changing chairs, remarking on the hardness of the one he had been sitting on due to his being bony, merely commenting 'Carlyle was a great man. A beneficial influence on Dickens.'

Q:

'What are your views on Solzhenitsyn?'

FRL:

'*The First Circle* is a great novel, but one *feels Dr Zhivago* more,

147

down here', he expostulated, holding himself in the guts.

Q:

'Nineteenth-century Russian novels?'

FRL:

'*War and Peace* is undoubtedly a great work, but' – with a knowing smile – *Il y a des longueurs*, you know. *Anna Karenina* is Tolstoy's greatest novel.'

Q:

'Dostoyevsky?'

FRL:

'*The Devils* is his best novel. In general I am not in favour of Dostoyevsky. That brand of religion.'

Q:

' Do you admire *The Idiot*?'

FRL:

'No.'

Q:

'Did you find *The Brothers Karamazov* disappointing?'

FRL:

'Yes, extremely so.'

Q:

'And what about Spanish literature?'

FRL:

'I have no intentions regarding Spanish literature. One mustn't spread oneself too much. There is not much time left: one must be selective. I did help Wilson translate the poems of Gongora.'

Q:

'What do you plan to write in the future?'

FRL:

'"Nor Shall My Sword", inspired by Blake. Blake is a believer in creation, a writer of immense complexity, as opposed to Swift, who is anti-creation like Eliot. I also intend to write on Wordsworth.'

Q:

'Byron?'

FRL:

'Byron was a great satirist, but not a poet of great force such as Blake. Great writers are great men, which Byron was not.'

At this stage, Father Santa-Maria leaned forward and breathed in my ear: 'He'll go on all night. I must go.' – getting up and giving the lead to all the others, for it was half an hour past midnight. But the audience had been spellbound. And not a little astonished. And if one thinks over the events of the day, Leavis's stamina was so extraordinary as to be hardly credible.

Tuesday 18 April 1972

'Three hundred and ten' that well-known gritty voice intoned on the Hotel Tamarises phone at 1.30p.m.

Watson:

'What about lunch today, Dr Leavis?'

FRL:

'With you?', the voice queried unenthusiastically. 'Well, no, I think not; you see, I can only eat steamed plaice. My wife gets it for me three times a week.'

I suggest meeting for tea between 4.00 and 5.00p.m.

FRL:

'I should like that very much.'

4.30 p.m. He was waiting when I arrived.

Watson:

'Would you like to go for a short walk first or shall we go to my house at once?'

FRL:

'I'm indifferent', he replied in a friendly way, and we set off along the sea front towards the old port. I mentioned Ion Williams, an academic who had applied to me for a job in my department, having written on Meredith and now wanting to do research on Cervantes.

FRL:

'Ah, must be an Oxford man. Yes, I think I've heard of him. At Warwick. Not much of a place. No one to know about *there*'.

Watson:

I've now had another application, from Michael Wilkins: he's written a thesis on "Dickens & High Society", supervised by Kathleen Tillotson.

FRL:

'Yes, they're a pair.' Referring no doubt to the Tillotsons.

Walking up the long steep hill from sea level to the house I slowed in case he had difficulty, but he was straining to go faster, eagerly saying: 'Ah, yes, I remember the way.'

I put him in the more comfortable of the yellow chairs in the window alcove above the sea, and when María had brought tea and Leavis had settled himself with the outsize cup, I asked him about the notorious Snow lecture. It was as though I had offered a relished bone to a hungry dog. With a gleam in the fixed look he fastened on me he began:

'I gave the lecture in Downing, and had given the porters instructions to keep journalists out. But early next morning when I was in the Combination Room a phone call was put through from the *Spectator*: Might they print the lecture? I answered "No". But the editor (was it Iain MacLeod, no, was it Ian Hamilton, I can't remember) insisted, saying it had been reported in *The Times*. So I told the editor to hold on while I read *The Times*. The article was on the page facing the leader, in the centre, you know, as you open the paper, and I found a mal-informed, malicious report. So I went back to the phone and told the editor he could have the article if he printed it entire. The editor asked how long it was. I replied that it was an hour's lecture, so I supposed it would be between six and seven thousand works. The editor agreed to print it all. But I informed him that the text was available only in manuscript. The editor said he had good compositors and sub-editors, and if I would sent it by express, they'd deal with queries by expressing it back and I could give corrections by telephone, reverse charges. This was done, so that the article could appear that Friday.

'Then Snow wrote,' Leavis recounted triumphantly, 'demanding the text. He was told there was none available, but could find it in that Friday's *Spectator*.

'Immediately after the lecture I walked into the combination room (or at any rate the room adjacent to the lecture room) and met the Master of Christ's. "Was it very bad?" I asked. "You were very rude, but I shan't cut you" was the reply. Several scientists wrote to congratulate me, and said it was time someone put C.P. Snow in his place.'

Watson:
'There were some very nasty letters in *The Times*, weren't there? People bearing old grudges.'

FRL:
'Yes, there were', he replied, but he seemed to feel that the

weight of opinion was on his side rather than Snow's. He added with zest 'Those who attacked me at least conceded that Snow was objectionable. Edith Sitwell, who plagiarised me almost verbatim – her reviewer pointed it out – wrote one of the nastiest. I had decided not to take legal action, but I wonder why Chatto didn't.'

Watson:
'You had, hadn't you, used some very strong language criticising Snow. Didn't you describe him as being 'as unintelligent as it is possible to be'?'

Leavis seemed pleased, either that I should quote from his lecture, or that he might have said, or be thought to have said, that.

FRL:
'No, it was "intellectually as undistinguished as it is possible to be". I understand Snow had been considering legal action for defamation. How could he? He was of course utterly undistinguished. Low class.' Leavis slopped tea into his saucer, and, afraid that he would dribble it all over his suit that he was to lecture in, I asked María to mop it up with a napkin.

'My wife does that', he remarked, sitting contentedly in the spring sunlight as he ate a biscuit or two: 'I can digest these.' I called a taxi to go to the university and Dr. Leavis began looking for his tie, which he eventually found in his coat pocket. After some fumbling he asked me if the broad green wedge of woollen material was central.

'My wife urges me to wear these flannel shirts', he confided, wonderfully unworldly in a pin-stripe suit mottled with biscuit crumbs and brown suede shoes.

'Hush-puppies,' he exclaimed with satisfaction, 'they're most comfortable.'

We got into a battered little taxi while the Basques as ever stared, and Leavis damned the disgusting state of British society as a purely mechanical materialist world until we reached the university garden or what was left of it. Some aspens had just been cut down to make way for an asphalt car park. The rector's work.

Watson:

'It reminds me of "Binsey Poplars".'

FRL:

'Yes, Hopkins was a very good, if not a great, poet, infinitely superior to contemporaries such as Meredith.'

Watson:

'Even Hopkins shows traces of Keat's longing for ease, the typically Victorian desire for escape from the sordid reality of contemporary life.'

FRL:

'Yes, but there is a division in Hopkins.'

Watson:

'That tension between duty and desire is perhaps what made him the poet he was. Perhaps if he had not been a Jesuit, he would not have been a poet.'

FRL:

There is a similarity to Keats in "The Habit of Perfection".'

Watson:

There is a stanza in Shelley's "To A Skylark" which had something of Keat's sensuousness, but "azure" moss is something Keats could never have written.'

FRL:

'Yes. My Shelley essay may have been too extreme. It was written in reaction against Victorian adulation. Shelley was a genius. I may read him again. I insist on the right to contradict myself. And so modify.'

When we got to the lecture room Leavis looked in perhaps anxiously, and there were fewer there than last night; I held him a while to let stragglers arrive.

The lecture took up the theme that T. S. Eliot's attitude to love was suspect – *La Figlia Che Piange* – and *Portrait of a Lady* – 'Is the man not Eliot?', Eliot's Dantesque love, and his over-reliance on Dante. As a critic, Eliot's essays were sometimes pretentious, and his tendency to toady to the establishment and lack of editorial integrity betrayed the other side of Eliot – the anti-creative side, the antithesis of Blake – of Eliot the insecure, unsure, betraying his inadequacy as a man.

Leavis stood at the lectern, reading without glasses from manuscript notes with a firm, clear voice and drinking water copiously, yet very much with an eye on the audience. He had said he would gauge audience reaction and act accordingly. He read poems out 'not that I regard myself as a virtuoso with a golden voice but because it is essential to focus on the text', and seemed very conscious of time, even subdued this evening. He had been concerned about his thought and conversation sequence last night; couldn't remember whether the dinner in my house had been before or after last night's lecture. But his lecture was as good or even better than last night's, and as good as any I heard him give in Cambridge.

It was moving seeing the old man, defiant, at times bitter and scornful, but alert and vital – in many ways he was younger than any of us. His eyes would light up, he would smile with the innocence of a child, his skin brown and healthy, his tufty side-whiskers straying out from his ears, upper lip protruding. He would die soon, of course, and there seemed to be a certain finality about the close of that lecture.

And so there might have been. As we came downstairs past the statue of Christ there was a scuffling – and there was Dr Leavis lying spread-eagled on the stone floor.

I bent down to lift him – he was so light he was hoisted into the air before being put on his feet, exclaiming, with a great bleeding gash in his finger, covered in dust and still sprinkled with biscuit crumbs, 'I'm quite all right. I'm used to falls, sprinting in the gloom in Cambridge.'

Wednesday 19 April 1972

When the university car arrived to go to the airport, remembering his car sickness I opened the front door for Leavis, but he declined, saying 'I want to sit in the back with you as it's the last chance to talk.'

His conversation was about his family: his concern for his son's future in an unjust world, his wife's sensitivity to adverse criticism, but his consciousness that theirs had been a struggle in adversity that they had overcome.

At the airport I asked him if he would like any Spanish drinks to take home, and with childlike hopefulness he replied; 'I should like a bottle of brandy. Do you think they have Martell? And perhaps a bottle of sherry?'

These were procured, the maw of his Gladstone bag opened wide and clamped shut with gusto.

'I must tell you,' Leavis said, 'that some weeks ago in Cambridge I saw some cut-price brandy in a shop window and took home three bottles. My wife suggested that perhaps I was taking an untoward interest in what might not be good for my health.'

The imminent departure of the plane was announced; an IBERIA representative appeared to escort Dr Leavis to the plane before the other passengers. Leavis gave me an earnest, almost expectant look as we shook hands. Was he wondering whether he would ever come back again?

He did not die soon. *Laus deo.* And he did come back.

24 March 1975

THOUGHT ART AND LANGUAGE LEAVIS

The characteristically laconic telegram stated: the third of a series of lectures whose general theme was, on 8 April, BELIEVING IN THE UNIVERSITY, on 9 April, THE PARADOX OF ELIOT and on 10 April, the telegraphed title.

He describes his intentions in a letter of 2 April:

I'm not offering a sustained argument in three instalments. I saw no solution but one of making three attacks, & hoping that my audience would see that, put together, they defined the problem and my responsible attitude towards it. I've lived for half a century with it, & watched it getting more & more hope-destroying. Now it's an immediate crisis of civilization & humanitas. But it's a time for going to the root of the malady: perhaps some of my audience may credit me with having done that; and recognize that, while I can't be an optimist, neither am I a pessimist.'

Dr Leavis's plane was to arrive on 7 April. María and I had made a rapid sortie to the Highlands to buy a hotel we reverted to a private house, reaching Spain after midnight on the eve. But there were to be no problems. This time he was to stay in our very primitive croft house high on a hill above Orduña, at the border between the Basque country and Castile. It was a typical Basque 'caserío', with pens for animals on the ground floor (we had had sheep sleeping the nights there, so that one slept to the sound of urinating and the strong smell of ammonia, while lambs bleated and raced round the compound), floors and furniture riddled with wood-worm, cracked walls and nothing but the most basic amenities. The house was reached by a muddy track and set amongst beeches, walnut trees and a few aspens.

It was soon obvious that Leavis was delighted with the place. No television, a ten-year-old fridge being the only concession to modernity. He would get up in the night to make himself tea in the kitchen by the vast 'Wuthering Heights' type of fireplace, and felt himself free as he had not in a hotel.

By day, he would go out and sit for hours on a stone in the snow lit up by sunshine, high over the valley, ruminating on his lectures and contrasting, no doubt, the urban industrial 'civilization' of England with the aspects of primitive life: the donkey passing loaded with milk churns, led by an astonished red-faced Basque farmer's wife; a half-crazy cow-herd cursing his animals in diabolical language Leavis did not understand; and shepherds unknown to him to be thieves directing their flocks with volleys of stones at the stragglers.

We went in and out to the lectures in the evening by train from

Orduña, but otherwise the days passed quietly, María stayed at home to see to anything Dr Leavis might want. To his own surprise, he ate daily bigger and bigger breakfasts she served him, of smoked Serrano and York hams, local wholemeal bread, tomatoes, goat's milk and sheep's milk cheeses, boiled eggs and orange juice. QDL may have had difficulty with him when he returned, his normal diet being a few morsels of steamed fish. He radiated contentment sitting there in a room with a sagging wooden floor, a view over the sierra, and silence. He wrote to us on 12 April:

"The whole visit was very enjoyable: I felt the pains I'd taken over those lectures wasn't wasted, & I certainly profited. Psycho-somatically, staying with you was positively remedial: my works are practically "normal". And please give my warmest thanks to Mrs Watson."

The lectures were fundamentally a development of 'Believing in the University' (in *The Human World*); 'The Living Principle'; 'English – Unrest and Continuity' (a lecture at the University of Wales, 1969) and themes in 'Nor Shall My Sword'. That is to say, the urgency of a cultural renaissance (with University English faculties as the pivot) so that once again an educated public – necessarily a minority – may be formed to regain our cultural heritage and be vitally concerned with moral and spiritual values. Eliot, as the major poet of our time, implicitly denies human creativity through his 'profound conviction of the utter abjectness and worthlessness of humanity'. Leavis is conscious of an impending cataclysm, as our society's standards fall, and materialism triumphs, but retains the faith that moral and spiritual renewal are possible, although this means, as Lawrence put it, 'The whole great form of our era will have to go.'

The lectures were a great draw, for we now had first-class students and afterwards ('afterwawrds' as he would say) Leavis had eager and intelligent questioners (though he sent a Spanish journalist packing with the retort that he had absolutely nothing to say to him); even a sycophantic lecturer, the kind of creep Leavis loathed, who polished the passenger seat of his car when asked to transport the head of the British Council in the hope of a job offer, stood in awe of his evident sincerity, fervour and selfless dedication to the ideal of awakening society to a civilization beyond the crass hedonism and materialism of our age. I have never known a man so absolutely dedicated to his calling. He had the simplicity and obsessive vital absorption of a great man. To be in his presence was undeniably to feel that.

After his last lecture (he was to catch the plane next morning) the reception went on too late, ardent questioners keeping the old man locked in interminable discussion, so that in the end María and I had to break it off and hurry him to the station for the journey to Orduña, some 40 kilometres. Our taxi reached the station just as the guard was blowing his whistle for the last train to start, and it was at least a hundred yards up the platform. Without thinking, we sprinted for it flat out, and it wasn't until we were sitting in the train, having made it by a second, that I realized what we had done. But Dr Leavis, 79 ¾ years old, sat panting with a triumphant smile.

I'm an old distance runner. Got the distance runner's perfect heart.'

MANOLO

Manolo had had a long, hot journey from Jerez de la Frontera to Seville. He felt confused by this change from his home in the country and wished he could go back. But they said "*Quien va a Sevilla, pierde su silla*". Whoever goes to Seville loses his place.

He disliked the noise, the traffic and the blaring brass band music in the streets. Yes, it was true, he supposed, what he had heard. Those who go to Seville never come back.

He was meditating on all this when he became aware that a woman had stolen up on him and was staring at him. He stared back unblinking at this insignificant-looking creature. What did she want? He wasn't used to being stared at, least of all by a woman whose perfectly rounded features amounted to nothing.

Thank Providence she soon turned away and went off through the busy streets. She returned to her hotel room and watched herself on video. She must perfect that smile. It wasn't quite right. She posed in front of the great mirror on the bedroom wall and smiled frontal and sideways until she was satisfied that she was irresistibly alluring. Then she tried on her frilly white silk blouse and drew her glossy black hair back in a tail. Yes, that tail flew out in the wind when she was mounted on *Casilda*, the dappled grey she rode. She was eventually convinced that she looked almost queenly, dignified and yet very alluring as she practised a little wave. A little wave to the crowd, a jubilant, light, triumphal wave, but ever appealing to those who watched her. She solemnly crossed herself twice in the mirror, showing her seriousness and female delicacy. Appearing submissive before God. Then, quite certain that she would be the idol of the crowd, she went out into the streets again, joining her boyfriend in the gipsy Bar *Traga*.

Next day Manolo heard much louder and more vulgar military

brass bands blaring from very nearby and extraordinary shouting, besides a booing sound that reminded him of the cows mooing about his place in the country near Jerez de la Frontera. He supposed that was typical of town people.

All of a sudden he was taken by surprise when two men came up to shave him. He'd never been shaved before. Before he knew what was happening, they beat him over the head with a heavy wooden club that left him stunned. Then they stuck a short spear into his shoulder so that blood poured down his side. Enraged but dazed Manolo was propelled into a dark passage with light at the end of it. Bewildered, he emerged from the dark into the blinding sunlight and looked about him. He was astonished. Why did they do this to him? What was going to happen now?

He looked round in amazement at the hundreds of two-legged mandrakes seated in ascending rows that seemed to reach into the sky, and at the thunderous roar they let out at his appearance.

And then he saw it. That female figure who had stared at him now mounted on a dappled grey horse was galloping towards him. What would she do to him? He wasn't taking any chances, so he charged at her, his head lowered with its blunted horns. He went for her with all his might but she swerved and just as she bypassed him she stuck another of those spears into his shoulders, a barbed one this time, the red and orange streamers fluttering in the wind as the hot blood poured down his flank. Manolo was furious at this non-entity getting the better of him, and stopped to watch her as she put on that well-practised smile at the spectators in answer to their roar of approval at her dexterity, waving her little hand in the air as she cantered round the ring, her wide hips going up and down, up and down, up and down.

Manolo glowered at her in disgust, a female that attacked him. No cow had ever done anything like that. On the contrary they had admired and loved him in the campo of Jerez de la Frontera. And there she was, coming at him again. This time he would get her, unseat her from that horse and gore her to the ground. Disembowel the bitch. He let out a roar of rage and went for her in a wild gallop. She tried to swerve but this time he got those blunted horns under the belly of the horse and lifted it off the ground, almost knocking

Mari Luz, the Virgin of Light, off her mount. She clutched desperately at the horse's neck. If only they hadn't 'shaved' the points off his horns he'd have done for that horse and she'd have been his victim. But she regained her hold, and the horse turned away with a bleeding gash on its under-belly. Mari Luz wasn't smiling now; at least he'd wiped that smirk off her characterless face.

With a glance at the crowd, Mari Luz crossed herself twice. Then she came galloping at him, and he rushed to meet her in a valiant charge. But once again she succeeded in turning *Casilda* aside at the last moment and sticking another barbed spear into his shoulder. The spectators roared approval and those little white handkerchiefs fluttered in the women's hands. Once again Mari Luz did the round of the arena, crossing herself as she came to a halt and smiling up at the spectators. Manolo followed her gaze and maddened by the uproarious cheers and fluttering handkerchiefs charged at the spectators' stand, the barbed *banderillas* hanging down from his shoulders. He went for that stand with demonic energy and managed to clamber up to the first row of the petrified audience, the women shrieking in terror as Manolo's great head swished in the air right by them. He straddled the first row of benches, vapour pouring from his wide nostrils, his eyes blazing with rage.

But at that moment a posse of effeminately dressed figures rushed out of the tunnel, surrounding and dancing round Manolo, distracting him with capes, some pushing, others pulling his tail until they succeeded in forcing him down onto the bloody floor of the arena.

He struggled back onto his legs, and when the effeminately dressed figures retreated behind the safety of the barrier he looked wildly round. Yes, there she was, cantering round again with a mien of self-assurance that drove him mad. Up and down, up and down went those wide hips in the saddle. So he went for her again in a furious rush, but again she swerved just as he was on the point of unhorsing her. As she bypassed him she plunged yet another barbed *banderilla* into his bleeding shoulder, to the cheers of *¡Bravo! ¡Toro bravo!* from the wine-soaked throats of the men, and again those damnable little white handkerchiefs flashing in the brilliant sunlight, the brass band blaring in accompaniment to the bloody spectacle.

Would he be pardoned by the President for his bravery? By this time he had five *banderillas* hanging with triumphant streamers of red and yellow from his body as he stood still, glaring round. But the President made no move to pardon him, though the men kept shouting *"¡Toro bravo! ¡Bravo toro!"* in thunderous applause. Manolo had never flinched for a moment. He had gone for that female figure on horseback with all his brave bull's heart.

But now, at a signal from the President's box. Mari Luz cantered over to collect the sword to strike at that brave heart. With the long sword shrouded in a flag, its point gleaming in the harsh sunlight, she galloped up to Manolo who gallantly raced to meet her, as fast as the horse itself.

Mari Luz deftly managed to turn aside just as Manolo's great horns were about to sink into the horse's flank again, and as he was brought up in his rush and stood impotently rooted to the spot, she plunged that sword into his body. It caused Manolo to stagger, fall on his knees coughing up great quantities of blood from his throat, but it did not kill him. To howls of derision at Mari Luz's failure from the spectators. Manolo struggled to his feet again, glaring defiantly as his persecutor, 5 *banderillas* and a sword hanging from his body.

"¡Ahora! ¡Ahora!", roared the crowd. "Get him now! Now!"

Mari Luz cantered round again to collect another sword and came again at Manolo as he swayed on his legs, panting for breath as cascades of gore flowed from his throat. But just as she veered round to stab him mortally, Manolo managed to raise his great head and knock the sword from Mari Luz's hand with a side swipe of his great horns that entangled that sword and wrenched it away from that delicate hand, letting it fall harmlessly to the ground.

Once again the crowd roared disapproval, making booing noises that made Manolo think they were cows. But he had no time for reflection, for having collected yet another sword, Mari Luz advanced on the staggering bull and again plunged that sword into his body. But her aim was not true, and went wide of Manolo's heart. So wide that the sword entered to only half its length.

The spectators were now derisively shouting abuse at Mari Luz as she went for a fourth sword. She manoeuvred her horse to stand over the bull in his agony. Once more she crossed herself before taking careful aim and drove that sword into the body of the stricken bull, this time to the very hilt. Manolo turned a moment and then his legs collapsed and rolled over on his side. The deed was at last ignominiously done. As the blood filled his eyes, Manolo, amidst the agony and the humiliation, had a momentary vision of the Elysian fields replete with virgin cows that his brother bulls at Jerez de la Frontera had told him about. Then the blood clouded his eyes. He shuddered, and the darkness overcame him.

Mari Luz dismounted and ran weeping into the waiting arms of her gipsy boyfriend, leaving *Casilda* standing alone and bleeding profusely from her wound.

But there were to be many deaths to celebrate later that afternoon, with an ear, two ears, and even two ears and a tail awarded to the matadors, with the fluttering of many white handkerchiefs and the sipping of cool *vino fino* on the stands, young girls wreathed in smiles thinking of the impression they were making with their well-brushed *sombreros de Cordoba* on the callow male youths.

Meanwhile, on this Easter Sunday, Manolo – Immanuel – was dragged off to the butcher's on this his 5th birthday, on that glorious celebration of the Resurrection.

VENGEANCE

The gangling dreamer was regarded with some derision by the local Scottish farmers and shepherds. He lumbered along by his flock howling "How! How! How!", which the bemused sheep tolerated with good-humoured detachment, one or two quizzically eyeing the unaccustomed spectre flapping his arms with all energy.

Olaf had sat about people's homes for years in the west end of Edinburgh, mostly by the Dean bridge, enveloped by the beguiling odour of the local brewery. He drank whisky far into the night propounding schemes which by dawn had evaporated. Yet beneath the dreaminess there had been a shrewd and sharp eye for the property market. Some of those years ago he had spotted a FOR SALE sign on the vast neglected tenement block that had been the YMCA building. On discovering the required price he had made an offer of a fifth of that; getting a written response advising him that his offer was an insult. He had forgotten all about it when two years later he received a printed communication that his offer was accepted. His reply intimated that that offer had expired but that he was prepared now to buy the building for half of his original offer. And the deal was done.

And yet he had continued to haunt his friends' homes as though…. When was he going to do something? But of course there was his fortune, the hundreds of thousands he had made on the sale of the YMCA building to a developer.

He lived alone in a converted doocot, or dovecot as the English call it. But to everyone's surprise, one day he sent out invitations to an engagement party. His own engagement to a pretty actress a little past her prime, but still what would be called vivacious: dark, petite, with sparkling eyes.

Those invited were architects, university lecturers, lawyers:

decent upper middle class Edinburgh citizens who maintained the old values of times gone by in an age of rising hedonism and generally rather pointless existence.

So it was with some curiosity that they looked on the twenty-nine year-olds which both were: the shrewd dreamer and the vivacious, witty actress.

"But how" everyone asked, "was Juliet going to live the life of a shepherd's wife, on a remote small-holding in the Perthshire hills?" For Olaf had taken it into his head to become a shepherd and bought a croft. When asked why he had decided at length to devote his life to sheep he would reply facetiously but unsmiling "Because they're difficult to catch."

Well, the Edinburgh burghers didn't need to speculate for long. The actress left the marriage bed at four o'clock in the morning of her first and only night in the croft house Olaf had painted in pastel pinks and turquoise with soft amber lamps, besides dangling cords that at a gentle tug dispensed the perfumes of Arabia. All supposedly to enchant the little actress. The local farmers and shepherds had naturally observed all these preparations with dour derision.

So here he was, stranded in the Perthshire hills, his only companions now the 'assistant' shepherd he had employed and several hundred sheep. All the effective work was of course done by the 'assistant', who regarded his patron with a mixture of amused contempt and despair.

"How! How! How!" wailed Olaf at the sheep dip as he ran alongside the bewildered creatures flapping those long arms.

"Wid ye no be getting' a collie?" the assistant enquired. "A dug that'd save ye all yon runnin' aroun?"

Olaf pondered the matter for a day or two before setting off in his Land-Rover on a tour of the Highlands in search of a collie. In the event he went all round the Highlands and the Lowlands twice until he reached Easter Urray by Inverness. There he was lucky enough to find at last the dog he had been searching for: a very handsome pup of three months old, son of a working mother and father. The owner gave a display of the parents' prowess, ordering them to corral a small flock of sheep, and then to leap over five-barred gates and fences, to lie low, to 'come by' and just about every manoeuvre a well-trained sheep-dog could perform. The young pup was not yet trained, but Olaf could see he was eager to join in the fray. He looked the arch-typical Border Collie: a shaggy black and white coat, with a white ruff round his neck that reminded Olaf of Phillip II of Spain.

Olaf paid the £10 asked for the collie, which jumped into the back of the Land-Rover and set off for his croft, deciding on the way to call him 'Lucky' in view of his at long last fortuitous find. Olaf had been as shrewd in choosing a collie as he had been in making a fortune speculating on a building.

It didn't take the dog long to respond to his name and to learn the rudiments of sheep handling, although he was still far from full-grown. Even the 'assistant' shepherd, to his great surprise, had to admit grudgingly that Olaf could not have found a better collie.

In a year or so Lucky was herding the sheep for their dip, lying low when necessary so as not to frighten them, and responding to Olaf's 'come by' and all the other commands. He was a very quick and eager learner, and what's more he was brave and affectionate. "Indeed I have been lucky" Olaf frequently said to himself on his lonely rounds of the Perthshire hills and dales in a silence broken only by the haunting call of curlews, the chatter of oyster catchers and the high-pitched mew of peewits.

Olaf himself had been both lucky and unlucky in his short life. His Scotch father and Norwegian mother had been killed in an air crash over Bergen when he was twelve. But he had been adopted by his eccentric Aunt Marion, who lived in that converted doocot near the Haymarket in west Edinburgh. Aunt Marion had a curious bird-like appearance and a very sharp tongue, but she was devoted to her nephew and entered into his boyish interests with extraordinary enthusiasm. She took him to the castle esplanade to see the monstrous cannon 'Mons Meg', and told him to listen for the one o'clock gun that boomed out as Edinburgh's speaking clock. She accompanied him to the Camera Obscura that gave close-up aerial views of Edinburgh's monuments, and they went into the Princes' Street gardens with little bags of corn to feed the birds that perched on their shoulders.

Aunt Marion was the widow of a beach-comber who had posed

as a kind of buccaneer on the Spanish Mediterranean and her house was cluttered with relics of their time in Malaga: wide-brimmed sombreros, leathern wine bottles, a variety of cruel-looking daggers and knives, and what most fascinated the boy, a sword-stick with a serpent's head.

There was quite a collection of Spanish books too, and Aunt Marion insisted on teaching her bright nephew Spanish, so that he could read in the original 'Platero y Yo', travels with a donkey, the wild dramas of Lope de Vega, Lazarillo de Tormes and other picaresque tales, and of course, Don Quixote, which the boy read in bed at night, laughing and crying, before switching off the ceiling light-switch by the door by the ingenious system of pulleys Marion had devised to save him getting out of bed.

And then, when young Olaf was seventeen, Aunt Marion died suddenly in his arms just as she was showing him photographs she had taken of fairies at the bottom of the doocot garden. She had left Olaf the doocot and a small legacy. And quite desolate, for she had been his best friend.

Olaf was then a first-year student of Spanish and French at Edinburgh University and shortly after graduating had fortuitously made that fortune that had allowed him to dream for years before becoming a sheep farmer. To everyone's surprise the croft produced some champion black-faced sheep, and Lucky won several sheepdog trials, becoming the most famous collie in all Scotland. The ineffectual dreamer had unexpectedly made good. He and Lucky lived some twelve enchanted years through the changing seasons.

And then catastrophe struck. The Russian nuclear reactor at Chernobyl exploded, sending radio-active clouds over the central highlands of Scotland. Right over Olaf's croft. The authorities ordered the slaughter and burning of carcases of contaminated sheep, and the sale of lambs from Olaf's croft was at first prohibited and then permitted only after government inspection. Which offered a bleak future.

In his lonely and now disastrous life, Olaf took to drinking whisky to wild excess in the evenings after his work as he tried to plan how to overcome his desperate situation. And then one evening, gazing mournfully at Lucky's beautiful Philip II ruff, he shouted "Spain!" as he tramped up and down his long sitting-room in the pouring rain with the melancholy cries of curlews outside.

"Spain! Isn't the Basque country famous for its shepherds? Of course it is! I'm going to leave this benighted place. To Spain! Viva España." From his corner by the peat fire Lucky gave a doubtful slow wag of his tail as he gazed fixedly at his exuberant master. In his plan to go to the Basque country nothing could have been less appropriate than that "Viva España!"

Olaf sold his croft for what he could get for it and boarded the ferry for Bilbao with Lucky in his Land-Rover. When they docked he headed south to Orduña, the small country town by the frontier of Biscay and Castile. He parked in the colonnaded main square and, calling Lucky to follow him, went into the Bar Llarena. It was full of farmers and shepherds with great black berets overlapping their heads.

As he edged his way through the throng to the bar followed by Lucky, who detected the aroma of sheep from the trouser legs of the assembly, Olaf found that he had barged between two stalwart Basques and a small, wiry figure whose outsize beret was ludicrously overlapping. He had begun to step aside when a great rough hand clapped his shoulder.

"Que pasa, hombre? Quedate entre nosotros. What's up, man? Stay with us. Don't go away. You've only just arrived!" laughed Viktor, a big shaggy shepherd. Lucky examined the three figures dubiously.

"I'm looking for a flock of sheep and a croft house" said Olaf when they had shaken hands. "You don't happen to know of any for sale, do you?"

The three looked Olaf over closely as he stood somewhat bedraggled under his battered black balmoral with tattered streamers; and then at each other.

"Unza" said Juanjo, the cowherd, wild hair protruding from under his great 'gorra'. "Old Sergio is giving up." Then turning to Olaf he said "Dying of cancer of the liver. His woman's trying to cope, but it'll be too much for her. Though Sergio's stubborn, still takes his flock up to the sierra" he added, turning again to his companions. "He won't let them go cheap."

"The devil he won't!" said Viktor. "They're Merinos!" as he called for Txakoli for the four of them; which the three Basques tossed straight down their throats as Olaf dubiously sipped the sour immature wine. He noticed that they drank only half the glass, as though disdaining to appear beggarly.

"Let's go then" Iñaki, the smallest and thinnest of the three said impatiently. Two intense eyes looking out nervously from under his immense Basque beret. "What're we waiting for? Let's take this Scotsman up to Unza so he can see Sergio's flock for himself."

"We're waiting for you to order a round, you miserable bugger" laughed Viktor, having to shout above the cacophony of the boozers and the television, which already very loud was suddenly turned up to full volume. Immediately there was silence among the crowd. The newsreader announced that twelve Civil Guards had been killed in an ambush by ETA between Vitoria and Orduña. At once the hubbub began again, wildly animated now as the peasants celebrated the news.

"What's happened?" asked Olaf, who had not quite caught what had happened. "What's it all about?"

"We've cleaned up a dozen of them" said Iñaki" tersely, "Civil Guard bastards, got it now?" He gave a fanatical glare at Olaf, then raising his glass to Viktor and Juanjo, as one or two neighbours came over to celebrate the kill. One of them tapped Iñaki on the arm and took him aside for a moment.

"But that's terrible" gasped Olaf, shocked. "I heard the newsreader say all the Civil Guards were from Andalusia. You can't mean the people here are celebrating."

"That's right" commented the crazy-looking Juanjo, "they'd be poor villagers who couldn't find work. That's what happens. They send them here to 'pacify' the Basque country."

"Pacify's not the word" spat out the tense Iñaki. "They're sent here to torture and kill us. To make sure we don't speak in our own language and to repress our hopes of independence."

"It's a shame" said Juanjo, quietly mournful. "But you must remember what the Basques have suffered. Guernika dive-bombed by the Fascists and as Iñaki says, our language forbidden, and many of us killed and beaten up by those Civil Guard bastards. Still, it's no good, it's a shame. Bloody revenge is no good."

"What the devil d'you mean" Iñaki shrieked hysterically, "It's the best thing that could have happened. We're at war, and in war you have to kill or be killed. Isn't that so, Viktor?"

"That's enough" barked Viktor gruffly, "pay for your round and let's get to Unza!" But knowing Iñaki was penniless Viktor handed over the money to the barman.

It was near sundown when the two Land-Rovers reached the top of the pass and arrived at Sergio's rambling house on the edge of a precipice. Old Sergio was approaching slowly and shakily, tottering at the head of his flock, the apparition seeming to stream straight out of the sunset. Lucky caught sight of thirty vultures preening on the cliff face as Sergio's wife came out of the ramshackle house, smoothing her apron and her hair as the four men came up.

The deal was eventually concluded over many copas in the smoky kitchen, Sergio's yellow eyes cunningly fixed on Olaf as the old shepherd drank heavily to ease the pain of his rotten liver and so bringing on death. What else had he to look forward to?

"Where are you going to spend the night?" Iñaki asked Olaf as they left the warm kitchen in the encroaching darkness. "If you've got nowhere I can put you up in my hut. It's up over the ridge beyond Sergio's place and there's a spare bed. Then in the morning I can show you an old caserio – a croft house – that's to let." He didn't divulge that it had been his own house.

"Yes, and I can show you another" said the hulking Viktor, "though it's a long way off in a deserted village."

"I know the one you mean" put in Juanjo, "but I'm not sure if it's to let or for sale. Anyway, I'll be glad to come along too. Between the three of us we'll get you fixed up, Olaf."

So it was agreed that they would all meet at Unza the following morning as Juanjo and Viktor rumbled off to their caserios for the night.

When they had gone, Olaf collected Lucky and a bottle of Scotch whisky from his Land-Rover, and they trudged up to the top of the sierra in intermittent moonlight towards Iñaki's chabola. All of a sudden Lucky shot off several hundred metres to the west of the track and then stopped, barking at something in the wide expanse of the sierra. He was just visible in the sporadic moonlight breaking through the scudding clouds, but when Olaf whistled to him he came bounding back and then made off in the same direction, beckoning his master to follow him.

It took Olaf and Iñaki a fair time to catch up with Lucky, who was standing looking down into a grotto a metre and a half deep with steep sides, in which a wretched black-face sheep was trapped. Olaf quickly pulled the sheep up by her small horns. Whereupon the jubilant sheep did a hop, skip and a leap of joy before being tethered by Iñaki.

"By Christ! It's one of mine. She wouldn't have lasted long. Been missing several days now. What a wonderful dog you have! My own'd never have found her. And just as well, too, for I'm down to twenty beasts now. We've scarcely enough to live on and have to send them to market."

"Yes, and look down there" said Olaf, shining his torch on the bottom of the narrow grotto where lay a sheep's skull and bones. "Not cheerful company for the poor old girl."

"It's not much of a place" complained Iñaki as they arrived, going in first and lighting a paraffin lamp, "bit it's better than nothing, I suppose." A mangy half-starved mongrel cringed in a corner, not daring to let out more than a pathetic moan as Lucky sat down by his master.

And then, to Olaf's astonishment, a girl came out from behind a partition and glanced at Iñaki with a look of terror. She was slight with a round head like a doll, her black hair plastered close to her scalp. Everything about her was diminutive: her nose was small and straight, her ears peeped through her glistening hair like the finest shells, her eyes like those of a frightened rabbit staring suddenly at Olaf with a look of wonder, even of appeal. But no words came from her trembling lips.

"What the hell are you staring at us for, Itxiar" snarled Iñaki. "Get to bed, you bitch. Go on, get to your bed and out of the way."

Olaf was embarrassed, not knowing where to look or what to say. But again the slip of a girl gave him a quick beseeching glance as she disappeared behind the partition silently.

They sat for hours over whisky. As the wind got up, Iñaki diluted his with water from a butt outside, the rain soon pattering on the corrugated iron roof.

"Wife's got my house" Iñaki muttered angrily. "The usual settlement. Bitch of a judge treated me like a criminal. Got a divorce" he added with a dark look at Olaf. "Had to. I've three boys. The first was alright. Then the second arrived with blond hair, which surprised me a bit. When the third turned out ginger everyone called him 'el Irlandés'. My woman's hair's as black as coal. A cleaner, she was – still is – at Dow Unquinesa, the chemical factory at Erandio. Just a short journey on the local train. We desperately needed the money. Can't make a living out of sheep. Well the boss of Dow Unquinesa was, is Irish" said Iñaki bitterly, blushing to the roots of his sparse jet-black hair.

In spite of the whisky and Iñaki's confession, Olaf was too ashamed to recount what had happened with Juliet, other than that he was divorced also. But the thought of it made him blush too, as though it would set fire to his ginger beard.

Iñaki looked at him curiously for a moment, and then asked

"Is Scotland part of England?"

"It certainly is not" replied Olaf, his hackles rising. "They're two separate countries."

"Where's the government of Scotland, then?"

"It's in London" stammered Olaf. "You see, there was an act of union in 1707."

"Then you ceded the government to the English" sneered Iñaki

"Well, I suppose in a manner of speaking we did" answered Olaf defensively. "Actually, the English call the country England; unless it's a case of English football hooligans, when they become British."

"Then it's just as I said" Iñaki insisted. "Scotland is just a part of England. But if you Scots were a separate nation, how is it you put up with the English being your boss? Are there no Scots nationalists? Don't you want independence?"

"Trouble is," Olaf answered "That the nationalist party has no votes, I mean only a minority."

"It seems to me they have no balls" Iñaki jeered. You say you were an independent nation but you allowed the English to steal your nationality."

"The problem is" said Olaf evasively, "that much of the Scottish middle class is Anglicised. Speak with English accents, send their sons to English schools and English universities. They're ashamed of their own language and their sons get better jobs with an English education. And of course the Scottish aristocracy has always been with the English, the absentee landlords living in London, forced the highlanders out of their own country by introducing hundreds of thousands of sheep for the new fortunes to be made from woollen mills, destroying the highlanders' cattle small holdings. They brought in the army against them, and got the church to tell them it was God's will they should make way for the landlords' sheep, forcing them to emigrate to Australia, New Zealand, Canada and America."

"Are you telling me the Scots put up with all that?"

"They had no option. English bayonets forced them out of their own country."

"Pathetic! That's what it is. Pathetic! We Basques are fighting now for our independence, and we keep the government in Madrid on the run. And we're only a small nation, much smaller than the Scots. We kill the bastards. That's all I've got to live for now. So you saw in the Llarena how we rejoice when we kill them. It's good to see their families suffer too. Let them learn. Treat us as a Spanish colony, they do. But in our history we had fueros, privileges that set us apart."

"I'm absolutely against killing" said Olaf. "The only way to settle these things is by the ballot box, by votes. And you're killing innocent people, aren't you?"

"So you're prepared to give up your Scottish independence because of some soppy middle class snobs and an aristocracy that of course will vote for its own interests. And what about the working class?"

"They're just apathetic. Used by the Labour left who need their votes to get power in England. If Scotland got independence they wouldn't be able to form a government in England because they depend on the great mass of working class Scots who vote Labour."

"Well, then" countered Iñaki, "That's just the situation where you have to fight for your ideals and freedom because the ballot box that you worship will never give you back your country. And if that fight means killing a few innocents, or a great many, so what? There's no alternative. Isn't that how the Irish got their independence from England and English imperialism? Juanjo'll tell you, he's always reading history books and I don't know what all."

"Yes, but what kind of leaders emerge from terrorism?" demanded Olaf, irritated by Iñaki's dogmatic fanaticism. "Wasn't Hitler in effect a terrorist in his street fighting days before he got power?"

"You're on the wrong track there" said Iñaki triumphantly, "Hitler was voted into power by your beloved ballot box. So what d'you say to that?"

"Well, I'll have to concede that's true. But what about Stalin, in effect a hired assassin in his young days, and as you know, a mass murderer once in power, murdering not only millions of peasants, but picking off his own henchmen one by one at the slightest suspicion of what he saw as disloyalty?"

"Right you are" Iñaki sneered, "but didn't you English, sorry, British intellectuals praise Stalin in the twenties and thirties, saying they'd seen the future, and it worked? So even your people were in favour of terrorism if it led to a desired end. And didn't Churchill describe Stalin as a wonderful leader? You just ask Juanjo. He knows."

"Alright" answered Olaf weakly, retreating to a new argument, but look at the African dictators, almost all ridden to power on the back of bloody murders and massacres. And what about South American leaders? It's the same with the Arabs and the Jews. Weren't the Israelis governed by ex-Stern gang leaders and other terrorists?"

"Well, so far as the Israelis, and come to think of it the Irish, are concerned, you've given me the argument" retorted Iñaki, quick to pounce, "Because who says the Irish and the Israelis are not civilized? Aren't their countries and their leaders recognized by the United Nations? But they got where they are by terrorism."

"But where are you getting with your violence" Olaf queried. "Tell me where it has got you?"

"Listen. The Spaniards will never give us independence through votes. Even if the majority of the Basques vote for a separate state.

They throw us some scraps, some sops which they hope will satisfy us and we're supposed to grovel and pick them up with gratitude. All they try to do is con us out of our birth-right. Didn't we tell you about Guernika? Our sacred emblem of Basque nationality was bombed to perdition by fascists. German fascists but ordered by Spanish fascists. The town destroyed with dive bombers by General Richthofen, countless civilian Basques killed on Spanish orders, get it? Like your highlanders being bayoneted by the English. We Basques can't forget that. And we don't want Spaniards governing us, because we hate them."

There was a long silence broken only by an outside gate banging against its post in the wind. Iñaki scrutinized Olaf sardonically.

"I think we've reached a dead end" yawned Olaf, sleepily gazing at Iñaki through his grubby glasses. "We just aren't going to agree."

"You're dead right we aren't" said Iñaki with a scornful smile. We'd better turn in for the night."

It was just after two in the morning when they went to bed, Olaf sleeping on a bunk in the corner, fully clothed as usual. He didn't bother with pyjamas. Not since that night with Juliet.

★

Next morning Iñaki and Olaf tramped down to Unza to meet Viktor and Juanjo. Lucky raced down the hill, barking madly at a strange apparition at the side of the track leading to the village of three houses, Odio, on the way. There was a man's head and shoulders sticking out of a culvert inspection shaft, a concrete box a metre and a half deep. It was Juanjo, sheltering from the wind and reading a thick tome about the Carlist wars, oblivious to their approach. At Lucky's bark Juanjo jumped out grinning and patting the astonished collie.

Just then Viktor drove down in his lorry for transporting sheep to market, with VASCONGADAS, PAIS DE HOMBRES emblazoned above the driver's cab.

When they had all shaken hands below the vultures sweeping above their heads on their vast outstretched wings in the wind they followed Iñaki to what had been his caserio before he lost it to Maite, his wife, in the divorce court. But Maite had left it empty, preferring to share a flat with her paramour in Erandio. So Iñaki was ready to let it clandestinely to Olaf.

It was a typical Basque caserio, with a huge sloping roof and exaggerated overhanging eaves to keep the walls clear of the almost perpetual rain. Just like the overhanging gorras the Basques wear on their heads. Though it is said Basques are born with umbrellas.

The ground floor was all for sheep or cows, the house benefitting from the heat generated by the animals in winter. Upstairs were four crude rooms and a kitchen with an enormous fire-place. The kitchen being the room the Basques inhabit as sitting-room and dining-room, where the woman of the house dominates; in spite of the proclamation on Viktor's lorry the Basque country is in reality a matriarchy. But the women take good care of their men, always serving them first at meals. Nevertheless, the men make their escape on holidays to what they call txokos, where exclusively male gatherings in huts, garages or wherever, cook up vast meals of beans, black pudding, spice sausage, cod, lentils, and endless other heavy dishes that would fell lesser men. Washed down, of course, with prodigious quantities of alcohol, followed by the smoking of farias, very dark brown cigars.

The caserio had three corrals and a byre besides, and Olaf was almost beyond believing he could get anything so ideal for himself, Lucky, and the sheep he had bought the night before.

"How much?" he gingerly asked Iñaki.

Iñaki, equally uncertain, said "Cinco mil?"

Olaf could hardly believe his luck. Five thousand pesetas a month, about £25 sterling.

"The bitch'll never come here" said Iñaki, so you just pay me on the quiet and there'll be no trouble."

Olaf was so anxious to close the deal that he whipped out five thousand peseta notes from his wallet at once, which were gratefully grabbed by the impoverished Iñaki. "If I moved in myself, she'd find out and have the Civil Guard onto me in no time" he spat out. "As it is, if it comes to the worst I can offer her half."

When Olaf drove his Merino sheep up from Unza, Lucky keeping them in unaccustomed order, and they were corralled, Iñaki watched with rancour in his heart. Why should this ninny of a foreigner have such a magnificent flock with a wonderful dog, and now the run of his caserio, while he himself had nothing but twenty assorted sheep and a more of less useless mongrel, with only a hut to live in? Still, the Scotsman hadn't got a woman. "I can't imagine a woman wanting that gangling, bespectacled creature" he muttered to himself.

It wasn't long before Viktor and Juanjo came up from their caserios that formed the base of the triangle of the 'village'; only three houses on a muddy track rejoicing in the name Odio; Hatred. What incidents in the dim past would have earned it that name? And what would have happened in a three-house village 'Tortura' not so very far away?

Iñaki slunk off when Viktor lumbered over with a big sheep's milk cheese, and Juanjo brought a billycan of milk and a huge round flat loaf of bread.

"Just to get you started, Olaf" said Juanjo jovially. "And to wish you luck in your new life with us as your neighbours" added Viktor, clapping a huge hand on Olaf's shoulders.

"What about a dram of Scotch water?" Olaf offered, bringing out a bottle of whisky and three glasses.

"Slainte!"

"Oh, that's too strong for us, we're not used to it" spluttered Juanjo, after downing his dram in one draught.

"Your very good health" said Viktor, sinking his more circumspectly seeing Juanjo's discomfiture.

★

When Olaf had installed his few belongings in the caserio, flung three rather smelly blankets onto one of five beds and stowed the cheese, milk and bread in the kitchen cupboard after making a sandwich, he set off across the sierra with Lucky and his new flock of some two hundred very fine Merino sheep. He took them a long way, over towards the Orduña pass, stopping to watch with astonishment a solitary bull attacking two small cars parked beside the road, which it had more or less demolished. Fortunately on the other side of a stout fence; but he had to restrain Lucky who was game for an encounter with the anti-industrial monster.

Olaf then turned the flock northward into a narrow track that led through a beech wood, where they rested in the shade while Olaf ate his cheese sandwich, giving Lucky half of it. There was a hillock by the track which one of the sheep climbed, only to be deposed by another which ran at it with lowered head, leading to a resounding skull cracking. Both then retreated three or four paces backwards and ran at one another again until one remained victor on the hillock.

"Just like humans, Lucky" laughed Olaf, as another silly sheep challenged the proprietor of the hillock.

Towards evening, as they were coming near the edge of the great beech wood there was a right angle bend, and there, at twenty metres, with its huge horned head lowered and steam spouting from its nostrils, was the great bull. It charged, leaving Olaf no time to get up a tree. "Get him, boy, get him!" he ordered Lucky, who leapt at the head of the disconcerted beast, causing it to turn tail and run back along the track until it was out of sight.

"Saved my life, you did" murmured Olaf as the valiant dog jumped up, clasping one of Olaf's thighs with his fore paws and gazing at him steadfastly as Olaf caressed his white ruff.

★

When the sheep had been corralled that evening Olaf went down to Juanjo's house to return the billycan. As he approached he could hear the most diabolical language coming from the byre, although the door was closed.

"Hija de puta, Moreno, daughter of a whore, you've kicked over the milk pail again, you shameless bitch. Damn it all, you're a lot of idiots. I shit on the great whore mother that begot you! And you, Blondie, get out of my way before I hang you from that great hook there. Make no mistake, that's what I'll do!"

Olaf decided to avoid the byre for the moment and went to the door of the house. An ancient white-haired crone opened the door cautiously but on seeing Olaf standing quietly there asked him to come in. "No, I won't come in, thank you" said Olaf, handing her the billycan with many thanks. "You must tell me what I owe you for the milk."

"Well now, you won't be thinking I'm going to take money from our new neighbour, would you?" she intoned in her gentle high-pitched voice. "But here's Juanjo come out of the byre from the milking."

"Hola!, Olaf, how are you getting on? Yes, I know about that wild bull, it's been roaming about the sierra for weeks, but nobody knows where it's come from or who it belongs to. But won't you sit down on this bench a few minutes and join me for a copa?" invited Juanjo, sweat pouring down from his forehead under the wild fuzzy mat of hair now liberated from his great gorra.

"By the way" said Olaf, "Iñaki says you know Winston Churhill was an admirer of Stalin. Is that really so?"

"That's right. I've read his history of the Second World War and at both the Teheran and Yalta conferences he said Stalin was a great man and even called him a friend. I think he was besotted by Stalin, with serious consequences for those Russians who fought with the German army against the communist government."

"How could that be?"

"Well, many of them were taken prisoner by the British army and after the war Churchill authorized their repatriation to the Soviet Union. And you can guess," he said, scratching his head under the disorderly tufts of hair, "what happened to them once Stalin got his hands on them. Tricked, they were, I'm sorry to say, into believing they were being transported to Italy in railway carriages with guards and locked doors. Many who sensed what was going on had to be forced onto the trains with rifle butts.

"I can't believe Churchill authorized that", said the bewildered Olaf.

"But I'm sorry to say it's true. He sent a communication to the Foreign Office in October 1944 clearly instructing them to take action."

"But if that's true it negates our 'honourable' war to a great extend."

"I think it's due to Churchill's being in thrall to Stalin. He even wrote to his wife that he liked Stalin more the more he saw him. But it seems incredible that he wasn't aware, through his intelligence men, what sort of a barbaric monster Stalin was."

"So Iñaki's right then," said Olaf despondently.

"I don't know about that, but democracies can be as ruthless as totalitarians when it's a question of expediency."

There was a sound of crashing and banging from the byre, so Juanjo excused himself, saying he'd better impose order on his rebellious cows.

"What a lot your son knows" said Olaf to the old woman once Juanjo had gone.

"Oh yes, my son has great wisdom. He could be a government minister. He's always reading, even under an umbrella in the rain while his cows are munching on the sierra."

★

Feeling a bit lonely and having run out of whisky, Olaf headed down to the bar Llarena in Orduña. It was as usual crowded but there was no one he knew. After downing a solitary dram or two he was about to leave, when once again that silence fell throughout the bar. The TV newsreader announced that an army colonel had been shot in the back of the neck as he left Mass in a Bilbao church. It was pouring with rain and apparently a girl had sat behind him during Mass and then, as he left in a sea of umbrellas, put a pistol to the back of his head and killed him. There was a glimpse of the scene with a girl making her escape through the crowd. As Olaf went close to the screen he dropped his glass in amazement. For the shadowy slip of a girl was, could it possibly be, Itxiar. The fleeting image was so phantasmagorical that he was incredulous. And yet ….

At that moment, while the loud babbling of the customers in the bar resumed, Iñaki appeared white-faced. He ordered a brandy, and it seemed to Olaf that his hand was unsteady. But he would not look at Olaf or speak to him, and left as soon as he had downed his coñac.

★

Olaf got another glass of whisky and went over to a table where he sat down in great perplexity. He was almost sure the girl was Itxiar. He sat on in the bar until near closing time, when he noticed a burly Basque was staring at him. Olaf ordered another whisky and stared back, with his balmoral streamers down his neck. The more the man stared, the more Olaf stared back. And so it went on until closing time.

When he got outside, the staring Basque, who was with a group of friends, came up to Olaf and said "Are you English?" Olaf didn't answer. The man then said "The English are cowards!"

"I'm not English, I'm a Scot" replied Olaf.

"D'you want to fight?" demanded the Basque.

"All right" said Olaf, "if you want to, start it!" and took off his jacket, handing it to a bystander in the circle of the curious now surrounding them.

"You're a coward!" the Basque snorted, "or you'd start yourself!"

At that, Olaf went up to him and hit him hard in the face. Which produced a whirl of blows from the Basque. But Olaf had practised boxing at Edinburgh Academy and learnt how to duck, weave, deflect and hold, which he now did with the wild swinging blows of the Basque. So that gangling and thin as he was, and more than a little drunk, he managed to land some straight lefts to the hulk's jaw, nose and an eye.

When both were exhausted, noses bleeding, eyes blackened, lips cut and swollen, they stood panting opposite one another, too tired to continue. At that moment, the Basque went up to Olaf with hand outstretched and said

"Tu eres muy noble! You're a very noble fellow!" They then shook hands. It was a performance that could only happen with a Basque.

The little crowd had dispersed and Olaf walked down a narrow lane with the Basque at his side. He was perhaps thirty years old, and looked like a farmer of some kind. As they passed the high iron gates of a rich man's house a huge Alsatian rushed up to the gates snarling furiously. The Basque pressed himself close up to the bars and urinated over the dog, which made a hasty retreat in silence. "That's a risk I wouldn't take!" said Olaf. "You might have lost your masculinity!"

"Es psicología!" the Basque answered as he bade good night,

saying he had to attend to his loaves. Leaving Olaf with a sensation of amazement and joy as he went for his Land-Rover and returned to the caserio in high spirits.

But the image of Itxiar came to him in a nightmare.

★

Olaf was woken in the early hours by Lucky's growling from his corner of the bedroom. Then he heard a very light tapping at the outside door. Rousing himself he opened the door in bare feet and gasped in amazement. Itxiar stood there trembling with her head downwards as though in supplication in the drizzle. Olaf hurried her into the kitchen, lighting a paraffin lamp.

"My God, what has happened to you?" she cried, staring at Olaf's bruised and still bloody face.

"Just a friendly tryst" Olaf managed to laugh. But then, turning to her he asked "What brings you here?"

"I think you know. Did you see it about the colonel on the TV? It was me, Iñaki made me do it. He was behind me with a pistol. But the pistol was trained on me. It's terrible. I should never have acceded. I wish now I had died. It if happened again, I would. I would have refused. You are the only person I can turn to. I heard what you said about hating killing that night at Iñaki's chabola and I could see from a glance that you are a good person. I beg you to help me, to save me from myself. I cannot bear it… the remorse I feel. You see, I was already an Etarra from conviction… but I never thought it would come to this. Once in, you can never escape. Do you know about Pertur?"

"No, I don't."

"He was a young idealist, horrified to discover what ETA is. Well, he tried to leave ETA, but they killed him. He has never been seen, alive or dead. They take care of that.

She looked up at him in the shadows of the lamp and began to cry desperately. Olaf took her in his arms and held her close from an overwhelming sense of pity; pity that overcame the shock and revulsion at what she had done.

After a while she calmed down, and looking into his battered face said "I must clean you up, bathe your bloody wounds."

"It's nothing; as a matter of face I'm rather proud of them" said Olaf looking at himself in the mirror. I think it's likely they'll turn out to be nothing once washed, except for the black eye."

But Itxiar was adamant, and got a sponge and water and cleaned him up, as she put it. And while she did so, Olaf felt a terrible pang of pity for her. Pity which instinctively he knew was dangerous. He had a premonition that it would lead to… He dared not think, he dared not speculate. But before he knew what he had done he had kissed her, and she put her arms tight rough his neck like a child. In the morning he looked at her doll's face asleep on his pillow and it was a face of innocence, of weak, childish innocence. How would she ever get free of what she had done? Of course she never would.

After a quick breakfast she left in the rain.

★

Iñaki found out. While Olaf was tending his flock with Lucky next day, high up on the sierra, he happened to look back at the caserio, just visible in the distance. From it a spiral of smoke rose into the sky. Olaf abandoned the sheep to Lucky and ran over the rough ground faster than he had ever run. When he reached the caserio there was a crowd of peasants making a chain with pails of water from the nearby spring and a couple of Civil Guards watching. Juanjo and Viktor were foremost among these attempting to douse the fire, at once joined by Olaf. A demented peasant was screaming at the fire-fighters not to ruin his hay which he had stored in the adjacent byre, but which was now an inferno.

"Do you think we can save the house?" Olaf anxiously asked Viktor, next to whom he had joined the human chain. "Not a chance. There isn't enough water. But we can at least try."

"That's right" shouted Juanjo, who had got up onto the roof, "we'll do all we can, all we can, Olaf, but I fear we won't save it."

And they didn't, they couldn't, for the wind got up and roused the flames into demonic fervour, roof beams crashing in, the fire raging until nothing was left but the walls, and even those were in danger of caving in.

★

Everyone suspected Iñaki, but Iñaki had disappeared. And so had Itxiar. A search and capture warrant was set up by the Civil Guard, without result. Yet the crazy peasant whose hay had been burnt screamed that he knew it was a cowherd in Lendoño de Abajo who had tried to get his hay cheap and got in a rage when refused.

As Juanjo was a bachelor, Viktor having a wife and four children, Juanjo took Olaf in for the night with his collie into his big caserio, and tomorrow they would go over to Llorengoz to see the caserio Viktor had said was to let. Viktor joined them in Juanjo's byre that evening, after they had accommodated Olaf's sheep in his corrals. It was warm and convivial in the byre, but it was no good Olaf offering them whisky from his Land-Rover.

"Too strong for us" the two Basques excused themselves, and so they drank Juanjo's coñac.

Luckily for Olaf his possessions had amounted to very little in the burnt caserio, and his Land-Rover had been parked in the so-called plaza of Odio, some fifty metres below.

★

As it was a long tramp to Llorengoz they drove up the Puerto de Orduña in Olaf's Land-Rover, through Villalba de Losa where they turned off on the narrow road to Llorengoz, overlooking the Puerto de Angulo. Llorengoz was eerie, a village of mostly deserted caserios and the whole place was run down. It was like a village of the dead and when they walked over to the caserio supposedly to let, Lucky seemed to be possessed by Scotch superstition, barking furiously at the front door swinging in the wind.

There was no one visible except an old woman with a bucket of swill, but she told them the owner lived in Berberana. So they looked round the house, which was in much worse repair than Iñaki's wife's place had been. It had broken windows and inside the walls were damp and the plaster peeling. The kitchen had a table and a couple of chairs but there were no beds or any other furniture.

When they found the owner's house, having asked at the bar in Berberana, Viktor told Olaf to wait in the Land-Rover while he and Juanjo went to bargain with the man Viktor already knew.

184

"The moment he realizes you're a foreigner, he'll charge you at least double" Viktor advised. So Olaf waited.

"I don't want to let it" Manolo said sleepily "what I want is to sell it. If I'm to let it I'll need to repair the windows, put in beds and so on, so I'll need to charge 6,000 pesetas a month."

And there was no budging him from that price, though Viktor and Juanjo tried to get him down to five.

Manolo was the Berberana baker and having done his morning rounds was anxious to get to bed. He had to be up all night in the bakery, with the twenty cats he kept to keep the place clear of rats and mice. Yawning now, he asked "And who is this that's wanting to rent a place in that village of the dead?"

At that moment, Olaf, tired of waiting, walked in.

"Caramba! Por el amor de díos" exclaimed Manolo, rushing up to Olaf and enthusiastically shaking his hand. "Don't tell me it's you, my friend! Yes I see you've still got a bit of a black eye! And what about the cut on my nose! Come on, come on, I can still spare time for a couple of copas in the bar, to celebrate. And don't think I'm going to accept rent from you, my noble friend. I'll do the repairs, furnish the place, and all you have to pay is for electricity. How's that?"

And there was no persuading the hulking Basque of the 'tryst' in the main square of Orduña to let the place on any other terms.

★

So once again Lucky took charge of the sheep for the long trek over the wild sierra to Llorengoz. Although he was to miss Viktor and Juanjo, Olaf felt some relief in leaving Odio. It was all too close to Iñaki's chabola. He could not help wondering what had happened to Itxiar in the long days and nights of isolation at Llorengoz. The place was strikingly rugged and seemed almost like the end of the world. He had tramped down the next day to Odio to collect his Land-Rover and some provisions for his 'new' caserío and now, once again, took to heavy whisky drinking in the solitary evenings and late into the nights.

One evening, some ten days later, he went down to the bar at

Berberana. There were only two or three customers in the bar, one of them inevitably Manolo, the baker, before his long arduous night producing his loaves. When he had left after a couple of convivial coñacs – there was no whisky – Olaf was ruminating on the extraordinary events that he had been involved in during the short time he had been in Spain. Berberana being in Castile, he was glad to get away from the oppressive fanaticism of the Basques. But just as he was drinking his fourth coñac he got a shock. When the owner of the bar had left to deal with something in the back premises, a small, dark girl appeared behind the bar. It was Itxiar. They stared at one another silently for a moment, and Itxiar clearly wanted to get out of sight; but it was too late. When the other customers had left, and the owner was still out at the back. Olaf asked what she was doing there.

"This bar belongs to my parents" she said, "and I help out here. But what are you doing here?" she asked timidly.

Olaf explained what had happened at Odio.

"Of course it was Iñaki. He hated you for harbouring me, and he hates his wife who owned that caserio, so he got revenge on the two of you."

"But where is he now?"

"I can't tell you" Itxiar answered with a look of terror, "but he's gone on some mission, as he calls it. He's forbidden me ever to see you again."

The owner of the bar now came in again. "Aren't you the foreigner as was looking for a house at Llorengoz?" he asked in a desultory sort of way.

"That's right" said Olaf. "Well, I must be going. It's getting late."

★

It wasn't long before Itxiar joined Olaf in the caserio. It was a fatal attraction. Both of them knew it. But neither could resist it. Itxiar joined him in the caserio as though she was his wife.

"You're in a desperate position" Olaf said to her one night as he took his dram after corralling the sheep.

"Nothing can be done about it" Itxiar replied hopelessly.

"You may be damned, but there just might be a way out. I'll pit my brains to see if anything can be done."

Itxiar said nothing for a while. Then she said "I deserve perdition for what I've done. Only Iñaki and you know, but sooner or later they'll get me."

"Who'll get you?"

"Either the Civil Guard oe Iñaki"

They agreed to forget the horror in so far as possible and lived the healthy life of shepherd and mistress. Olaf once or twice took Lucky to a sheep-dog trial, and in spite of his age, for he was now well over twelve, he won first prize each time, succeeding in corralling groups of recalcitrant sheep, one or two always escaping from the little flock, but always by Lucky's skill and pertinacity being reunited with their companions.

Numerous shepherds came up to Olaf asking him to sell Lucky to them, in spite of his age. But Olaf always politely refused saying "I would sooner sell my soul than my best friend" and would join the shepherds for a txakoli in La Llarena at Orduña.

Olaf met Viktor at one of these trials and they arranged to have a txoko lunch al fresco with Juanjo, in Viktor's garage with the usual succession of heavy dishes cooked by themselves and, of course, washed down with much wine. Viktor's lorry, with the proclamation VASCONGADAS, PAIS DE HOMBRES, was parked outside, as though celebrating this escape from the matriarchy.

Another day the three went to a Basque equivalent of Scotch Highland Games, with log-chopping competitions, stone throwing and Basque dancing, accompanied by the txistu, a kind of penny whistle and a drum. They told Olaf that Iñaki was a wonderful dancer, with his white shirt and trousers with red sash. But the three didn't like to speculate where Iñaki was or what he was doing. "Nada bueno" said Viktor, 'nothing good', he's good-for-nothing, that boy and he'll come to a bad end, you mark my works." Olaf shivered, but said nothing.

When it came to log-chopping, Viktor, with his colossal size and strength, won the competition, which the three celebrated with much alcohol. But this time Lucky was outshone by a well-trained

Alsatian and came second only, to his obvious chagrin. He was getting on in years, even if he was remarkable, and on a good day could face any competition.

★

And so the summer passed in the Basque country, with many a wet and dismal day; the climate, Olaf found out, was similar to that of the Scottish Highlands, even if generally warmer; but not much.

One day as Olaf and Itxiar were having breakfast before taking the sheep out on the sierra, Itxiar got up, came behind Olaf's chair and put her hands over his eyes. "Guess what, Olaf" she said timidly. "I can't guess" Olaf laughed, "you'll have to tell me."

"You're going to be a father, Olaf" she said, giving him a little kiss on his left ear.

Olaf jumped up and embraced her with tears in his eyes. "Oh Itxiar, I am so happy, so very happy. Are you sure?"

"Yes, I'm sure. I've been to the social security clinic and they did a test. It should be in about, let's see, six or seven months."

"Oh, heavens" Olaf gasped. Itxiar, we must resolve your…. position with ETA. Listen, I've been thinking about this. The head of Iñaki's and your comando, is in Vitoria, but it looks as though he's joined the Madrid comando from what I've been able to pick up, though you can't rely on it. It's all so dangerous. What I want you to do… is ……"

"Yes, tell me" said Itxiar anxiously.

"I think you should ask for a meeting with the head of your comando, explain all your circumstances and ask to be allowed to relinquish your affiliation with ETA."

"Yes, Olaf, but remember what happened to Pertur. He asked for just that and was never seen again. Of course they killed him. It's too dangerous for them to have a renegade, who might at any time betray them to the authorities."

"Yes, but Pertur wasn't a woman, and wasn't pregnant." said Olaf. "And I don't need to tell you this, Itxiar, forgive me. Supposing you don't even try to get out, they'll order you to kill again. And if you refuse, they'll kill you anyway. Isn't that the norm?"

"It is. I know it is. But the idea of appealing to them terrifies me. They'll never let me go."

"Well, Itxiar, why not at least try. You never know, they may agree under certain conditions. Please, Itxiar, for your own sake and for your unborn child, think it over and see if you don't agree it's worth at least a try."

"But then they'll know I'm disaffected. And they know how to deal with the disaffected. You don't know how utterly ruthless they are. And 'they' include doctors, lawyers, teachers as well as the criminal class. Not to mention priests."

They left it at that for the time being. After a week or two, however, Itxiar determined that she would make the attempt, perhaps by promising to renew her vows if they would not let her go.

★

A few days later there was a tremendous explosion in Madrid and a Government Minister was killed in his chauffeur-driven car on his way to the Ministry. Olaf had to go to Bilbao later that day to collect some papers from the Town Hall. As he approached the ugly grey building he saw that he would not be able to get into the Town Hall. There was a huge crowd of Basques in front of it gesticulating with clenched fists and roaring "ETA, estamos contigo – ETA we're with you" – as though in a delirious frenzy.

He just managed to squeeze through the mob by keeping close to the parapet of the bridge and then following the river down towards La Salve, where he knew there was a bar that sold roast chicken. It was, as he supposed, quiet at the time, with only two or three customers, one of whom was a Civil Guard. Olaf ordered a beer and leaned against the counter vaguely interested in the conversation between a stalwart Basque and the Civil Guard. After a few minutes he realized that their encounter was becoming unpleasant. The Guard was in fact menacing the heavily built working class man.

"Are you saying you are not Spanish?" demanded the guard.

"Soy vasco y nada mas" stolidly answered the other.

"I didn't ask you if you were Basque" rapped out the policeman, "I asked if you deny having Spanish nationality."

"I told you before, and I tell you again, that I am Basque and nothing else."

"You'd better come with me to the Cuartel."

And they went out and into the Civil Guard barracks which was right next to the bar. Olaf wondered what would happen. He had been told by a newspaper seller of a similar incident, when the man had been taken to the local Civil Guard HQ, and repeatedly knocked to the floor and then brutally hauled to his feet by the hair of his head. He was then asked if he had changed his opinion.

★

Next day Itxiar was bundled blindfold into the boot of a car in a layby in Berberana and driven to a dank building in Vitoria where she was led into a room lit by a penumbra and placed in an upright chair opposite a dais at which three figures were seated. Had she been able to see them she would have been struck by the terrifying visage of the presiding figure of this tribunal.

His broad face was almost fat, with a small but horrible triangle of beard which reached from just below his lower lip to the point of his chin, which formed its apex. It was jet black, as was the thin but broad moustache over it. His eyes were cold and hard, and his expression was set in what looked like a permanent scowl. There was no hint whatsoever of humanity in that face which looked as though it had never smiled. The black hair plastered back over his head was all of a piece with the harsh and cruel mien he presented to the world. What horrors had he seen, what monstrosities had he perpetrated, what hatred had corroded his inner being? For it was obvious that hatred was the leit motif of his self.

"Why have you come here?" his harsh voice demanded.

"I beg to be allowed to withdraw from ETA" said Itxiar in a low, faltering voice.

"For what reason? Do you believe in the struggle of the Basque people for independence?"

"Yes, I do."

"What then?"

"It is the methods, I cannot bring myself to …. to kill."

"But you have killed."

"Yes, but it was not I who did it. It was …."

"Do you mean some alter ego?"

"Yes, partly that and partly because I was forced to do it."

"Did you not willingly join our organization for freedom, freedom which will never be conceded to us by the Spanish Government? Was it not made clear to you that only by violence can we ever achieve our end?"

"Yes, that is true, I mean that I vowed to support the ideal of freedom for the Basque Country…. but I did not realize fully what this would involve."

"You are saying that you did not know that ETA is at war with the Spanish State and that the norms of warfare are our methods?"

"I have felt infinite remorse for killing that colonel with a shot in the nape of the neck as he left Mass. That does not seem a norm of war, but a cold-blooded murder of the most cowardly kind."

"Then why did you do it?"

"I suppose because I am weak and was in effect forced to do it."

"What would be the consequences if you were now to be released from your vows?"

"I would remain for ever silent about my participation."

"What guarantee is there of that, that you would not be treacherous?"

"You have my word. You may kill me if you so think. But I am to have a child, and for my child's sake and its father's sake…. I would hope to live…. in repentance."

There was a long silence, broken only by the gentle sobbing of Itxiar. "Yes, we know about the foreigner and his influence on you. The 'President' nodded to the figure on his right, an elderly bald man with gold-rimmed glasses and a rather scraggy neck.

"Hija mía" he began, "do you not understand that our liberation movement is like an old-fashioned watch, in which all the parts are dependent one on another, and in which the malfunction of even the smallest cog-wheel will bring the whole to a stop?

Can you not bring yourself to promise that you will henceforth, as in the past, obey any necessary order or fulfil any allotted task for the good of our liberation movement and of the Basque people?"

Again there was only the sound of Itxiar quietly sobbing.

The 'President' now turned to the short-haired woman on his left.

"You are a disgrace to Basque womanhood" she said slowly and deliberately. "But your case will be carefully considered. Within forty-eight hours a determination will be made. You may now return to your home."

Itxiar was taken out and once more bundled into the boot of a car, which drove off and deposited her, still blindfolded, on the outskirts of Berberana.

★

Just before dawn three masked figures broke into the caserio at Llorengoz and succeeded in handcuffing Olaf and Itxiar before they were fully awake or realized what was happening. Suddenly Lucky sprang ferociously on the figure handcuffing his master, biting through his wrist. He was shot out of hand, causing Olaf to let out a heart-rending howl of anguish. Two of the figures quickly gagged him, while the third did the same to Itxiar.

They were taken out and thrown onto the floor of a Land-Rover and driven to the beech wood almost exactly where Lucky had saved his master from the bull. There each of them was tied on either side of a great beech tree, face to the trunk. Two simultaneous shots rang out as pistols were held to the nape of their necks.

By midday the vultures had descended. At about the same time the subordinate members of the Vitoria comando celebrated with Catalan champagne and king prawns, with the toast "ETA, Basque Homeland and Freedom."

THE MISSING ZURBARAN

"Get up, get dressed, and get out of here" was all Salvador said, leaving a valise of new clothes procured by his sister on the hospital bedside chair. Inmaculada's having been surreptitiously removed. Inmaculada obeyed, sensing from his tone that it was urgent.

Salvador took the trembling Inmaculada the four or five hundred metres to her home in that small university town. Trembling physically but calm and resolute as usual. There was that morning one of those winds that seemed as though it would carry them off into the sky whirling noisily overhead and battering their eyes with sharp eddies of dust. Salvador had to put his hairy mouth close to Inmaculada's ear to be heard. Instinctively she edged away from the furry face impinging on her as he shouted:

"You know they wanted to have you confined to a mental home. Your junior colleague at the university, my sister, overheard the plot."

"That doesn't surprise me" she gasped faintly against the wind, giving him a wan smile.

"Inmaculada" he spluttered through his black beard flecked with grey as they approached the Plaza Mayor, "you must have someone to look after you full time."

"Yes, I think you are right" Inmaculada answered quickly, fearing that he was about to propose himself. "But I have got a strong character, you know. It is only that I am physically a little sensitive."

Salvador thought of the fable of the princess and the pea. 'She'd notice it under nine mattresses' he reflected wryly.

Inmaculada had, it is true, had a brief brush with Salvador, the bespectacled lecturer in French literature, but the liaison, if it could be called that, had been strictly correct, and the bearded man had eventually drifted away muttering to himself 'Cold meat!'

Yet he had been unable to banish her from his mind, and her dire predicament now impelled him to act. He had to save her.

"Although I have not met her personally, I am thinking of a Basque woman who has been a housekeeper and cook." He paused a moment as they reached the heavy stone steps that lead up to the gallery of the Plaza Mayor.

"She's visiting relations here. She's the sister of our hall porter and goes back to Bilbao on Sunday. He tells me she's out of a job as her employer in the north died recently. She would from all I hear, be a trusty companion as well as cook and housekeeper." He hesitated. "Shall I send her to you?"

"Well, alright" Inmaculada assented, not ungratefully but from exhaustion and to get rid of the assiduous attention of Salvador as they got to the door of her flat. "Yes, please do send her, and thank you so much for everything. I think perhaps you have saved my life. I can't thank you enough, Salvador" she gasped, just managing to give him her slender hand before slipping into the irreal world of her home, hastily closing the door. But not before the doors of the neighbours' flats had opened an inch or two, and then silently closed.

★

The next door flat was the long time residence of the famous Dean, Zorrillo Cartero, perpetual purveyor of "es muy profundo y fundamental" at every point in all his lectures. A man despized by her father, in spite of his membership of the Royal Spanish Academy, as an ignorant pedant and a poseur. They had never spoken or been invited into one another's residence. Though as Zorrillo had said to a visiting professor from Oxford by way of excuse "In Spain men meet in bars rather than at home, in the Moorish tradition which allows no man to enter his wife's dwelling. You English are a people of the house, while we are people of the street. This distinction between our races is very profound and fundamental."

All the flats were situated on the galleries that spanned the four sides of the Plaza Mayor, below which were innumerable bars and shops.

★

There were only two men in Inmaculada's life. Her father and Jesus Christ. But Don Aurelio had died a widower years ago, a famous eye surgeon and Professor of Ophthalmology at the University of …… Inmaculada had worn black, silk, satin or velvet, depending on the season, for seven years and visited his grave, an impressive marble vaulted tomb, every day in the torrid heat of summer and in the bitter winds of winter from the Castilian plain.

Inmaculada and her elder sister Concepción had been educated at the Irish convent school in nearby Valladolid and family life had always meant constant religious devotion for the girls; and of course for their mother. They had attended morning and evening Mass in their black veils while papa gave early lectures at the University and later attended to his private and extremely lucrative practice. Patients travelled from all over Spain to his surgery, and even some from other European countries, such was his renown.

Neither the girls nor their father would agree to the fashionable and familiar abbreviation of their names to 'Inma' or 'Concha'. Together their names signified what individually they also meant: Immaculate Conception. And to Inmaculada, any other form of conception was repugnant. Besides, as only their father knew, Concha, or shell, has gross connotations in South America.

When the girls were young their father had taken the family to Seville on holiday, where he had teased Inmaculada, telling her that she bore a striking resemblance to the Virgin in Zurbarán's presentation by the Virgin of the portrait of the founder of the Dominican order, when they visited the Church of the Magdalen. Which no doubt was true when Inmaculada was a young girl. Now, however, her visage had the very faintly sceptical expression of the Saint Margaret in the National Gallery in London: a suggestion of scepticism that was banished whenever her enchanting smile broke out.

After their father's death, Concepción, who like her sister was something of a dreamer, had gone to Madrid, where she moved for some time in artistic circles before marrying a wealthy Count.

So Inmaculada was left alone in the second floor family flat overlooking the magnificent Plaza Mayor. Inmaculada had quite recently, through merit but aided by her father's prestige, become Professor of History of Art in the Faculty of Philosophy and Letters at the venerable university. She had by now discarded her black weeds and almost always dressed her tall, elegant body in scarlet with a silver crucifix at her throat, and a white silk scarf thrown over her shoulder. Whether she wore skirts and jackets or long gowns with corded belts pendant like a nun's they were always of the best quality, bought on her bi-annual shopping expeditions to Madrid. They set off superbly her glossy black hair, the pallor of her cheeks and her luminous dark brown eyes. Not to mention the elegance of her slender legs as she walked at a leisurely pace with a thoughtful expression, her eyes occasionally illuminated by a beguiling slow smile on meeting acquaintances. Intimate friends she had none, being of a decidedly independent character and inclined to be somewhat solitary. Indeed so solitary and of such deep religious devotion that she would spend the long summer vacation at the convent in Valladolid, whose damp climate, trapped as the town is between the rivers Pisuerga and the Duero could only exacerbate her pulmonary weakness.

Inmaculada had, after months of careful but inspired reflection, transformed her father's typically gloomy Spanish flat with its heavy ornate furniture, dingy curtains and a general air of solemnity if not pomposity. Every window was now of stained glass; not, as might have been expected, of religious scenes, but of her own bright abstract designs, principally in blues and reds or blues and yellows. The effect was arresting, and in spite of the vividness of the colours gave an impression of otherworldliness, irreality or even of a mausoleum. But a jolly mausoleum.

The exception to this extraordinary design was what would now be called the master bedroom. The bedroom her parents had inhabited all their married life, and which was now Inmadulada's. It remained severely austere, its only furniture an antique ebony wardrobe and two hard-backed ebony chairs, one on either side of a marble-topped chiffonier on which Inmaculada kept a large silver-framed photo of her father in his handsome youth.

But what struck one on entering was the huge portrait of Christ towering over the stark brass bedstead, dark and forbidding as many a Zurbarán painting. Yet this Christ, in contrast to those of his later period, was like a young poet, slender with a fine Grecian nose and a scanty beard with the silkiness of youth.

Every morning on getting up and every evening before going to bed Inmaculada knelt in her nightdress and bare feet on a little Persian mat on the marble floor and prayed fervently, her white alabaster hands with long delicate fingers clasped over her bosom before Christ.

Strong as she was in spirit, the hostile climate of Castile affected Inmaculada's health. She always had a little cough, and could detect a lighted cigarette in the History of Art Department at twenty metres and would insist on its being extinguished. Some of her colleagues at the university said it was hypochondria; others with relish affirmed that she wouldn't last long. For while Inmaculada was admired and even loved by her students, in spire of her strictness, the other teachers were deeply jealous of her position, her elegance and her wealth. The fact that she sometimes coldly, if unconsciously, ignored or rejected their fawning attempts to ingratiate themselves with her, led to her being generally alienated. Which she scarcely noticed or minded.

When she walked sedately, her skirts rustling, up the long dark corridor to her own room as Head of Department and heard the falsetto voice of the ancient woolly-haired French language teacher enunciating "sensibilité, sensualité", or the drumming of girls' feet in the Spanish literature department as they uncomprehendingly chanted Calderon's lines

La vida es sueño
y los sueños sueños son

as though they were savages in the African jungle, an ironic smile would break out on her lips as though involuntarily.

As she approached her room Inmaculada had heard with amused irritation the Dean, the pedant Zorrillo Cartero, Member of the Royal Spanish Academy, booming from the dais of his lecture room

"La diferencia entre masculine y femenino: eso es muy profundo y fundamental"

in his wine-soaked voice. She wondered why he did not elaborate. After all, he was only pontificating about adjectives and nouns, on which scholars of Latin languages must spend endless hours memorising genders: say of a knee, which is feminine, and an ankle, which is masculine. Spanish is said to be logical, but who can explain why the prostate gland, the essence of masculinity, is feminine; or why, in colloquial Spanish, the most intimate part of the feminine body is masculine? So perhaps the Royal Academician had a point.

But these were still the old-fashioned days of Spanish university education, when books might be chained to the library shelves and the lecturer would be the only one – to his great advantage – with a text book. These pompous pedants of the old school, when university wages were pitifully low and when at Salamanca teachers were even paid in coal three months in arrears when cash was not forthcoming from the government, were in their absurd way perhaps little worse than the slick fashion-conscious computer-orientated generation who replaced them, with their card indexes and the latest jargon about 'infrastructure', 'unreconstructed post-modernists' and all the rest of it. Spaniards take easily to extremes.

On entering her office at the end of the passage Inmaculada had been pleased to find a Telex from the British Council confirming that the exhibition of paintings by Francis Bacon she had requested would shortly be dispatched from Madrid. She had infuriated her colleagues in all departments of the Faculty by what they regarded not so much as exhibitions of art as her own exhibitionism.

They could not understand that such things might be staged simply for the enlightenment of the students. Otherwise, what was there in it for her?

Her first had been of Turner, whom the Spaniards regarded as immensely inferior to their own national masters, an Englishman who had never learnt to draw and whose watery scenes were merely so much indefinite wish-wash. Later she had gone even further with some French Impressionists, indubitably following Turner, but which the Spaniards, with their obsequious idolatry of all things French, had tolerated. And which, of course, they had soon learnt assiduously to imitate. Nevertheless, when Inmaculada had introduced a display of Matisse her integrity was called in question.

And now, when a week later the somewhat shocking and grotesque Bacon canvases were put on show in the Faculty auditorium, there was uproar. Inmaculada was accused of leading her students into dangerous uncharted territory. Consequently she was now the talk not only of the university but also of the town.

It was at the time of one of those harsh winters when spring never seems to come. To that university town might equally be applied the refrain of the Madrileños regarding their climate:

Nueve meses de invierno
y tres de infierno

Nine months' winter,
and three of infernal heat.

Strong of character though she was, Inmaculada was deeply upset by the insulting comments regarding her Bacon exhibition, with which she was trying to bring modern European art to Spain. She sensed the manoeuvres of jealous rivals in her own department and the general air of satisfaction throughout the Faculty that she had incurred the disapproval of the Dean and even the Rector. So concerned was she that it affected her always delicate health and led to her having to go to hospital unable to breathe normally. One doctor saying she suffered from pleurisy; another that she had pneumonia; a third that she had asthma; the consultant, not to be outdone, intimated that she suffered from all three simultaneously.

This was the very moment her envious colleagues had been hoping for. Meetings were held hugger-mugger in the History of Art department where all the teachers were women except for an effeminate male nick-named 'Slaverer', and a couple of pygmies well skilled in the arts of slander and familiarly known as the eunuchs of the seraglio. Which, alas, had no Sultan. Hence the ceaseless feminine intrigue.

A petition to the Dean was got up accusing Inmaculada not only of attempting to introduce licentious tendencies into the pure girls' souls, but insinuating that she was actually of unsound mind, as they delicately put it after two or three other versions, including one baldly accusing her of insanity, were deemed to be possibly counter-productive. There had been much debate, too, whether to refer to the "pure girls' minds" but it was felt that "souls" would be more moving and therefore more effective.

And then delicate reference was made to a notorious incident. 'Slaverer' had been excluded from these machinations, perhaps because he had been valiantly defended by Inmaculada when involved in a scandal. A telegram had arrived at the Faculty one morning for this effeminate teacher and a porter was dispatched to his flat to deliver it. The door was opened by a pansy boy student dressed only in a dish-towel, the disconcerted 'Slaverer' breathlessly appearing behind him in a hastily flung on dressing-gown. The porter thought it his duty to report this incident to the Dean, who summoned Inmaculada to his office, and with undisguised relish confronted her with the shameful report. But Inmaculada, regarding the question with distaste, had insisted that the teacher must be given the benefit of any doubt.

"What proof is there" she had countered the Dean's demand for his dismissal. The Dean felt obliged to take the matter no further.

Of course this had left Inmaculada in bad odour with the authorities. While those colleagues, and there were several, including 'Slaverer', she had defended against the machinations of the Dean's cronies and the ultra-conservatism of the Rector were among the first to turn when they believed the wind was propitious. Having been marked for dismissal they were all too aware of the weakness of their position, with only Inmaculada to defend them. If she should go, all the more reason to get in with whoever should take over. And just such a person there was.

The weak and the waverers were skilfully manipulated by a middle-aged lady whose husband was Professor of History. She herself being a native of this city and on only temporary secondment from the University of …….. in the south of Spain, was avid to get Inmaculada's coveted Chair and so join her husband permanently in her home town. And she knew how to insinuate that if by chance she should be appointed to that Chair favours would be granted to all and sundry, including Inmaculada's enemies and the waverers.

By contrast with Inmaculada, Doña Matilde was an ugly, yellow-faced woman, but she dressed ostentatiously, which of course was in perfect keeping with her character. She had made a point of keeping in with as many important personages of the University and political circles of that small town as did not see through her very accomplished flattery. After all, one never knew what circumstances might arise. And now that the opportunity seemed to have arisen, it was planned by this lady, who took care that the scheme was well concealed and could not be traced back to her, actually to have Inmaculada declared mentally ill, now that she was virtually a prisoner in hospital.

So a fairly eminent psychiatrist distantly related to Doña Matilde was, not altogether willingly, inveigled into agreeing to make an apparently impartial investigation of the state of mind of Inmaculada and to declare her suffering from schizophrenia. The psychiatrist was plied with what seemed abundant evidence to that effect. She was said to be morbidly religious and inhabited an unreal world of her own fabrication. There was the extraordinary fact that she had no friends, choosing to incarcerate herself in her luridly decorated flat. Clearly she had not what was known as a well-balance mind. Indeed she might well have suicidal tendencies and need protection from herself. Matilde had laid special emphasis on this last point, demonstrating her compassionate concern for the unfortunate patient. Indeed, Matilde had convinced herself that this really was the case; which coincided comfortably with her personal ambition.

Collateral evidence of her divorce from reality was only too prevalent. Her confronting the young students with sinister abstract exhibitions, polluting and confusing their impressionable minds instead of instilling into them the beauties of art. While her taking the part of a teacher clearly culpable of gross indecency with a student indicated her moral ambivalence.

Once such an official medical diagnosis was made, it seemed certain that Doña Matilde, given her influential backers in town and gown, would be appointed to the Chair of History of Art.

And as Inmaculada languished in her hospital bed the plot had almost come to fruition. But on that very morning when the psychiatrist was to carry out his examination and proceed to certify the patient, Inmaculada had been astonished, as she lay dreamily half asleep, to find quite suddenly Salvador, the one who thought of her as "cold meat", standing beside her bed.

★

When Inmaculada's door had so firmly closed against him Salvador had walked gloomily back to his lodgings reflecting on what seemed his hopeless relations with her. How could he aspire to the ideal that her father was for Inmaculada? As for the Christ that he had glimpsed through the half-open door on his one brief admittance to her sanctuary, when he had in the past called to accompany her to a concert of baroque music, he could never hope to penetrate her virginal religious armoury. Her father and Jesus Christ. How could he, a bespectacled thirty-three year old assistant lecturer with a scraggy beard dream of competing with a world-famous Professor and the tragic figure of Christ? He was in competition with ghosts from the past. Ghosts that to Inmaculada were as real as if they were alive.

Salvador had written two poems dedicated to Inmaculada but had not had the temerity to deliver either of them to her. In the first he envisaged her as an unattainable ideal. But in the second he had composed a frivolous lyric on an untouchable angel who could never repose, disdaining a speck of dust inevitable on any earthly mattress.

Although he was thirty-three Salvador had never had any other 'amor'. Even if he had had Platonic friendship with a very few youngish women of the town who regarded him with detached amusement. Salvador's tendency to idealize women invariably left him with broken-mirror images when less than angelic features became evident. In fact, he lived the life of an academic recluse whose only release from adust academe was to put into poetic form his necessarily rather abstract conceptions of love. And finding solace in playing classical sonatas on his battered upright piano. But for the moment he was only too glad to have even some vicarious contact with the ethereal Inmaculada by at once telling the porter to send his sister to Inmaculada's flat.

★

Early next morning Inmaculada was woken by a tremendous hammering on the outer door of her residence. Arantxa, buxom, Basque and boisterous had arrived with her baggage. As she stood waiting in the gallery after thunderously knocking on Inmaculada's door, the uniformed maid of the Dean, the famous Zorrillo Cartero, appeared in his doorway. She wore a little frilly cap like a pastry perched on her head and a white apron with crossed bands over her black dress and stood staring at Arantxa, arms akimbo, with a scornful expression on her pinched face. Even the tabby cat at her feet looked disdainful.

"What are you prying into with that long nose of yours?" bawled Arantxa. "Cotilla!" Nosy Parker!

"We have to watch out for itinerant gypsies like you" jeered the maid. "I suppose you're a street vendor with those enormous melons under your blouse."

Astonished at the uproar, Inmaculada slipped out of bed in her shimmy, opening the door just in time to hear Arantxa guffaw "Just because you haven't got an ounce of tit on you there's no need to be jealous, you dried up old stick."

By this time all the doors in the gallery had opened and Inmaculada hastily begged Arantxa to enter; which she did panting breathlessly as she lugged her cardboard suitcase tied up with string into the hallway.

When they had exchanged formal greetings Arantxa, still gasping with pleasure from her encounter with the Dean's maid, exploded with a gurgling laugh "Díos mío! Good heavens! What's this? A church, is it?"

And then, noticing Inmaculada's shivering, she enjoined "You've got the shakes, my dear, you're trembling like an aspen leaf. You'd better get straight back to bed."

While Inmaculada gratefully complied, there was a clanging of pots and pans in the kitchen before Arantxa appeared in the doorway of Inmaculada's bedroom with two steaming mugs of caldo, thin meat soup.

"Madre de díos!" Arantxa exclaimed. "Mother of God! What a stupendous Christ! Never seen one so good-looking! It must be centuries old. What will it be worth?

"Yes," Inmaculada answered as she gratefully sipped the boiling broth, watching Arantxa gulp hers, "it belonged to my father, and before him it was in the family for generations. It's a Zurbarán of his early period."

Arantxa seemed abstracted for a moment as she gazed fixedly at the Christ.

"Tell me, please, Arantxa, what made you leave your employment in Bilbao?"

"The widow died, Señora. Some kind of food poisoning. I think she ate some oysters that were off at a dinner with some ladies at Neguri, the estuary where the great Basque shipbuilders built their turreted mansions. She was the widow of a multi-millionaire shipbuilder herself and one of the closed society of the upper-class clique of that elegant enclave. Her own house was a veritable palace. But as I was saying, señora, she came home rather late from a tertulia complaining of pains in her stomach, but she said it wasn't anything to worry about, and went to bed after taking a little glass of bicarbonate of soda. Yet by the morning – so help me God! – she was delirious. I called the doctor but when he arrived there was nothing he could do. She was stone dead, señora."

"Oh, how dreadful!" sighed Inmaculada. "And had she sons and daughters?"

"That's just it, señora, she was childless."

"So what became of her fortune?"

"Well, would you believe it, señora, I'd been with her only two years, but she left it all to me."

"So then you're a rich woman, Arantxa! How is it that you're looking for work?"

"That's just it, señora. After she died they did an autopsy, which confirmed that it was food poisoning. But then there was a judicial enquiry and the judge said that because of a technicality that emerged from the autopsy her will was not valid. So her fortune went to a long lost and distant relation she'd never even seen."

"Good gracious, Arantxa! So you were left with nothing?"

"You've said it, señora. But seeing as I'd never expected anything, I couldn't really de disappointed, could I?" answered Arantxa with a disarming guffaw.

The solitary Inmaculada did feel reassured by the presence of the jolly Arantxa and her resilience in the face of ill fortune. There was something that seemed to her protective in this woman's bearing. Feeling sympathy for her and thinking of Salvador's recommendation, she spontaneously engaged her as house-keeper and cook on the spot. Though she begged her not to have any more altercations with the neighbours.

"It was her fault. She started it. And if she tries it on again she'll get what's coming to her. You didn't hear the insults she launched at me, the impertinent hussy. We Basques don't take kindly to cheek from our inferiors, señora."

From her Spartan bed Inmaculada contemplated this paragon of womanhood. Arantxa indeed wore a low-cut blouse that scarcely concealed her magnificent bosom with all the menace of a heavily armoured tank, not to mention her broad shoulders with jutting breast bones. Inmaculada gazed from her pillow now at her heavy arms, dimpled at the elbows, and at the array of massive rings with coloured stones on her stumpy fingers. She could see that she had a colossal backside as Arantxa sat with sturdy legs, stocking rolled up just above her knees and held there by elastic bands causing the flesh of her thighs to roll over downwards, legs firmly and widely apart on the marble floor, her full round face grinning indulgently under the thick brown locks of her unkempt hair. Arantxa was jolly in a conspiratorial way. Yet behind her bluff manner was evidently a shrewd mind.

"But why are there no carpets?" Arantaxa enquired looking round. "Que frío! How cold it is in here!"

"Because dust doesn't agree with me" Inmaculada replied with a stifled cough. "But let me get dressed now, and I'll show you to your room. It's just beside the kitchen."

"Don't you dream of getting up, señora. You'll catch your death of cold. Let me take over. I'll bring your meals to your bedroom. I can't wait to get things in order. There are a lot of changes to be made in this flat."

With some misgiving, Inmaculada replied: "No, Arantxa, dear. I don't intend to languish in bed. I think my indisposition, and it's no more than that, is partly psychosomatic."

"Psycho what? What's that?" asked Arantxa.

"It doesn't sound too good. You rest in bed, Doña Inmaculada."

"Arantxa, would you please leave me now. I am going to get up and when I do I'll show you the house and tell you where we buy provisions.

As soon as Arantxa left her, Inmaculada hastily knelt on the small Persian mat by her bed in the shadow of the great dark Zurbarán and gave thanks for her deliverance from the hands of her enemies, adding a short prayer for Arantxa. Then she clasped her slender white hands under her chin and remained for some time transfixed in adoration of the beautiful Christ.

When Inmaculada was fully dressed in a long scarlet robe and sitting on a dark blue velvet sofa in the big salón, which was suffused with the red and blue light from the stained glass windows, Arantxa, after knocking discreetly at the door, entered to enquire what Inmaculada would like for lunch.

"Madre de díos! Es Vd. preciosa, Doña Inmaculada! Mother of God! How beautiful you are!" she exclaimed ecstatically as she lumbered over to kiss Inmaculada on her velvet cheek.

Inmaculada was somewhat taken aback by this, but she retained her habitual composure. "I know how famous your Basque cooking is and can't wait to taste it. Do tell me what your specialities are."

Arantxa remained once more standing by the door, arms folded under her bosom, and eagerly answered "Well, for a cold day like this I can do mangel wurzel soup, conger eel with peas or dogfish stew, unless you prefer horse mackerel, or cod in green sauce which is the great Basque speciality. And when it comes to meat, one of my best dishes is pigs' trotters. How about it? What do you think? Perhaps you would prefer another Basque favourite, snails with spice sausage sauce. But there wouldn't be time for that today as the snails must be purged previously."

Inmaculada was dismayed. With her delicate constitution she was accustomed to the lightest dishes. A few oysters, grilled lemon sole or possibly a few slices of Serrano ham. And sometimes a soufflé or sherry trifle for postre. But using all her tact she said such marvellously robust dishes might be a little on the heavy side for her just for the time being, until she had completely recovered from her ordeal in hospital and the shock of discovering the manoeuvres of her colleagues. Not only of Doña Matilde but also her own protégées, those she had literally protected and nurtured in her department.

"Just let me get my hands on them" burst out Arantxa, alarming

Inmaculada even more and making her regret her narration of her problems at the University. But she did need sympathy and support at this time and Arantxa offered these in super-abundance. Yet the tranquillity and dreamy atmosphere of that flat were routed irrevocably.

It was settled that Inmaculada would have sherry consomé followed by fresh grapefruit and a small plate of York and Serrano hams for lunch, but no postre today. Meanwhile, Arantxa set out to buy supplies for the kitchen before, as she announced, getting the daily woman who arrived in the afternoons to wash the slightly dusty marble floors.

Inmaculada had just settled down with some examination papers she had to grade when the door bell sounded. Deeply concerned for Inmaculada and only too glad to have an opportunity to be with her even for a fleeting moment, Salvador had come with further news of the manoeuvres at the University. He carefully knocked out the ash from his rather ridiculous little round pipe filled with 'picadura', a kind of camel dung produced by the State Tobacco Monopoly, waiting outside the door observed by several concealed eyes in the gallery above the Plaza Mayor. Inmaculada opened the door and giving him her enchanting smile begged him to await Arantxa's return. It wouldn't do for her to admit a single man alone to her residence, or indeed a married man for that matter, as it would cause a scandal.

So Salvador strolled up and down the gallery apprehensively waiting to be admitted. But Arantxa soon came wheezing up the stairs festooned with bundles of artichokes and strings of onions and garlic pendant, her arms round a large yellow marrow parked on top of the shelf formed by her heaving breast, spiced sausages and black puddings trailing from her belt. On reaching the top step she looked Salvador over from head to toe, rang the bell and demanded of Inmaculada when she opened the door

"Quien es? Who is it?"

Inmaculada quickly assured her he was the colleague from the University who had recommended her, and urged them both to come in.

"But I've never even seen him" Arantxa protested. "He must

have spoken to my brother. Will he be staying to lunch?" she snorted before depositing her load in the kitchen as Inmaculada ushered Salvador into the big salón. Salvador politely declined, but Inmaculada insisted.

"What will the gentleman be having for lunch then?" enquired Arantxa, appearing at the door of the salón. "He'll need something more substantial than consomé and a few morsels of ham. What about bean stew with blood pudding?"

Salvador told Inmaculada that would be fine, and soon Arantxa could be heard singing with gusto as she busied herself in the kitchen.

"You must put in an appearance at the department" whispered Salvador anxiously, wavering when he noticed Inmaculada's glance of disapproval.

"Why should I go?" Inmaculada replied. "I didn't take part in any manoeuvres, as you know. I intend to behave perfectly normally and carry out my duties just as though I was unaware of any subterfuge. I think I am entitled to a little time for convalescence."

"Sorry, Inmaculada" said Salvador, closing the salón door and sitting down on an elegant silk covered chair opposite Inmaculada, who was now reclining languidly on a golden chaise longue. "I must tell you that Doña Matilde has been trying to get the students against you, telling them that you fail the highest percentage of candidates in examinations."

"Well, I can't say I'm surprised that she should stoop to that, after all that's been going on" laughed Inmaculada. "But I don't think anyone would succeed in turning my students against me, and ...."

"Excuse me interrupting, Inmaculada, but if you are not there I have heard the plan is to fail them all in your absence, alleging that you don't follow the normal learning by rote and the regurgitation of the standard text books on the subject."

"Yes, of course, Salvador, I try to get them to think for themselves, although given the traditions it is very difficult. But there, I think Arantxa's knocking at the door. Let's go to the dining-room."

"But just before we go, Inmaculada, let me warn you Matilde has already got the teachers to sign a letter to the Dean claiming that you don't treat them with respect and that when they want to consult you in your office either you're not there or you tell them you're too busy to see them. I know all this is untrue, but when people are after a little job or are promised this or that they'll lower themselves to things you wouldn't believe."

"Yes, you are right, you are quite right, Salvador. I shall go tomorrow without fail, even if it's only for an hour or so. I am sure I shall be well enough by then, what with a day's rest and Arantxa's company and the way she's already looking after me. I can't thank you enough for getting the porter to send her. And knowing of your moral support, Salvador, you have been an angel" she said, pouring him a glass of manzanilla, "you really have."

Salvador was beside himself with joy, though he took care to maintain his usual rather solemn deportment. He wanted to take her in his arms and kiss her; but he knew that was out of the question.

At Arantxa's insistent beckoning, they withdrew to the elegant dining-room, seating themselves at opposite ends of the long mahogany table, while Arantxa came bustling in and out. Having dutifully served Inmaculada her consomé and grapefruit with ham she placed a steaming casserole before Salvador, who set about it with all the gusto of a hungry bachelor.

But a certain awkwardness fell like a curtain between them and the lunch passed of inconsequently, to the disappointment of both. Perhaps in part because both had the sensation that Arantxa was intent on overhearing them.

When Salvador had left, a little lugubriously and blaming himself for not having been more forthright, in this, one of his rarest opportunities for intimacy with Inmaculada, Arantxa burst out

"I hope that lecher will not be coming back again. I've heard all about his reputation from my brother. I didn't realize at first it was him. As the porter of his block of flats my brother tells me he has endless streams of girlies going up to his place. Most of them go up at night and come down in the morning. They pass Carlos with their noses in the air. Who do they think they're fooling?"

"I don't believe it" answered Inmaculada, raising an eyebrow, but with a twinkle of interest. No woman is ever shocked by a man's excesses. They take it, rather, as a compliment to their sex.

But there was no silencing Arantxa's determination to keep Inmaculada and Salvador apart.

"You can see by his face the life he's been leading. Debauches, wassailing, that's what he's used to. He's not your type, Doña Inmaculada, and if I were you I'd get shot of him. There's only one thing he's after, and I needn't tell you what that is. Don't be taken in, señora. He's no angel."

Inmaculada blushed a deep crimson, for Salvador had aroused unspoken, unacknowledged sensations in her soul. And, dare she confess it even to herself, in her body.

She wondered for a moment: had Arantxa been listening at the door? Inmaculada *had* called him an angel, she recollected. But she felt a spasm of shame at her suspicion of Arantxa and put it out of her mind as something unworthy of her.

★

The following morning Inmaculada walked at her usual sedate pace to the Faculty of Philosophy and Letters. As she passed the open door of the French department's main lecture room she saw Salvador invigilating the final examination of the year and, to her bewilderment, felt once again an involuntary palpitation of the heart. But she deliberately suppressed the alarming sensation.

To the discomfiture of her colleagues, Inmaculada walked unexpectedly into the History of Art Department where Doña Matilde was presiding over a departmental meeting. In considerable confusion Matilde vacated the Chairwoman's seat while Inmaculada demurely, with a smile, sat down in her place. All the renegades immediately transferred their allegiance back to Inmaculada, greeting her effusively and enquiring with feigned sympathy after her health, seeing how the scheme to remove her had failed.

★

"I've got them, I've got them, Doña Inma!" Arantaxa burst out exultantly, having hastily climbed the stairs to the gallery above the Plaza Mayor. "I had to wait, while they set the new line of print."

"New line?" queried Inmaculada, noting with displeasure that Arantxa abbreviated her name, which she had never in her life permitted anyone to do. "What new line?"

"Look" said Arantxa proudly, holding out one of Inmaculada's cards she had been sent to renew before her reclining face.

A look of dismay overcame Inmaculada's expression of languid serenity. Instead of the Gothic script of her previous visiting cards in the name of the Professor of History of Art, now two bold and vulgar lines proclaimed

INMACULADA DIAZ DE ENTRESOTOS
ARANTXA ARAIGOICOECHEA GALLETEBEITIA

Inmaculada passed her hand over her eyes and remained silent.

"Isn't it good? Don't you like them? It's much better to have both names. People will know what they have to reckon with" Arantxa insisted, gurgling with malevolent laughter. And congratulating herself on tightening her hold over her mistress, just as she had done in Neguri.

"Yes, perhaps you are right" Inmaculada sighed, "but leave me now please. I feel a little faint and need rest."

"But what about your dinner? You must have your dinner. Listen, Doña Inma" – Inmaculada drew in her breath sharply – "you must have your dinner. Why don't we both have meals together. It's much jollier in the kitchen, and it will be so good for you to have company. You have become very isolated, isn't that so now?"

"Yes, that may well be so" sighed Inmaculada, putting an alabaster hand over her eyes again. "Yes, all right" she agreed, "for dinner, anyway, but please Arantxa, leave me now, would you?"

And so it was agreed that Inmaculada should join Arantxa for dinner in the conviviality of the kitchen. After a day or two it seemed quite natural. Arantxa's raw humour cheered the pensive and slightly melancholy Inmaculada, and her energy seemed vicariously to bring her new life. She was entertained by Arantxa's tales of her encounters in the market, recounting anecdotes that somewhat shocked her mistress but made her, unwillingly as it were, laugh.

Even if it was only just a laugh, an extension of her charming smile. But by one anecdote she was disgusted.

"That Salvador, d'you know, he goes through the fish market every day to buy his bachelor's lunch. When he had passed me unseen between the stalls one fishwife shouted to another

'Who's that little weed that comes here every day?'

'Him!' called back the stall-holder opposite, 'we call him the ball-less wonder. Looks as though he'd faint if a lassie lifted her skirt to him.'

'Right y'are' yelled the first fish-wife, 'he'd likely run to his mummy and tell her the lassie tried to pee on him.'

This caused a general convulsion and screaming with laughter," alleged Arantxa, gurgling with malevolent glee herself.

Inmaculada maintained a frigid silence as Arantxa scrutinized her face for the expected effect. Inmaculada was deeply offended; but instead of alienating her from Salvador, as intended, she felt drawn to him in sympathy. Besides, she wondered whether the tale was not a fabrication. It didn't tally with his alleged promiscuousness.

Nevertheless, after some days, Arantxa persuaded Inmaculada to have her lunch in the kitchen too, where she kept her plied with further, seemingly unending, rollicking accounts of her escapades. Which were more than a little tinged with vainglory. But Inmaculada was resolute about having her early morning coffee and a magdalena in her bedroom, which Arantxa placed, attempting clumsily to tip-toe into the room, on the marble-topped chiffonier by her bed. Inmaculada took her coffee cold after she had knelt to say her morning prayers in the shadow of Zurbarán's beautiful Christ; before getting dressed for Mass.

Arantxa gave a backward glance at the Christ as she left the room, muttering to herself 'I'll deal with that idolatry; just give me time. I'll put an end to this worship of that Christ of Zurbarán's, see if I don't.'

★

It was now getting on for the summer vacation at the university. Quite suddenly there was one of those changes in the weather characteristic of late spring in Castile. From the chill of winter, spring seemed to be bypassed and the torrid heat of summer arrived. The dreaded scorching wind blew mercilessly as Inmaculada walked in such shade as there was to the Faculty of Philosophy and Letters. She still had some students' 'tesinas' to assess, literally 'little theses', or monographs, which the students tended to copy out of text books if a sharp eye was not kept on them. Inmaculada also had plans to make with her colleagues for the autumn term. The meeting to which she summoned them passed off without unpleasant incident. All the signs of rebellion had subsided, Doña Matilde had returned to the University of …… in the south, and life seemed to run smoothly again after the dreadful tribulations Inmaculada had undergone.

When she returned home, exhausted by the heat, she found a note from Arantxa saying she had gone out to market. Inmaculada reposed on her chaise-longue, reflecting "I don't know how I ever managed without her. Or what I would do if she left me." Although she was calm, her little cough always irritated her and the doctor's diagnosis of asthma proved correct. Asthma exacerbated by subliminal tension.

After quite some time there was the sound of a tremendous commotion in the gallery outside the door of her flat. Inmaculada rose quickly and cautiously opened the door; in time to see Arantxa chasing the Dean's maid down the long gallery in a cloud of dust. Arantxa was whacking her on the backside with the wicker carpet beater she had wrenched from the fleeing maid, who had tied the Dean's carpet on a line suspended from the window grills, even to a grill of Inmaculada's window, filling the gallery with the deserts of Arabia.

Inmaculada at once retreated from the suffocating dust with a fit of coughing, hurriedly half-closing her door. Meanwhile the fleeing maid's frilly cap fell off as Arantxa gave her resounding whacks, bawling in time to the blows

"I'll teach you – whack – to fill the gallery with dust – whack – you imbecile – whack. You know the lady Professor is allergic to dust – whack. You did it deliberately – whack – deliberately – whack – deliberately – whack" she shouted, delivering yet another swing of the carpet beater that landed on the maid's meagre buttocks.

As Arantxa came swaggering back to the flat, a grin of satisfaction spreading over her broad and rather swarthy face, while the maid was cowering still at the far end of the gallery, the Dean emerged, his normally crimson complexion as black as thunder.

"What the devil's going on?" he demanded, as Arantxa scuttled rapidly behind Inmaculada, who stood nonplussed at her doorway with a handkerchief to her face.

When the Dean's maid had given a hysterical account and Arantxa countered with her version, the Dean insisted, turning to Inmaculada, that Arantxa should be dismissed. But Inmaculada pointed out the maid's provocation, and seeing that it was a light carpet beater and no physical damage had been done, proposed a mutual apology. However the incident ended inconclusively as neither would back down.

Inmaculada hurried Arantxa into her flat, Arantxa protesting "I'm not going to apologize to that bitch, whatever the consequences" before Arantxa made the situation even worse.

Inmaculada was concerned about her relations with the Dean. He had, after all, ignored the manoeuvres of her colleagues, even if he had done nothing positive, preferring as he did an easy life. It wasn't until that evening that she hit on the solution.

As she and Arantxa were having dinner in the kitchen, Inmaculada confided in her servant "I've got an idea. You know what, Arantxa?" she said with that alluring smile of hers. "I'll invite the Dean to lunch."

"Invite the Dean?" queried Arantxa incredulously. "But you can't invite him alone; that would cause a scandal. Anyway, he won't come."

"Don't worry, Arantxa, I shall invite one of my colleagues from the Faculty. Salvador is on friendly terms with the Dean, and I'm sure he'll come" she added with a sparkle in her eye.

"But didn't I warn you about his debauches?" protested Arantxa. "And that Dean wanted me sacked for defending your interests."

Nevertheless, it was arranged. Salvador, still by turns attracted and dispirited by Inmaculada's apparently cool aloofness, agreed to come with alacrity and persuaded the dubious Dean to do likewise.

But Arantxa remained sullen. However, when Inmaculada

begged her to be her usual jolly self and to bear in mind that it was the maid who had caused the trouble and not the Dean, Arantxa somewhat reluctantly promised to be on her best behaviour; while making up her mind to get even with both: with Salvador because he was an interloper; and the Dean because he wanted her dismissed.

★

The lunch went very well. The windows of the spacious dining room faced north, and what with the red and blue stained glass and the white marbled floor the room was cool in spite of the torrid heat of the Plaza Mayor. The Dean was jovial in that boisterous manner of so many Spanish academics of the old school, and Salvador acted as a perfect foil to the Dean's cumbersome humour. So well did everything go that by the time they had drunk chilled manzanilla with caviare, and bowls of iced gazpacho, the Dean grandly announced that a little trivial misunderstanding should not come between them,

The Dean spoke with that grating, gritty voice sustained by decades of wine swallowing, every phrase ending with a guffaw and an "Eh?" He even glanced appreciatively at Arantxa as she came waddling in and out with each succulent dish, her buttocks seeming to grind like mill stones under her floral cotton dress. She seemed curiously jubilant, all sulkiness vanished.

After lobster mayonnaise accompanied by an exquisite dry French white wine, Inmaculada asked Salvador to uncork a twenty-year old bottle of special reserve rioja to let it take air before the main dish: rabbit stewed in sherry.

When Arantxa came in bearing a huge steaming casserole which she placed, with a wink and a grin, in front of Salvador – not unnoticed by Inmaculada – asking him to serve it with a big silver ladle. The two men were in the most genial spirits, not least on account of the excellent and plentiful supplies of wine. Inmaculada both ate and drank frugally as always and excused herself from the rabbit stew as being a little too heavy for her.

"Have you heard" asked the Dean, beaming round at each in

turn, "have you heard about the European parachutists who were afraid to jump? You haven't? Well, let me tell you this little anecdote. Quite true, of course.

There were four parachutists, an Italian, a Frenchman, a German and a Spaniard aloft in a big plane under the orders of a British sergeant. The door was wide open, but the trouble was that none of them dared jump. Yet the sergeant was a clever fellow, so he got hold of the Italian by the shoulder and pointed down to a field below. 'Look there,' he said, 'can't you see that beautiful girl all alone by the bushes?'

'Mamma mía!' called out the Italian and jumped.

Next the sergeant turned to the trembling Frenchman and called out loudly 'Jump, mon vieux, pour la grandeur de la France!' The Frenchman, intoning a few bars from the Marseillaise, hurled himself into the air.

But even the great brute of a German was shaking with fear, so the sergeant shouted 'Not to jump is strictly verboten.' The German stood to attention, clicked his heels and was gone.

Now the sergeant was puzzled for a moment how to get the jittery Spaniard to jump. Then he had a stroke of genius. Scowling at the Spaniard he spat out 'You are a coward!' The Spaniard quickly unhitched his parachute and jumped without it. "Ha, ha, ha" roared the Dean, "a wonderful illustration of the different national characters of Europe, eh? Muy profundo y fundamental!"

Even Inmaculada politely joined in the general laughter; Arantxa, who had waited by the door to hear the story outdoing even the Dean's exultation at his own anecdote.

"Magnificent! Absolutely magnificent!" the Dean chortled, equally pleased with himself and the stew, sherry sauce dribbling down the napkin he had tucked into his collar.

"Quite delicious!" echoed Salvador, eyeing Arantxa ecstatically, "such a delicate but pronounced flavour. It's the best rabbit stew I've ever …."

But he was interrupted by a loud crunching crack and a howl of pain from the Dean.

"I've broken a tooth on a bone" he screamed, thrusting his fat hairy fingers into his mouth and pulling something out. Examining

216

it closely he exclaimed "My God! it's not a tooth, it's a stone." And then, wiping it on his napkin, he growled "But it's metal, it's shining. For Christ's sake, it's my cat's bell. It's Tiger's bell."

There was a suppressed belly laugh from the kitchen as he got up enraged from the table bellowing, blood running from his injured gum, "You'll take the consequences of this, Doña Inmaculada. Just wait! I see now why you didn't eat any stew. I had forgiven your servant but you will be made to pay for your conduct."

The apoplectic Dean marched out of the flat, slamming the door, followed by the resonant crash of his own front door.

"Arantxa! What's this? What has happened?" called out Inmaculada in alarm. "What have you done, Arantxa?"

"It was cat stewed in sherry" spluttered Salvador, "wasn't it, Arantxa? How could you? The Dean was complaining in the Faculty the other day that his beloved cat had disappeared. You monster, Arantxa! You shameless hussy!" he yelled, bolting from the flat with a withering glance of reproach at Inmaculada.

"Arantxa, dear, explain" said Inmaculada with unwonted coldness. But the irrepressible Arantxa answered with her rumbling laugh

"I forgot to tell you, when you asked what Basque specialities I could cook. Cat in sherry is one of my best!"

Next day Inmaculada received a summons from the Dean, whose face, Inma noticed as she entered the Decanato, was quite swollen on one side. As she sat opposite him at his huge desk he received her with pained coldness, saying that he regretted the action he was compelled to take.

"Although I am prepared to overlook those complaints from your colleagues, I'm afraid I can no longer have confidence in your integrity."

"I did not know about the cat. It was a horrible surprise to me, and I am truly sorry and ashamed for what happened."

"I should think you are! But then in that case you should get rid of that cook."

Inmaculada made no response.

"But it is curious, is it not, that you ate no stew."

Again there was no response from Inmaculada.

"Doña Inmaculada, I fear you are no longer fit to hold a responsible position as Head of the Art Department. Accordingly, I have sent a telegram to Doña Matilde offering her the post, and she has accepted. But of course, as you disclaim responsibility for your cook's action, you remain free to work under Doña Matilde's supervision. It appears that you are not mistress of that cook's actions, and are therefore not competent to control a department."

Inmaculada got up from her chair and drew herself up to her full imposing height. "Clearly you made this decision before hearing what I have told you. I deeply resent your insinuation regarding my integrity, and do not wish to continue working under your jurisdiction. You have my immediate resignation."

As she reached the door she half turned and added haughtily "In case there should be any doubt, that resignation includes my position as teacher. Adios."

★

'Not mistress of your cook's actions.' The accusation rankled. But it was true. Inmaculada had become enthralled by Arantxa, allowing herself to depend on her for all practical purposes. Her loneliness, her isolation, her very unworldliness made her an easy prey, as did her innocence and her religiosity.

Inmaculada could not bring herself to think badly of Arantxa. She was conscious of the many instances of Arantxa's concern for her well-being. As for the question of the Dean's cat, she put it down to her Basque background. Who has not heard of Basques chasing cats through the alleys as quarry for dinner; just as those from other regions think of rabbit. 'She might well have thought the cat a stray' she told herself, forgetting, of course, the bell, which with diabolical malevolence Arantxa had deliberately dropped into the stew.

★

On returning home, Inmaculada knelt by her bed on the little Persian mat, and gazing a moment at her beloved Christ Crucified,

218

intoned "I beseech you, Lord, to give me strength to rise above this calamity." And then, as an after thought, "And I pray you forgive Arantxa."

To Inmaculada's surprise, following her initial angry reaction, she felt a curious sense of relief. The interminable spite, envy, back-biting and the lowest of all possible manoeuvres that she had constantly to beware of at the Faculty were more than the job was worth. In spite of her absolute dedication to her work, to her students and to the University. She had brought the level of her Department to a height where it was acknowledged to be the foremost and the vanguard throughout Spain in its approach to art. And it was this, of course, that had occasioned the jealousy of her colleagues. Envy being one of the Seven Deadly Sins lurking in the Spanish character.

Arantxa had at first lapsed into a state of tremulous tearfulness, fearing she might be dismissed when Inmaculada said

"I shall be glad, Arantxa, never to go back to that den of iniquity. But, my dear Arantxa, we shall have to be just a little careful from now on. The salary was only a pittance, nevertheless …."

But when Inmaculada added "Thanks to Papa's provision for Concepción and for me, neither of us could ever want", Arantxa dried her eyes and assumed her former exuberance.

"I'll haggle harder in the market" she bragged, "no one can beat them down as I do. I've always got an eye for a bargain. And for a windfall. What about the Dean's cat, eh!"

"Don't ever mention it again, Arantxa, never, never even think of such a dreadful thing."

So they practised a little economy, Arantxa triumphantly declaring how cheaply she got strings of onions and garlic, fresh prawns and even occasionally oysters. Inmaculada, however, was accustomed to the very best in clothes, in the little food that she ate and in furnishing her exquisite flat. She could not resist a beautiful antique escritorio, although she already had one of extraordinary elegance, that she espied soon after these tribulations and she had no intention of relinquishing her expedition to Madrid to replenish her wardrobe.

★

No one called to see Inmaculada. Not even Salvador. He had been shocked by what happened at the lunch for the Dean and could not believe it possible that Inmaculada was innocent of what transpired. And yet …. Despairing of his relation with Inmaculada he had already applied for a lectureship at the University of Seville and had been appointed to take it up in October.

Meanwhile, the heavy heat of summer meant idle days for Inmaculada, lounging on her chaise-longue, quaffing sherbets that Arantxa plied her with and pondering various aspects of the history of art. She had intended, she reflected, gazing at the beautiful inlaid design of her latest escritorio, to write a monograph on Francis Bacon. But thinking that this would entail a visit to the London galleries to bring herself fully up to date, she gladly resigned herself to the curtailment of the project.

And then, one late morning, the translucence of the stained glass shadowed by the Persian blinds lowered at midday, inspiration came to her. "Why didn't it occur to me before?" she asked herself. "University monographs and articles are ephemeral. And in any case, they would never publish anything of mine here; or, perhaps now, in any Spanish university. But I can see it all so clearly now. I shall devote my life to a major work of art history, and I shall call it THE MISSING ZURBARAN.

The Christ Crucified that had been in her father's family for generations immemorial had never been put on public exhibition. The family had always shunned publicity, although certain distinguished art critics and painters had viewed it privately. But always as friends and never in a professional capacity. Nevertheless, some speculation had arisen in Spanish, European and even American artistic circles, leading to controversy regarding what had become known as ' The missing Zurbarán'. The painting in Inmaculada's flat had an uncanny likeness to the other early Christ Crucified of 1627, now in the Art Institute of Chicago. But it was markedly different from the Christs of Zurbarán's later work. Some of those who had seen it were of the opinion that it might have been painted in 1628 or even 1629. But all were certain it could not be later. It was something of an enigma, particularly as it was not signed by the artist; although it was well known that several of Zurbarán's paintings of his Seville period were sold unsigned. This was what Inmaculada decided she must explore. She was even prepared to investigate the possibility of its pre-dating the Christ Crucified in the Chicago Art Institute.

Inmaculada was now ecstatic at the prospect, and as she reclined in her chaise-longue in these languorous days she already began to plan in outline the form her work would take.

But one curious thing began to impinge on her consciousness. She was becoming aware that Arantxa would leave the flat for much longer than her normal shopping expeditions, lengthy as these were. Furthermore, Inmaculada noticed dreamily that Arantxa sallied forth always in the same low-cut floral dress, with lips brightly painted and her normally wayward hair in unaccustomed order.

Then one day she gave a little start. Could it mean, she wondered, that Arantxa was meeting …. a man? Inmaculada roused herself in some perplexity at this suspicion, pacing the shadowy rooms oblivious of the distant cries of street vendors in the great Plaza below. And when Arantxa, with armfuls of fruit and vegetables noisily returned she meant by discreet allusion to divine what these lengthy excursions implied. But she could never bring herself to penetrate that cheerful busyness.

Even when she had joined Arantxa in the kitchen for lunch and dinner she had to laugh at Arantxa's anecdotes about the fishmongers and butchers, and, when alone again she would wonder what would become of her if Arantxa left. She had become so used to, so dependent on Arantxa's ever cheerful company that …. She didn't allow herself to speculate, now that she was quite alone in the world.

And then an unworthy, an unwanted thought intruded on her dreamy musings. Could it be, might it not be that she was somehow involved with Salvador? Salvador never visited her now. She remembered the wink Arantxa had aimed at Salvador when she placed the so-called rabbit casserole before him. And one or two other suggestions of intimacy. She also recalled the porter's reported allusion to Salvador's promiscuousness. Inmaculada forced herself to abandon such base thoughts, though the persistence and regularity of Arantxa's absences, at the same time, in the same dress and for so long, day after day in the torrid heat, left her helplessly dreaming. For she herself left the claustrophobic if comforting seclusion of her flat only to attend Mass, morning and evening, in her black veil.

Inmaculada took to praying ever more ardently beneath the beatific Christ of Zurbarán, begging forgiveness for her unworthy suspicions and for fortitude to overcome the loss of Arantxa, if it should come to that. She prayed for Arantxa's wellbeing, come whatever might. Oh thank God for her beloved Christ. Who gave her strength to endure, love such as she had never known.

Inmaculada was growing ever paler; although she reclined on her chaise-longue most of the day she felt exhausted. Until one day in late July she determined to shake off her lethargy and visit Concepción in Madrid. They would as always go shopping for elegant clothes together, at the very best establishments, and they would visit the Prado besides other galleries and museums, not to mention the religious establishments where works by Zurbarán were still to be found. And so she would begin the research for her book, mixing that with the pleasure of concerts and the theatre. And meantime Arantxa would look after the flat.

Arantxa accompanied her to the railway station where she installed Inmaculada's fashionable calf-skin suitcase on the rack, considerably disturbing the other passengers in the first class compartment by her bustling attention to Inmaculada's comfort, brusquely moving aside any luggage which might impede it, laughing loudly and hoarsely at her own repartee in answer to any feeble protest from Inmaculada's companions for the journey.

When lingering farewells had been exchanged and the train was trundling south-eastward, to her surprise Inmaculada felt not only chagrin at leaving Arantxa but also a certain sense of relief at being free of the constant bombardment of her attention. So it was with serenity that she looked out over the arid plain gliding by, punctuated by an occasional uneasy qualm as she speculated on Arantxa's mysterious absences.

She awoke from a spell of daydreaming to find they had long passed Avila, now approaching El Escorial, and her fellow passengers were beginning to collect their belongings in anticipation of their arrival. The Rápido was thundering along with a melancholy wail as though it would be unable to stop, the carriages swaying perilously to the high-pitched cry of 'Madrid! Madrid!' from a boy in the corridor.

Inmaculada eagerly and a little anxiously looked out for Concepción and her husband in the jostling crowd at the Estación del Norte; but the Count had already espied her from the platform and came swiftly up with a porter, followed by Concepción. After a rapturous welcome, the sisters shedding a tear or two, they were borne along the Castellana in the Count's chauffeur-driven limousine to his magnificent house in the Paseo del Prado.

Inmaculada spent a delightful month with her sister and the Count, visiting the couturiers with Concepción almost every day. In the early mornings and evenings Inmaculada went often by herself to various art galleries and museums, including the Real Academia de Bellas Artes at San Fernando, where she spent a long time standing before Zurbarán's Vision del Beato Alonso Rodriguez. But the Prado being almost on her doorstep she was to be found there early most mornings. She was fascinated by Zurbarán's Christ with Saint Lucas as Painter, as it was almost certainly a portrait of the artist himself. But she felt deeply the inferiority of that Christ to the Christ Crucified in the ancestral bedroom. And she stopped before the Vision de San Pedro Nolasco, much praised by the critics; but it did not inspire her.

Her stay in Madrid was to include concerts of her favourite Baroque music and several theatrical performances, including work by Garcia Lorca and Calderon. All too quickly the month flashed by.

★

Inmaculada didn't know why, but it was with a certain sense of dread that she unlocked the door of her flat on her return. She had been surprised and concerned that Arantxa had not been at the station to meet her, and even more so when she opened the flat to find it empty. She was disappointed not to be able to give Arantxa a surprise with the presents she had bought for her in Madrid. Having looked into all the rooms, she opened the door of her bedroom to unpack the clothes she had with such enthusiasm bought in Madrid.

On opening the door she first gasped in astonishment and then fainted. Where the great Christ Crucified of Zurbarán had hung for countless years over the ancestral bed there was now an equally vast portrait in its place. Of Arantxa, broad, buxom and grinning with luridly painted lips in a cheap floral print dress.

When Inmaculada recovered consciousness, having luckily fallen on her bed, she noticed a scrap of paper and a little pile of banknotes on top of the chiffonier. With difficulty she drew the paper towards herself and read it with incredulity.

Doña Inma, preciosa, I am so sorry to miss your arrival. I have to rush to get the Zurbarán sent off to a dealer in Barcelona who has a buyer waiting in Paris.

You see, the artist who painted my portrait – which he did for nothing, just think of that – said the Zurbarán is certainly not authentic as it isn't signed by him. But he negotiated a price of ten thousand pesetas for it, so here they are! As we have been a little hard up I didn't want to lose the opportunity. He even went so far as to say the Zurbarán is a fake, so we're lucky to get so much for it. But there's nothing fake about my portrait, it there, Inma my dear. I dedicate it to you, in memory of happy times.

As I know you are in reduced circumstances I don't want you to have the added expense of my wages and keep. So I have decided I must sacrifice my well-being by leaving your employment. I shall try to find a little job in the north, and will be on my way there by the time of your return.

With all my best wishes for ever, from your devoted servant, Arantxa.

Arantxa had intended that her portrait should substitute the great Christ Crucified in Inmaculada's affection. But the overwhelming bargain she had struck had proved irresistible.

When Inmaculada had taken in all that this note implied she struggled shakily to her feet and anxiously paced up and down the length of the great salón.

After a while she made her way resolutely to the block of flats where Arantxa's brother worked as porter. When she arrived he was about to show some new tenants to their flat but asked Inmaculada to be seated meanwhile in his little office.

"I'll be back in a quarter of an hour, señora" he said as he set off up the stairs with two heavy suitcases.

Inmaculada waited impatiently, seated on the porter's hard chair in front of his desk, glancing at the pigeon holes cluttered with keys and letters. Then she noticed that the newspaper spread out on the desk was La Gaceta del Norte, six months old, and that a small article had been circled with a pen. With mild curiosity she looked it over and was then arrested by what she read.

ALLEGED POISONER FREED ON APPEAL FOR LACK OF EVIDENCE

The Court of Cassation in Madrid has decided unanimously in the case of the sudden mysterious death of Doña María Tejera, widow of the famous Bilbao shipbuilder Don Juan Cortázar, that her cook/housekeeper, Srta. Arantxa Garaicoechea Galletebeitia, convicted of poisoning her mistress for financial gain, should be freed on account of the unsatisfactory and inconclusive evidence. Doña María had left her entire fortune to the servant in her will, but the Court of Cassation upholds the decision of the lower Court that the said will should be declared invalid.

Inmaculada was aghast when the porter noisily burst open his office door. Noticing that Inmaculada was reading that encircled article, he hastily deposited a large bunch of keys on top of it.

Turning breathlessly, the little grey-haired man begged pardon for the delay and asked Inmaculada politely what he could do for her. She showed him her card, enquiring whether he knew the whereabouts of his sister.

"No, señora" he replied in some consternation, "I assumed she was with you."

Inmaculada thanked him and was on the point of leaving when a figure passed the office window, vaulting up the stairs two at a time. She caught a glimpse of Salvador.

"A colleague of yours, I believe, señora. Such a quiet, studious young man. Unfortunately he's leaving us tomorrow to take up a new post in Seville."

Inmaculada tried not to show any sign of the double shock she had received that evening, but trembling slightly she bade the porter goodnight and returned home.

When she opened the door of her flat the telephone was ringing. It was Salvador.

"I wanted to call to say goodbye. Could I come over for a few minutes this evening? I'm off to Seville tomorrow for good."

Inmaculada begged him to come as soon as possible, not caring what the neighbours might think. When he arrived they stood facing each other in the hallway for a moment in embarrassed silence.

"So you are leaving us" said Inmaculada, her lips trembling and in spite of all her efforts a tear rolled down her cheek. "May I ask why?"

"I have been offered a post as lecturer at the University of Seville. I have been unbearably lonely in this claustrophobic, evil little town and the fact that I .... after that dreadful lunch... I couldn't believe you could have allowed such a horrible thing... I had decided I could never ever see you again, but when Carlos said you had called I felt I must .... see you, in spite of everything, ... to say goodbye."

"But did you really believe I was privy to Arantxa's ... to her monstrous...."

Inma could hardly control the great emotion that overcame her, but asking Salvador to sit down a moment in the salón, she told him about Arantxa's disappearance, the vanishing of Zurbarán's Christ Crucified, and the article she had seen in the Gaceta del Norte. Then she opened her bedroom door to show him Arantxa's portrait. Salvador was for a moment transfixed and then rushed to the kitchen, returning in a fury with a huge cleaver. Inmaculada cowered against the bedroom wall, but to her amazement Salvador frenziedly hacked the picture to shreds, catching his breath with open mouth as he snarled "You wicked, evil witch!"

Salvador was speechless for some moments when the portrait

had been destroyed. Then, with a great effort he said, panting still "Inmaculada, if you only knew how much I admired you – admire you – how terrible that I should for a moment have believed …."

By this time Inmaculada's reserve had quite broken down. She wept uncontrollably as she rose to say goodbye. When she held out her hand, Salvador ignored it, taking her in his arms and murmuring "Inmaculada, I love you."

Inmaculada put her trembling arms round his shoulders, her whole body quaking with long pent up emotion.

"Salvador! Mi Salvador" she whispered. "O Díos mío!"

★

Salvador and Inmaculada were very quietly married in Seville cathedral by Canon Villalobos, only Concepción and the Count, besides Salvador's father, mother and sister being present.

They were lucky enough to find a small house in the Plaza Alfaro, with a mirador overlooking the Murillo Gardens. Inmaculada bought a small grand piano for Salvador that fitted neatly in the mirador, where he played classical sonatas that could be heard in the gardens many a night.

Inmaculada herself set to work on her 'The Missing Zurbarán', undaunted by the police report that the ancestral painting had vanished without any hope of recovery, having almost certainly been bought to order by a foreign millionaire aficionado of the arts.

Nothing could be proved against Arantxa, who had bought one of the grandest fish stalls in the market of San Sebastian, where she was well able to hold her own with the fishwives at ribald repartee.

With Salvador by her side, Inmaculada revisited the Church of the Magdalen, where Salvador was much moved to see The Apparition of the Virgin to Soriano, that virgin Inmaculada's father had declared her childhood likeness. Among others, they admired Zurbarán's Christ on the Cross at the Museo de Bellas Artes, although its attribution to Zurbarán is questioned by some. Inmaculada, certainly, found it disappointing, if only because the 'missing' Zurbarán was of such supreme power and pathos.

When the great heat of the Sevillian summer came they travelled to see Zurbarán's Inmaculada Concepción at Sigüenza, at the Museo Diocesano, before taking a plane from Madrid for Chicago.

This was the climax of Inmaculada's research. The Christ Crucified at the Chicago Art Institute bore an uncanny resemblance to the ancestral portrait that had been from time immemorial in the family. So much so that Inmaculada almost swooned before it, although Salvador's firm hand held her steady.

★

In due time Inmaculada's book, 'The Missing Zurbarán' was published and caused quite a stir in the art world on account of her eloquence and originality. Salvador too published some notable monographs on Corneille, Racine and Molière. He was never so happy, though he was astonished by the devouring passion of Inmaculada. "May the ancestral Zurbarán never be found" he signed contentedly to himself as he dropped off to sleep.

I must thank Cambridge University Press for permission to reproduce the following: Ivar Alastair Watson, 'The Distance Runner's Perfect Heart: Dr Leavis in Spain', Cambridge Review, Vol 116, No. 2326, November 1995.

Thanks are also due to the Times Literary Supplement, who published an abridged version of the above under the title 'Who's for lunch with Leavis? Entertaining the Scourge of the Academic World,' Ivar Alastair Watson, July 14th 1995, No. 4815, which was published by permission of Cambridge University Press.